PLANET FALL

LINE OF BATTLE SKIRMISHES

W. P. BROTHERS

ALENA PUBLISHING

Planet Fall
Line of Battle Skirmishes
Book 3 in the Line of Battle Series
Published by Alena Publishing, 2018

Cover Design by Creative Digital Studios

Copyright ©2018 by W.P. Brothers
All Rights Reserved

ISBN: 978-0-9977394-5-9

ACKNOWLEDGMENTS

I'd like to give my heartfelt thanks to anyone and everyone who supported me through this project.

Angela, Wesley, Mallory, and Oliver, for encouraging and supporting me when my motivation waned. Writing is a full-contact sport, and without you, it just wouldn't be fulfilling. Life has no reward if you have nobody to bring the bacon home to.

Mikki White, Pamela Clare, Benjamin Collins, and Mary Cutler, for their time and effort test-reading this work. Your ideas, feedback, and honesty were invaluable in refining the emotional embers of the final draft of *Planet Fall*.

Benjamin, my primary editor, advisor, and friend. Thank you for taking the time to help hone my craft especially whilst you are inundated with other projects. Without your attention to detail, knowledge, energy, and support, the Line of Battle universe wouldn't be the same.

My various friends and colleagues at Big Store Nine who make my days more interesting.

To all those people in my life who I can't mention by name —

family, colleagues, and acquaintances who have inspired or supported me: You have my thanks.

To Grandpa Vinny, who left us before this work could be completed. Thank you for always supporting me and sharing your wisdom. To all the men and women who have given their lives fighting unwinnable battles for the freedom of their families, their beliefs, and their countries: This one is for you.

IN ALLIANCE YEAR 836...

As the grueling cold war against the Milipa Empire grinds through its eighth century, the Royal Alliance Navy is desperate to hold the line. In order to survive, the Navy must transfer experienced captains to command new vessels and promote younger officers to take their place.

Six months ago, as part of this expansion, Captain Kim Morden received a promotion and her **FIRST COMMAND,** the battle-cruiser *RAS Verdun*. On a shakedown mission to Derek's Triangle to rescue a series of disappeared freighters, Morden and her crew faced and defeated a would-be invasion by the terrifying Frontin, a species of intelligent, ruthless arachnids hell-bent on consuming other space-faring species.

Her ship damaged and crew devastated, Captain Morden brought the *Verdun* to the remote Alliance **OUTPOST** of Kensington Station for rest and repairs. Without warning, a group of human insurgents calling themselves the United Worker's Legion attacked Kensington, forcing the *Verdun* and the station's small garrison to fight a desperate battle for control of the planet and their own survival. While Morden's crew prevailed on Kensington, a dozen other worlds fell to the Legion's growing war machine. The galaxy in turmoil, Morden's crew completed their repairs and set a course for Port Souville, one of the capital planets of the Alliance.

Now, with the *Verdun* in transit, the Royal Alliance prepares to take action against the Legion threat...

CHAPTER ONE

Major General Polis
Commanding Officer, 4ᵗʰ Infantry Division.
Admiralty Building.
London, Earth.
10 days until planet fall

Son-of-a-Bitch.
Major General Herman Polis checked his cellular band as he walked, the intensity of its light stinging his eyes.

0215.

He looked up toward the normally brilliant chandeliers hanging from the ceiling. Low power mode.

Polis zipped around the corner, stopping just in front of the final of the three checkpoints he had to navigate. At least there wasn't a line. That was the only upside of this early hour — that, and the absence of political refuse he normally tolerated there.

This checkpoint was reminiscent of the guard room protecting a combat vessel's bridge, the chief difference being the bullet-proof window set in the center of the ceiling-high wall. Next to the window was a single rotating body scanner that doubled as an entrance way.

He chuckled to himself as he stopped just shy of the biometric hand reader, returning the salute of the droopy-eyed duty sergeant. Marines, unlike Whitehall attendants, weren't known for pleasant interactions with VIPs. These checkpoints could do with a few more marines.

The attendant reached down, hitting some hidden button below the lip of the window.

"Early one today, sir?" The tinny tone of the speaker failed to cover the sarcasm in her voice.

Polis nodded, forcing what he hoped was a passive look on his face. She smiled, moving her unseen hands again. The biometric reader pulsed on, green light accentuated the smooth curves of the woman's face and body.

He fought the urge to smile, memories flooding his mind. In his youth, this was just the situation he lived for. The kind of beautiful young woman his good looks and swagger used to allow him to enjoy. He'd prided himself on getting to know women like this personally.

Polis sighed, pushing the memories away.

To be young again.

He pressed his hand against the pad, watching the small icon rotate as the computer processed his identity...

Slowly.

A small chime sounded. "Major General Herman Polis, Command Fourth Infantry Division. Logged in."

The hatch slid open. He stepped through, glancing at his cellular band for the third time in as many minutes.

Damn.

Mechanically, he lined his feet up to the marks on the floor. The room sealed. Its scanner powered on, clicking and whirling softly as it went. These damn checkpoints would waste less time if Parliament would just approve the funding to install an AI.

The historical preservation argument was crap, a political excuse to nickel-and-dime military spending. Whitehall had to function, regardless of age. Besides, the sensors, checkpoints, and other equipment had already begun the modernization process. Maybe the threat the Legion posed would force Parliament to pony up some dough for ground security, instead of the naval monstrosities that garnished all the headlines. Then at least some good could come from this civil war.

Civil War.

How the hell had this happened?

The scanner's cycle ended with a loud knocking sound. The pad turned, and the hatch opened to the large waiting room on the other side. Polis stepped out, returning the salute of another guard without looking back. He dashed towards the spiral stairway that led up to the Senior Admirals' Offices. He willed his legs to move faster. His tired muscles ached with the effort, his footfalls filling the otherwise empty marble hall.

Civil war.

Just the feel of the words over his tongue had turned his stomach during the initial briefing. Intellectually, he could make sense of the facts. It wasn't complicated. A rogue force of Alliance citizens had attacked several barely manned facilities along the old Black Star border. The sheer tenacity of the assailants and the ensuing shock had overwhelmed the defenders. Most of the outposts had fallen into the hands of the Legion.

Frankly, if it hadn't been for the brilliant actions of the captain of the *Verdun,* every one of the bases the Legion had attacked would be out of Alliance hands.

He reached the first landing, took a sharp right towards Admiral Edward Young's office. Polis tried to push the civil war from his mind. What the hell could the admiral want at 0200? Especially with Polis. He'd rarely seen eye to eye with Young on anything.

At best, Young was a hardnosed One Alliance Party advocate whose politics bled too far into his decisions. At worst, he was a power-hungry manipulator with delusions of grandeur, the kind of leader that drove Polis to gain promotion just to not have to take their orders. Unfortunately, Young was still his superior, and he didn't have a choice but to listen to him. They had clashed openly on the Parliament floor on more than one occasion.

Polis hated surprise meetings. Hated surprises. They rarely led to good things in this line of work. Before he left home, he'd tried to contact Admiral Knight, tried to figure out what this surprise could be. But Knight was still in transit from the second fleet's headquarters on Souville. The distance and early hour put him, and most of the general's other contacts, out of range. Whatever Young was up to, Polis would have to face it alone.

He came to halt just outside of the cracked door to Young's office. He straightened his uniform and nameplate. He was late, but he refused to look frazzled or anything other than pristine.

Polis opened the door, blinking as he stepped into the brightly lit room. Young's secretary, a balding, pale wisp of a man, looked up. The man, whose name Polis vaguely remembered as Hans, sneered at him.

Han's grating voice matched the thin line of his pursed lips. "Running late, general?"

Polis forced a smile. "Please let the Admiral know I'm here, with apologies for my tardiness."

"They're waiting, just go in." Hans looked back down at his keyboard.

Polis fought back the urge to slap Hans' attitude out the side of his head. Annoying cuss. He opened the door, stepped inside, cutting off Young's booming voice.

The Admiral was sitting behind his desk, his chair leaning back, his long arms crossed in his lap. Polis could remember when the man's crew cut and crisp, immaculate uniform had been the perfect, severe compliment to his tall, powerful frame, the austere trappings of a hardened professional. Now, combined with the high cheekbones in his aging face and rail-thin figure, they were cold, rigid, and sharp.

Polis' gaze moved to the four other people who were crowded into the office. Three had their backs turned, while another was leaning in the corner. Polis recognized him immediately. Colonel Don Tramo, a respected, albeit eccentric, member of the intelligence community. Tramo was a gaunt, short, well-built officer with light sandy hair and cold blue eyes. Although Polis couldn't say for sure, he suspected Tramo had been a Special Forces operator prior to his injuries — the same injuries that caused him to limp slightly on the side on which he was leaning now.

Both Tramo and Young looked up as he entered.

Young stood. "Come in, come in, and close the door."

Polis obliged, moving just behind the final three officers in the room.

Young smiled his overly toothy grin. "Now that you have graced us with your presence, General, we'll move quickly. Many things to cover. Since you clearly miss your bed, I'll try to get you back there before the sun starts shining."

Jackass.

Polis forced another smile. "Thank you, sir."

Young moved toward Tramo, reaching for a bottle of dark amber liquid sitting on the shelf to the Colonel's right. "Drink, anyone? Twenty-five-year-old Bourbon."

They shook their heads in a collective no. Young shrugged. He picked up the bottle and poured a small amount into a glass. "Suit yourselves. Colonel, go ahead and get the introductions out of the way so we can shove off."

Polis crossed his arms. This was so damn peculiar. Military life was no nine-to-five, but this kind of brass convention at 0200 was unusual. It smelled of classified action.

Or unsanctioned action.

Tramo pushed himself forward, using his arm to brace his weak leg. "For those of you who don't know me, I'm Colonel Don Tramo, current head of outer-rim intelligence."

There was a general course of hellos and tired nods from the three men in front of Polis. Tramo pointed toward him. "This is Major General Herman Polis, Commander of the fourth infantry division."

The three men turned, letting Polis see their faces for the first time. The man closest to Tramo was no more than thirty and easily the youngest among them. He had sandy brown hair, pencil-thin lips, and high, prominent cheekbones. A ranger, based on his uniform, the officer had dark brown eyes with the customary, unnecessary intensity Polis associated with rangers.

The man on his left was a tanker, and a good one judging by the medals plastering his chest. His salt-and-pepper hair and kind blue eyes contrasted with his hawkish nose. The final officer was the tallest, with black hair, green eyes, and chiseled features that screamed *marine*. The red dress uniform concurred with Polis' observation of his features.

Polis nodded.

Tramo continued. "This is Major Jeff Marshall, commander of the Seventh Ranger Battalion. Lt. Colonel Bradly Anderson, Fifth Armor Corps, and finally Colonel Fox Snider, 10th Marine Force Recon Division."

Polis opened his mouth to speak, but a laugh from Admiral Young cut him off.

Young sat back down, his cup empty. "I am encouraged to have such... talent assembled for this operation."

Tramo nodded. "Before we continue, I want to make it clear this is classified as top secret. You must not speak of anything you hear tonight with anyone outside this room, including your own staffs, until the mission is underway."

Polis' stomach tightened. Operations this classified were rarely fun, and with the Legion on the move, he could only guess what Young had planned for them.

Young scoffed. "Tramo, these are fine officers. Fine officers. I trust them implicitly. You worry too much. You're too cloak and dagger."

"Sir, with all due respect I..."

Young's tone hardened. "Tramo, sit down."

The intelligence officer never removed his eyes from Young, but eased himself back against the bookshelf.

Young turned to face Polis. "General, what do you know about Cross industries?"

Polis uncrossed his arms. "Nothing special. Cross is one of the largest manufacturers of small arms and munitions. The government just finished subsidizing a new state-of-the-art factory for him on New Utica in order to take on additional military contracts. Assuming those contracts clear the oversight commission..." Polis stopped himself from saying more. He'd never understood why trillionaires needed government assistance, especially when the administration was trying to rein in military spending.

Young clapped his hands. "Precisely. Archibald Cross has his hands in, around, and all over the damn pot. He has the ears of the right members of Parliament. Connected is the term. Worse, the rags-to-riches story he's always repeating is an inspiration to millions. His silly TV show has a massive following. It would be a major blow to the country's morale if something happened to him — and to our supply system."

Tramo shifted his weight, grimacing. "Not to mention the political dirt he could give up under the strain of torture." Tramo met the gaze of each officer in turn. "Unfortunately, we lost contact with his facility on New Utica. The last intelligence report we received showed several unknown ships entering the system. I believe the planet is under attack from the Legion."

Polis's breath caught in his chest.

The officers looked at each other, a murmur running around the room.

If the Legion was large enough to assault a colony planet, things had taken a turn for the worse. The last briefing had suggested that the entirety of the Legion's forces had been committed to assaults on the various supply outposts.

How could they have spread so quickly?

How could the Alliance's intelligence be so bad?

Young leaned forward. "We have to move quickly. If Cross is captured or killed, it will greatly undermine people's confidence in the government's control of the situation. If they can secure New Utica, it will give them a foothold dangerously close to the Milipa border. Fortunately, for the moment, things should be on our side."

The lights dimmed, replaced by the blue-green glow of a holographic image on Young's desk, a small island group that Polis didn't recognize.

Tramo's voice continued from the corner. "Cross's facility was built just off the southernmost continent here, at the edge of these islands." A building flickered red on the holotable, indicating its position. "The islands are connected by a series of bridges that lead back to the region's one spaceport."

Young held out his hands. "The bridges. This operation will hinge on them. To get Cross out, we will need to take and hold all five of the bridges that connect these islands and remove Cross via armored transport to the spaceport. The islands are too crowded with temporary worker housing and dense forest for a ship to land safely."

Polis studied the image, his mind working through the tactical situation. The islands were small, close together, with numerous, dense settlements. If Polis knew anything about that kind of terrain, he knew it would present any operation with obstacles — muddy or sandy terrain, buildings, and narrow streets that would favor defenders. Even combat landers and marine drop pods would struggle to touch down without flattening something. It would be hell under fire.

Almost impossible.

He looked up. "Our mission is to retrieve Cross? We aren't going to reinforce the territorials or evacuate the civilian population? This is about saving a rich asshole?"

Young shifted, his smile fading. "Parliament hasn't authorized any formal response to the Legion problem yet, especially so close to the Milipa border."

Marshall leaned back. "But the mission is sanctioned?"

"By the Admiralty, yes."

Polis's stomach dropped.

First civil war, now independent actions. Things really were going to shit.

"Sir, with respect, did the entire Admiralty sign off on this? It takes a unanimous vote to—"

Young's eyes flashed, his skin reddening. "None of your concern. This situation demands speed and secrecy. I — and others — won't allow the Admiralty or this government to suffer an embarrassment while we are waiting for committee hearings and votes."

Since when did Young care about the labor government's embarrassment?

Polis nodded. "I understand your feelings, but I am not comfortable—"

Young slammed his desk with his fist, making the holographic images flicker. "This is not a tinker-day parade. This is war. The Admiralty has the legal power to send in troops for limited actions. We are exercising that power. Period."

Polis could protest this through official channels. He wasn't going to argue with this asshole or ruin his career by being insubordinate.

Tramo interjected. "Besides, this is a small operation, with a huge reward potential. We estimate that you can be in and out in under 72 hours with an acceptable loss of personnel and supplies for the gains."

Young smiled again. "Correct, colonel. General Polis, you will have operational command. Three regiments of the Fourth Infantry Division will be accompanied by the Tenth Recon Marines, Seventh Rangers, and a detachment of armor. More than enough to break through the pitiful force of untrained insurgents you should be facing."

Tramo shifted the image again, and several more marks appeared on the image. "The plan is simple. Polis's forces and Marshall's rangers will go in and secure the spaceport. Snider and the remaining marines will be dropped in like a carpet over the bridges, capturing them. This surprise should limit the enemy's response and allow Anderson's armor to traverse quickly up the road to the Cross's facility."

Polis rubbed his temple. Against the Milipa, this would be suicide. Force Recon marines were tough, really tough, but they were lightly armed with limited ammunition.

If anything went wrong—

The holoimage disappeared as the room's overhead lights came back on.

Snider turned to look at Young. "It'll be hairy if they hit my people with anything big. These landing zones are narrow. Will we have any up-to-date intelligence? Air support?"

Young's lips spread, showing each one of his bleached teeth. "Certainly, there are risks, but I chose each of you for your superior skills. Your dropship, the RAS Hercules, will use drones to provide you with as much intelligence as possible."

Anderson nodded. "And combat air support?"

"Unlikely. We can't send in more than a handful of naval assets without alerting the Milipa."

Marshall leaned back. "And if they hit us from the air?"

Tramo pushed himself up. "There's little to no evidence of airborne assets. If the stolen vehicles encountered at Kensington are any indication, their air forces will be easy targets for our AA tankettes."

Anderson rubbed his chin. "What if the recon detachment is assaulted before we can get up the road?"

Tramo nodded. "All eventualities are planned for. Landers will drop one Henshaw CA-1 and two McGee fighting vehicles to help secure each bridge. More than enough firepower to keep our recon marines safe until your tanks arrive."

Young sat down. "Gentleman, I know there are concerns. There always are, but I can assure you our best planners have thought of every conceivable outcome. For now, get your troops together and be ready to shove off in three days. Tramo and I will accompany you aboard the Hercules. He can answer your questions then. Remember, this is top secret. You are to refer to it as a training exercise with your troops until you hit translight, understood?"

The three men in front of Polis nodded, standing to go. Polis didn't move. "Sir, we are being set up to lose men's lives. There are too many unknowns, too many questions. If anything goes wrong, we will be spread out with no way off the planet."

Young's face flushed red. "General, you have your orders. Dismissed."

Polis stood his ground. "Sir, I will execute your orders. However, I want my objection on the official record. I require written orders, along with your acknowledgment of my concerns. I want to be ready in case I must answer for a massacre after this thing is over."

Young eyes fixed on his. "What are you implying, General?"

Polis held the admiral's stare. "Implying? Nothing. I've made my position clear. There is no parliamentary order, no intelligence, and a God-knows-what disaster on the surface. You are unwilling to hear objections. Only the time frame and classified nature of our mission prevent me from protesting officially. Top secret or not, I will not be responsible for poor decisions above my pay grade."

Young didn't move for several seconds. He finally nodded. "Very well. Tramo will take care of it. Now get out of here."

With all pretense of cordiality gone, Polis turned and stormed from the room. He moved away from the officers now under his command, unable to shake the knot in his stomach. If this mission went south and his team was slaughtered, no written order from Young would bring back the dead.

Or ease his conscience.

FUCKING POLIS

Colonel Tramo shut the door to his office. He ignored the dull pain in his hip, collapsing quickly in the corner recliner. He was glad

Young had accepted his recommendation to put that ass-hat in charge. Polis's death would certainly make this deal worth-while.

Sanctimonious do-gooder.

The desk chair swiveled around. "Well?

Tramo's hand relaxed off his holster clasp.

Kline.

Tramo let out a breath. "You're supposed to be on New Utica. I told you never to come here."

Kline curved the corners of his lips into his perfect smile. "I have time, my good colonel. Besides, who will recognize me at this hour? I want to know what that bastard Polis said."

Tramo kept his tone sharp. "The computer, you halfwit. If Young looks too deeply —"

Kline laughed, turning the glass in his hand. "Young, seriously? That windbag won't know what hit him, let alone suspect foul play. Now, tell me everything."

Tramo didn't particularly like Kline. The man had little discipline and fewer brains. His character had all the substance of a slug and was just as slimy, despite his perfectly shellacked hair and smooth, tanned face. Or maybe because of it. Dealing with scum like this was a necessary evil for Tramo's work.

Tramo reached for a bottle and cup from the table beside him.

He forced his words to be even, calm. "Stop simpering. Confused about our roles again? Need I spell it out for you? You work for me. Your life is in my hand. You are a convenience, nothing more."

Kline's smile fell. "I am taking risks. If something goes wrong here, the whole plan may crumble on my head."

Tramo said nothing, letting the silence linger.

He poured a generous portion and set the bottle back down. The Legion had their agenda, he had his. They needed him far more than he could ever need money-grubbing assholes like Kline.

And they knew it.

Kline took a drink, tapping his ring against his glass. "Don, my friend, give me something. I need to know if the Alliance is committed. If the Legion movement fails, we stand to lose more than you appreciate. My associates will not give me the resources until I know the Alliance is on the path you promised."

Tramo laughed. "I don't care what you or any of those idiots of yours lose. I gave you a promise, and unlike you, I can meet a deadline without fleecing something for myself. They are coming."

"And Polis?"

Tramo took a drink. "As difficult as always. He has a rare gift for selflessness. It creates problems."

Kline raised his eyebrows. "But he is going? No risk of his contacting Admiral Knight or any of his other liberal allies?"

Tramo laughed again. "No idea. I would, if I were him. Hopefully his moral compass will prevent it. Young is convinced, which was the goal. Getting rid of Polis, Anderson, and Snider is a bonus. One, I might add, you may not be able to deliver even with their boots on the ground."

Kline slapped the table, the large ring on his finger knocking the wood. "Bullshit. You told me we couldn't take an Alliance facility. By my last count, we took four."

Tramo leaned back, ignoring the stiffness in his spine. "Smith was beaten on Kensington by a rookie captain with a smashed ship. Perhaps your child's mind has forgotten, but Kensington was the key. A victory means shit when you fumble the prize."

Kline went rigid. "Damaged or not, that ship was battlecruiser—"

Tramo jolted forward, a white-hot surge of emotion blasting past his reserve. "I don't need excuses. I have an entire department of subordinates for that. You promised victory and failed. We wouldn't need this operation without your blunders. That victory created heroes. Heroes are dangerous in a business like yours. You gave your opponents a rallying cry. In the long run, that could be enough to bring your movement down."

Kline didn't move. He was a coward and an idiot, but at least he knew when to shut up.

Tramo forced himself to calm down. "As for New Utica, Polis

may be a fucker, but he has made a career of winning hopeless battles. He will not die easily."

For the moment, Tramo needed the Legion. They could do what he couldn't without risking exposure. This was too delicate a time for that. Polis had already come too close.

Tramo took another sip. "Kline, I am counting on you to kill him. His dead body is the price of my continued support. Fail, and you won't live a week. That's a promise you can count on."

Kline gulped the remainder of his drink. "I know. That is why I am handling this personally. No Smiths to let us down. I won't fail."

He held the man's gaze for a moment. "See that you don't. Get out."

Kline swept out of the room without a whisper.

Tramo checked his cellular band.

0455.

He had a few hours before his shift, before his next task. Pushing Kline and the Legion from his mind, he leaned back and closed his eyes.

Soon his revenge would be at hand.

CHAPTER TWO

Captain Jordan Duncan
Bridge of RAS Hercules
15 hours to planet fall

Captain Jordan Duncan gripped the armrests of his chair, eyes fixed on his command screen. The *Hercules* was on target, the deceleration timer ticking towards zero. This wasn't the first time his crew had skipped a stone, nor the hundredth. They drilled this maneuver as often as combat drops. It was essential for tiptoeing into hot systems.

Timing was everything.

The size of this moon complicated matters, especially if they were to avoid detection. Drop out of translight too early, and the enemy would see them, wasting any element of surprise. The mission would be over before it began. Command estimated as many as twenty ships, rated as destroyers and cruisers. Duncan's ship wouldn't even have the firepower to reach the planet.

On the other hand, if they were even milliseconds too late, they would end up as a pancake on the surface of some shitty moon.

He uncurled his knuckles. "Commander Connelly, sound battle stations. Ready for close-orbit deceleration. Fighters and drones to launch stations. Time to skip this stone."

The ready indicators illuminated one after the next on Duncan's screen. Connelly was a short, balding man whose love of food was readily apparent. Despite his lack of physical prowess, he was the best executive officer Duncan had served with. Even tempered, reliable, and unflappable in combat. With the fleet's need for captains, Duncan was sure he wouldn't be enjoying Connelly's presence much longer.

The voice of Daryl, the *Hercules's* AI, broke his concentration. "Fifteen seconds to deceleration. All hands brace, brace, brace."

Here we go.

The number on his screen turned red as it hit five. Duncan closed his eyes, crossing his arms over his chest. He felt weightless for a second, before being forced forward, the safety belt pushing into his chest. The *Hercules* had begun reversing, the engines fighting the ship's inertia. Warning klaxons sounded as the strain on the superstructure increased. Duncan's arms went numb, his stomach turning as the g-forced squeezed it.

The ship stopped abruptly, klaxons still splitting the air.

Duncan shook his head, clearing his watering eyes. The ship's sensors were still offline, but based on the pressure readings, they were located just inside the top atmospheric layer of New Utica's furthest moon.

Perfect.

Duncan rebooted his monitor. "Ensign Ricky, establish a laser link with the Montalban, Tupu, Simcoe, and Horizon. I want zero risk of interception. Get me a status reports in two minutes."

Ricky croaked. "Aye, sir, establishing now."

Duncan zoomed his screen out. The sensors couldn't see beyond this planet's ionosphere. There were no satellite feeds available, no military transmissions, or beacons of any kind. The whole solar system was dark.

Damn.

Young was right. New Utica was under attack. In twenty-five years, he'd never entered a populated system this quiet. The *Hercules* shook several times as the Cerberus fighters and sensor drones took off from the launch bay.

They'd have answers soon.

They would have to be careful here. The drones needed to get close enough to give him a clear idea of what they were up against without alerting the enemy. He knew from reports that the Legion didn't have the most tactically minded captains, but he would not give them any freebies.

Duncan's jaw tensed. "Commander, manual control, all drones."

"Readout's ready, sir," Ricky called out.

Duncan's screen changed, an image of the *Montalban* replacing that of the *Hercules*. The cruiser was showing launch bays open and all systems green, its guns traversing upwards, engines firing in short bursts as the ship assumed position just above the *Hercules*.

He cycled through the three destroyers. All were in perfect condition, following the lead of the *Montalban*. Duncan typed in orders for his escorts.

Cerberus fighters only.

Manual control all drones.

Laser link only.

Silent running.

Acknowledge.

So far, so good.

He'd need the destroyer's guns if he wanted to reach New Utica.

The lead drones had reached the edge of the ionosphere on the opposite side of the moon, creeping upward on minimal thrust. He zoomed the screen out, studying the images playing across it.

New Utica, the sole inhabited planet in the system, had three other moons. According to the database, there were some scattered mining operations on them. No information was available about whether they were manned, automated, or even operational. The satellites that should be in orbit were gone, replaced with debris clouds and undetonated ordnance.

These Legion operators weren't neat or precise.

So far, Duncan could see thirteen cruisers and fifteen destroyers. They were spread out at random intervals throughout the area. Based on their disposition, he'd bet there were more destroyers just out of range. If the Legion used the Royal Alliance Navy as a template, they should have three destroyers for each cruiser. If not, Duncan would have nothing to go off beyond the *Verdun's* experiences.

Regardless, the Alliance fleet was outnumbered.

Most of the cruisers were clustered near Utica but had no clear formation or visible command ship. Many were drifting, the barest of power readings suggesting their engines were offline. That would give Duncan's battle group an edge, give them time to cut a hole in the enemy's gut big enough to drop the force and run

He fed the information to Daryl, asking for combat simulations. He watched the computer run simulation after simulation. Each time it ended about the same — forty-five to fifty percent of those fuckers survived and eliminated his ships.

Damn.

Young was right again. This had to be a stop and drop. Duncan had always prided himself on the support he provided his ground teams. There was a connection between dropships and the troops they carried. The *Hercules* had been assigned to the Tenth Marine Force Recon Division for longer than he had been in the service. The last thing he wanted to do was leave those marines stranded with enemy ships filling the skies.

Duncan saved the simulations. "Ricky, inform Polis this is a stop and drop. We need them ready to go ASAP. Daryl, send the general my findings."

Ricky replied, his voice light, cheerful. "Aye, aye, sir."

Duncan leaned back, pulled off his headset, and made eye contact with the young man. Ricky was the opposite of Connelly, fit and far too impulsive. He was enthusiastically ready for any fight the universe could throw at him.

He was also too young.

Duncan let out a sigh. The last time human beings had fought openly against each other had been more than eight hundred years ago when the *EE Dominion* had betrayed Emperor Harkler. That civil war had destroyed the empire, left a chip on the Milipa's shoulders, and thrown everything into disarray.

Millions dead.

Millions more homeless and in chaos. The tired, weakened newly formed Alliance forced to try to stop an onslaught of the Milipa's revenge machine.

Now, eight hundred years later, Duncan was about to unleash Alliance military forces onto an Alliance civilian planet. The idea turned his stomach. It was one thing to defend against a group of fanatics beating at your door, but a civilian population infested with traitors?

How would they recognize friend from foe?

Ricky couldn't see past the excitement of his first firefight. His first chance to test his mettle. Duncan remembered that feeling at the onset of the last war. Hopefully, Ricky could still feel that enthusiastic when the shooting stopped and this nightmare came to an end.

Assuming he would be able to feel anything at all.

Captain Franklin Reed
Hercules *Barracks*
7*th Ranger Battalion, 1st Company*
14 hours to planet fall

CAPTAIN FRANKLIN REED opened the door to the First Company's barrack. He stood for a moment, his shadow spilling from the doorway. He watched the quiet breathing of the men and women under his command. The action briefing was still a few hours away, but Reed wanted his team to be the first there. He sure as shit wouldn't let a marine recon unit beat him to the punch.

He activated the lights. Groans from a hundred soldiers filled the room. He smiled. One of the best parts of company command was not being in those bunks when it was time to wake up.

Reed started down the walkway. "First Company, rise and shine. Is it a beautiful day for a drop? A beautiful day for my rangers to get some!"

A blurry-eyed corporal from second platoon named Dean Harper tried covering his eyes. "Jesus, Cap. We're up already. The light's bad enough. Leave the sermon at the door."

Lieutenant Melissa Jade sat up, rubbing her head. "Yeah, Cap, this ain't even Sunday."

Private Walsh from Third Platoon chimed in. "This isn't the 'some' I had in mind."

Reed turned around, trying to hide a thin smile. "Is that so, maggots? Glad you're awake enough to find your funny bones. If you were marines, I'd give you time to wake up and get ready, but you're rangers. Rangers are always ready. Ain't that right, Jade?"

The lieutenant nodded, rubbing the back of her neck as she stretched.

Reed's smile broadened. "PT in five minutes. How's that for a sermon, Harper?"

There was another wave of groans. A couple of people tossed pillows at the corporal. Reed couldn't blame them. The Seventh had just rotated back home for leave. Two months of well-deserved rest before shipping back off to some shitty little base he'd never heard of for another year. They'd had boots on the ground for less than twenty-four hours when the recall orders hit.

Harper was supposed to be getting married. Jade was excited to spend time with her twins for the first time since the end of her maternity leave. Reed didn't want to know what Walsh had planned for leave. The kid was crazy, could drink whole towns dry.

There were a hundred stories like this throughout the company. Reed hadn't even finished his debriefing. Hadn't seen his son Charlie or his wife.

Or his bed.

One of the side effects of being a ranger. There was no such thing as work-life balance. His family was always second. It was the cost of being among the most elite soldiers in the Alliance, cramming a personal life into small snippets of time.

Why the hell the command needed *his* rangers for a war exercise on an industrial shithole like New Utica was beyond him. As good as the Seventh was, they were worn out. The Legion must have the heavy brass worried.

Who didn't they worry?

Reed personally knew officers who'd been killed in those cowardly raids. They'd hit the ranger detachments especially hard. Fuckers. Anyone willing to slaughter their own people in cold blood was beyond evil. Beyond cowards. They deserved no mercy. He didn't care what they wanted, or what political game was being played. He didn't care about the so-called 'tenement' conditions on which the news was focusing. The Legion had murdered good people. Terrorism like that was the act of cowards.

Reed took a breath, watching his troops.

He had to stay focused on the now. He'd get his chance to square things with the Legion. Right now, his company had to outscore his peers. He was close to promotion, maybe a battalion of his own. He'd finally be able to bring his wife and son to live with him on base.

Grab a little of the life he'd put off.

Reed started towards the barracks door. "Sergeants, give me four miles. Just enough fun to get their blood pumping. Then get them chow. Platoon leaders, meet me in the mess in five. Briefing after. Time to go to work."

Several people started barking orders, their voices disappearing into the noise.

Reed left the barracks, starting towards the officers' mess. It was

time to find out what kind of training had robbed him of his Charlie
fix.

––––––

Lieutenant Patrick Baxter
Hercules *Officer's Mess*
10th *Recon Marines* 2nd *Company,* 5th *Platoon*
14 *hours to planet fall*

LIEUTENANT PATRICK BAXTER watched a group of Rangers
shuffle into the officer's mess. He smiled. Rangers, always late to the
party. He took a deep drink of his coffee, the hot liquid perking up his
taste buds. He hoped the caffeine would have the same effect on
his body.

He wasn't counting on it.

The few weeks since their last drop were a blur. The majority of
his troops were fresh out of basic, replacements for promotions, trans-
fers, and KIAs. The Tenth Recon Marines were always in the shit.
They'd seen more action during the past few years than most, and
combat always came with a cost.

The war with the Milipa might be a cold one, but that didn't
seem to stem the killing. There always seemed to be a border area
with uninvited guests or a moon in need of surveillance equipment.
This was only Baxter's second tour, and he already couldn't
remember all the missions he hadn't been a part of.

Officially, that is.

This training drop had that same stink to it.

His platoon had been assigned by General Polis to load the transports prior to leaving orbit. In his experience, the only time a single
platoon loaded supplies was for classified operations. Fewer people
involved left a smaller chance of exposure. Plus, he'd never have
loaded that much ammunition for a training drop. Bullets cost money,
and money was the blood of politics. They never wasted money.

Baxter looked up, watching another stream of young army officers push through the door. This one wouldn't be easy, even if it really was training. The regulars were tired, especially after that shit on Holistad. The replacements were excited and nervous, driven to get into the fight. Baxter couldn't even rely on his sergeant, a transfer he hadn't gotten to know yet.

Lieutenant Johnathan Erga sat down next to him. He was a tall, lanky man with splotchy, sunburnt skin. The sun never seemed to agree with the man. He'd burn through armor, hats, and sunscreen. Next to white in the dictionary, it said, "See J. Erga."

Erga plopped his tray on the table with a clatter. "First as always, Patty. Do you ever sleep?"

Baxter took another sip of coffee. "No."

Captain Lauren Divina looked up from across the table. "Maybe you're always late, Erga. Lord knows your team can't ever hit their marks."

Baxter tied not to laugh, but the hot coffee had already gone up his nose, making him sputter. "He still beat the rangers, Cap!"

She frowned. "Who didn't?"

Erga pointed to the line. "The army."

Divina was the man's polar opposite, an officer on the fast track obsessed with her own image. She was short, well built, and way too prim and proper to be a marine. Since her promotion to company commander, she had been riding everyone's ass, especially Erga's.

Rumor had it they'd been an item in basic, but it had ended badly. The last drop hadn't helped. Erga's heavy weapon platoon had been surrounded by Milipa "pirates". Pirates, of course, referring to Milipa regulars their government swore did not exist. The bastards had forced Erga's platoon to pull back. Without Erga's howitzers, heavy machine guns, and mortars, Divina's company and Baxter's platoon had got cut up. Divina couldn't let something like that go easily — if at all.

Divina swallowed, refilling her fork with grits. "I bet even the army doesn't make it a habit to run away and hide."

Erga went red. "Lay off. Lotta guys died in that drop. You know full well—"

She dropped her fork, pounding the table. "Those were my soldiers, Lieutenant. We needed your heavy weapons. If your excuse for troops had held their ground, mine would still be here."

Baxter tensed. "Captain, that's wasn't John's fault. How the fuck could he have known those damn apes had flattened Fifth Platoon?"

Divina turned on him. "Was I asking you, Lieutenant?"

He held her gaze for a moment, not willing to further fuel her unwarranted anger. Erga wasn't moving, either. Based on the sound, the people at several nearby tables had stopped talking and were now watching the exchange. Baxter wasn't the high spit-and-polish officer Divina was, but even he knew this wasn't the place to make a scene.

Baxter purposefully took another sip of coffee, carefully lowering his tone. "I was in that shit storm with you. Don't forget that. It's the past. Focus on the next fight."

"Well said, Lieutenant. May I have a word, Lauren?"

The voice of Major Eli Stone made Baxter jump. Stone was a tough, hard-nosed leader who looked the part. Baxter considered himself fit, but he certainly wouldn't have picked a fight with the much older man.

Divina bolted up, her face white. "Yes, sir."

Baxter followed them with his eyes until they left the room, glad he wasn't in her shoes.

Erga took the first bite of his food. "Thanks, Patty."

He took the last sip of his coffee. "Don't thank me, brotha. She was out of line, but you weren't in that fight."

Erga swallowed. "No shit. I wanted to be. I kept hearing the calls, but if I had stayed put, I wouldn't be here to discuss it. I can only apologize so much."

Baxter shook his head, pushing up from the table. "The only apology that counts in this business is doing better the next time."

Captain Ursa Blomb
Hercules Officer's Mess
4ᵗʰ Infantry Division, 6ᵗʰ Regiment, 8ᵗʰ Company.
13 hours to planet fall

CAPTAIN URSA BLOMB sidled up to the chow line, narrowly missing two recon marines exiting the mess hall.

Damn special forces. Competitive, gruff, and always so edgy. Reminded Blomb of his thirteen-year-old sister. Never knew how to take advantage of good rack time. Rangers were the worst. Always running their mouths. Carrying on about their damn field guides and marksmanship.

Recon marines weren't much better. If he had to listen to one more recon marine go on about being the tip of the spear, he'd vomit. Regular marines weren't bad. He understood them. They'd get down in the blood and the mud with the best of them.

It's not that recon marines and rangers couldn't get down and dirty. Break some noses. In fact, he'd give his left nut to get his company functioning with half their skills. Blomb had gone through ranger training, but couldn't stand the attitudes. The army was the backbone of the fight. It took more than hiking and drop pod strikes to win wars.

He moved mechanically forward, bumping into a lieutenant he didn't know. He nodded his apology.

Blomb had to admit, those assholes had one thing right. They avoided these god damn lines. He glanced up at the clock. 0815. He only had forty-five minutes to eat and get up to the briefing.

The man behind him, a lieutenant, laughed. "I just did the same thing. Forty-five minutes isn't much for a hot meal."

He turned. The man was huge, at least a foot above his head and built like a tank. He had a long black beard and tattoos on every visible inch of skin. He held out his hand.

Blomb took it. "Ursa Blomb. No, it isn't. Maybe our last hot one for a while."

The man smiled. "Harlan Landro. Any word on what we are doing here?"

He shook a head. "Not a clue. Lotta special forces."

"That's for dead sure. This shit better be important. I want to be busting some goddamn Legion skulls. Got my furlough home denied. My wife's probably having our first baby right now."

Blomb picked up a tray. "Congratulations. I haven't managed to find a wife yet. Not that I've been looking, mind you. I'm happy with the quiet."

Landro slapped his back. "I get you there. Love my wife, but God damn, she ain't quiet. Sometimes I think I joined up for something quieter."

Blomb grabbed some cornbread, letting the servers pile his plate with whatever fit. "You must be confused. Gunfire isn't quiet."

"Quieter than her hollering." Landro moved in front of him, pointing to a spot in the back of the room.

They crossed the room, and slid down next to two medics. The Sixth hadn't brought their medical company. It was nice to see that at least one unit was available if someone hurt themselves. Every time the brass left medics out of the training exercises, something bad happened.

"Landy, who's the brass?" The first medic asked, his sleek black hair matching his narrow face and beady black eyes.

"That's not a major, asshole. He's a captain," the second, much shorter medic said. He had an oval face, with unusually large eyes, a tiny nose, and massive lips.

Landro rolled his eyes. "Guys, this here's Blomb. This is Corporal Marc Masters and Private Derek Blackburn. You can call 'em Snake and Spud. Before you blame them on me, I want you to know they're from the First. This is our third mission in a row with these fucking characters. Got to know them when we played in the shit."

Blomb took a bite of what he accepted as potatoes. "Pleasure."

Landro's milk carton looked small in his big hands. "Don't let their big mouths fool you. These two are top-notch medics. Last hoedown, my platoon got caught in a crossfire. Nasty shit. These two lug heads were right in the thick of it, pulling people out of goddamn no man's land."

Snake twisted his lips into a smile. "Don't forget it, bud. Me and Spud have the best record in the First."

Spud shook his head. "Not that you'll get to see us in action. People rarely need treatment during drills."

Snake hit Spud on the back. "Damn straight. Good thing, too. I am out, man! I'm not re-upping this time. I have a job lined up in a real hospital. No more blood, no more mud. No more shredded friends and cold meals."

Spud swung back. "Bull. You said that last time."

Blomb put down his spoon. "Don't know if I am with you there. Army's always been my home. Granted, I don't have skills like yours. I'd end up building tanks or consulting in some jackass office. I am here to stay, as long as my body doesn't fail me."

Landro tossed aside his milk carton. "Spud's all sad. You'd think he was the one missing his first child's birth."

Spud pursed his lips. "Worse. I already missed three of those. Now I'll have to get through another two years without this goddamn asshole." He pointed at Snake. "I am already getting, 'Spud, how you going to do your thing without your wife? Spud, who's cutting the umbilical? Spud, are you ready for you snakendectomy?' Buncha dicks."

Blomb laughed. "Two years will go fast. The wounded will keep you focused, busy."

Spud looked down. "I know."

The table fell silent.

Blomb checked the clock. Ten minutes. The only thing worse than remembering fallen friends was meetings.

Lieutenant Derek Hiltabrand

Hercules Lower Cargo Bay
10th Recon Marines 2nd Company, 3rd platoon.
12 hours prior to planet fall

LIEUTENANT DEREK HILTABRAND slid into the seat next to his platoon Sergeant, Marcus Oren, his lungs aching. It had been a bad decision to join in PT with the troops, but they were antsy, and he wanted to help ease them. He imagined he looked like crap. The look on the face of his CO, Holland Rayland, confirmed it.

His cheeks grew hot.

Oren smiled at him. "Glad you could make it."

Oren was a hard-charging old goat. Gray-haired, scarred, and covered in facial hair. He was tough as nails and hell on the enemy. Hiltabrand was happy to have him as his sergeant. The man knew his craft.

Hiltabrand ran his gaze around the room, avoiding Rayland's stare. This was a typical navy cargo hold. Lifts and straddle stackers filled one corner. Several offline androids and gun dogs lined the far right wall. Directly in front of the officers, covering the bay door, was a platform, podium, and holo-projector. He could see Major Stone and Colonel Snider on stage conversing with an officer he'd never seen. Presumably, this was General Polis, leader of this excursion. The room was filled to the brim with chairs, each with its own chattering recon marine officer.

The lights dimmed. Hiltabrand let his focus fall back to the platform.

Colonel Snider shook his head and moved to the podium. "Good morning, marines. Welcome to New Utica. Before we begin, I want you to know the information in this briefing is top secret. It is not to be repeated to anyone outside the expeditionary force. General Polis, Commander of the Fourth Infantry Division, will brief you on the situation. Please appeal to the better parts of your nature, and treat him with respect. General."

There was a brief chorus of laughter as the general walked to the stage.

Hiltabrand's heart leaped. Classified meant combat drop, and he was aching for a good fight.

Polis waved for silence. "Good morning. We have a situation that will benefit from your skills."

Hiltabrand joined his colleagues in shouting, "Oorah!"

Polis smiled. "Oorah indeed. The Legion has made its first move against a civilian population. Below us, a Legion strike force has landed. Our best intelligence suggests they are here to capture high-priority targets. One specific target would give them access to a large sum of money and put the Parliament in a position where they may be forced to negotiate."

An image of a man popped up on the screen. Hiltabrand recognized him immediately from the news. The stylish tousled hair that was supposed to look unaffected. The thin mustache and goatee surrounding a perfect, bleached smile.

Archibald Cross

"Our mission is simple," Polis was saying. "Extract this man and deal these assholes a blow they won't forget. Tomorrow you will drop, supported by army landers carrying AA tankettes and McGee Armored vehicles. Your task will be to take and hold the five bridges connecting a series of small islands leading from Cross's facility to the region's only spaceport."

Oren leaned over. "Bridges are never easy. Lots of blood for minimal gains."

Hiltabrand nodded. He'd only taken a bridge in training, but it had sucked, trying to get down a natural funnel while a dug-in enemy played pop goes the marine with their helmets.

"The McGees will be armed with machine guns to help suppress and push back any opposition," Polis continued. "The ranger battalion, along with three regiments of infantry, will take and hold the spaceport. With that objective in our hands, we will move armor up the road, crossing the now secured bridges and picking up Cross.

From this point, all elements will fall back to the spaceport and hold it until retrieval."

"Wait for retrieval?" Captain David Paxton, a tall company commander in the first row, yelled. "The navy isn't sticking around?"

Hiltabrand rolled his eyes. Golden boy Paxton had gained his platoon at the same time he had and somehow always received the best assignments. Paxton's platoon led every assault. If Hiltabrand had half the opportunities, he would have made captain, too. It didn't matter. Hiltabrand would get a company, no matter what it took. Maybe this operation would be his chance.

The worst part was Hiltabrand couldn't hate Paxton. The dickhead was genuinely nice. His wife was nice, his dogs were nice, even his goddamn toddler was nice.

General Polis leaned into the podium. "That's correct. The enemy has too many ships in orbit. This is a strike mission. In and out. We aren't here to coordinate with the territorial forces or push the Legion off the planet. The time for that will come later. All we need to do is give the Alliance a W and get Cross out."

Colonel Snider clapped his hands, walking to the podium. "Oorah. That's right, *mis amigos*. The Tenth Recon Marines get to introduce the Legion to the wonderful shit-filled taste of defeat. We have twelve hours for drop prep and ammunition loading. Company leaders, we have command pads available. Please see me after. I will expect this information downloaded and digested in three hours. Time to go to work."

The room burst into discussion as the meeting broke up.

Hiltabrand watched Rayland stand and walk towards Snider. He couldn't help but respect the captain. He was everything Hiltabrand should be, everything he wanted to be. A company commander, a hero, a dedicated leader. Rayland always had a story to go along with his pits and scars. He seemed invincible, and Hiltabrand was determined to learn as much as he could from him.

Oren tapped his shoulder. "Lieutenant, lots to do. Let's get to it!"

CHAPTER THREE

Lt. Colonel Bradly Anderson
Hercules Central Landing Bay
Fifth Armored Corps Detachment
6 hours to planet fall

Lt. Colonel Bradley Anderson watched the final McGee armored vehicle back up the Banshee's loading ramp. Its driver, Captain Beliard, commander of the McGee detachment, and two of the Banshee's crew jumped down. They began securing the vehicle to the deck, strapping down each one of its thick tires. Beliard was a tough guy, despite his short stature. He was an exceptional amour commander. He should have his own Ramsey, but no one in Fifth Corp had the ability to run a McGee column like Beliard.

Anderson couldn't help but grin. The team's speed was impressive, a testament to why anti-gravity crap would never make it into the military. That kind of tech could never compensate for the increased maintenance time.

Too fragile.

The fancier tech got, the more easily it broke. It couldn't take the abuse that good, old-fashioned equipment could. It didn't matter in the civilian sector. Technology kept improving and growing faster than Anderson was comfortable with, but civilian transports didn't need to be rated for torpedo impacts.

Anderson checked off the McGees on his pad. All ten locked down on the Banshee landing craft. It would be easier if this were a god-damned, stand-up fight. There would be fewer variables to consider.

He rubbed the back of his neck, placing his pad down beside him. The time crunch didn't help. He had forty minutes at best until this bay would be given over to the Army.

He studied the nearest enormous landing craft, trying to picture the images the drones had captured of the narrow landing zones they were heading for. Anderson adjusted his chest plate, wishing he'd requested something smaller. Normally, they used different birds to land. Able to accommodate two platoons with equipment, Banshees were great for landing troops on friendly installations, but maneuvered like tubs. Thank goodness they weren't headed into a hot landing.

Polis and Duncan had agreed to use the behemoths because of the landing window. It was small, ten, maybe twelve minutes round-trip. Fortunately, the *Hercules* was one of the few dropships large enough to carry enough Banshees to land the entire force, tanks included. She was old, built for planetary assaults during the Old Empire period, when the forces of the Earth were expanding in all directions

Anderson picked back up his pad, running his eyes over the inventory of the remaining vehicles. Most of the Henshaw AAs were already on board. The two Jacksons and ten Renard AP-4s were up next. Their crews were slowly finishing the pre-landing checklists.

Choosing what to bring had been difficult, the weight, size, and capabilities of each asset at odds with various aspects of the mission. Anderson had settled mainly on tankettes. Their smaller size and specialized abilities would give him maximum control if shit hit the fan.

Since the Kensington survivors hadn't reported many anti-tank weapons, heavy armor wouldn't be missed. They also hadn't reported any armor, so odds were the landing force wouldn't require the services of many battle tanks. This was going to be a drop and shop, not a knockdown, drag-out fight. Anderson needed speed and flexibility. This would be about suppressing massed infantry.

Poorly organized infantry.

He looked up. The silhouettes of the turrets of two Ramseys and two Whitmans loomed over the smaller vehicles. The Legion may not have armor, but Andersen wanted some insurance against the unknown. Anyone watching these monsters coming down the road would think twice about engaging them without serious backup.

The other issue he had to overcome with the banshees was their lack of dedicated tank compartments. He had to carefully balance the loads. He had considered bringing dedicated vehicle landers, but without air superiority or at least some fighter cover, they would be easy to pick out and easier to shoot down. Those tubs made the Banshees look like speed demons.

The Renards would be easy to squeeze in. Classified as anti-infantry tanks, their lack of a turret and fixed machine guns made them one of the smallest tankettes in his arsenal. They'd be crucial for maintaining defensive perimeters, especially in the tight spaces between buildings.

The Wittmans, lovingly named *Led Slinger* and *Howler* by their crews, where also anti-infantry tanks, built to bring maximum death to enemy soldiers. Their large size would hamper them in tight urban spaces and leave them vulnerable to flanking maneuvers.

Anderson stenciled in a few notes onto his command pad, sending the corresponding commands.

He frowned.

The barrels of the Jackson tanks were too damn long and would need to be locked down. Assaulting a planet called for big guns to punch through planetary defenses or other hard points. The 105-mm projectile the Jacksons threw was perfect. Normally meant for armored vehicles, they'd eat the kinds of defenses they could expect on New Utica for breakfast.

He sent another group of commands through.

Daryl's reply came back almost instantly over the intercom. "Lieutenants Milo and Agathorn to the landing bay for loading."

It had been difficult narrowing down the Jackson crews for this one. The Jacksons were easy to use, durable, cheap, and perfectly suited for officers and crews fresh from the Royal Armor Academy. Nothing seasoned greenhorns more than a few years dropping lead from behind the gun of a Jackson. The downside was the Army had figured that out, too — when you needed a Jackson for a mission like this, most of the crews were fresh.

Anderson had settled on Milo and Agathorn because of their crews. Milo had less than forty hours of drive time, but she had shown excellent aptitude so far. The *Striker's* seasoned crew counterbalanced her lack of experience. They were top notch, long-term tankers.

Agathorn was different, a true leader. He was the senior Jackson column commander for Fifth Corps. The man was due for a promotion, either to a Renard or possibly a Wittman. His six years with *Cannibal* had produced outstanding crews. This drop, however, would be this crew's first mission together. Agathorn would have to work fast to get them firing on all cylinders.

The two officers trotted down the stairs, both looking winded. Agathorn's black, untidy hair, and short stature were easy to spot at a distance. Milo, on the other hand, was one of the taller women in the Fifth. Her Amazonian good looks, strength, and unmatched poker ability had already earned her a reputation. Working with Agathorn would do wonders for her. If she continued to perform like she had, she could easily take over Agathorn's column one day.

He pointed to Bay Three. "Agathorn, help Milo get Striker loaded up, then get Cannibal loaded into Bay Six."

They nodded, then sprinted over to *Striker* without saying a word.

The last big hurdle would be the two Ramsey IIs. Ramseys were the biggest, meanest main battle tanks built by any army. These two, named *Bloodhound* and *Big Dawg,* were outfitted for use against infantry. The turrets had the standard anti-aircraft side mounts and main 178-mm cannon. However, the side sponsons had been switched out, trading the normal 105-mm guns for double-stacked .30-caliber machine guns.

The Legion would need massive firepower to deal with a Ramsey. None of the small arms the Legion had been known to use so far would pose a threat to them. Anderson had seen Milipa regulars break and run at the sight of one of these war machines approaching. Fear was a powerful weapon. Hopefully, they would even the odds if the landing force was outnumbered.

This mission was as much about intimidation as it was saving this jackass Cross. The Legion needed to know what fucking with the Alliance military meant. They had to show these bastards that beating a few tired garrisons caught off-guard meant nothing. Anderson had no clue what the Legion truly stood for, but the last thing humanity needed was an all-out civil war. Even if the government could hide it from the Milipa — and that was doubtful — the Alliance's infrastructure would be smashed and its populations gutted if the conflict spread.

If they couldn't hide it, the Milipa would descend upon the Alliance and rip it apart. There was no way the Alliance had enough ships and materials to fight back against both the Milipa and the Legion.

Anderson typed in the final commands, assigning both the remaining Renards and Ramseys to appropriate vessels.

There was very little time left.

The infantry platoons were already beginning to shuffle into the bay. He could hear the hydraulics of the marines' drop pods from the deck above. General Polis and Colonel Snider appeared at the room's far entrance.

The party was on.

The room was getting louder as the engines of the final tanks and the voices of soldiers filled the bay. Anderson turned off his tablet and crossed the room towards the two leaders. Polis caught sight of him and turned to meet him.

General Polis held out his hand. "Colonel, are your tanks stowed and ready?"

Anderson took it, nodded. "Last few are bedding down now. I'm worried about how narrow our landing zones are."

Snider tightened his helmet strap. "I'm more worried about flak, or armor. I don't believe for ten hot seconds they don't have something nasty waiting for us."

The hairs on the back of Anderson's neck prickled. "Agreed. Did you see the number of fucking ships out there? I don't care what Command says. We should see some action on the surface. The Verdun didn't face that many ships. If you have the resources to build that many destroyers without anyone noticing, tanks aren't difficult."

Polis rubbed his chin. "Watch yourselves down there. No one man is worth risking so many lives. I can't believe the majority of the Admiralty is behind this."

Snider smiled. "I was thinking the same damn thing. This stinks of military intelligence. That fuck Tramo is pulling some political strings. Or he's lying to get Young's buy-in."

Polis nodded. "Orders are orders. We will unravel this mess, but we can't accomplish that here. Let's wipe the floor with these bastards and get back home. Then I can go digging."

Snider checked his pistol. "Hopefully. I just can't get past the silence from the governor's mansion. We may be paying for that ticket home with body bags. Ours."

Polis frowned. "Gentleman, I'll see you on the ground."

Anderson turned, walking towards his designated ship. He took a breath. In less than an hour, they would be knee-deep in whatever bloody trap the Legion had planned for them. Right now, all he could do was hope Snider was wrong about the price of returning home.

———

Captain Jordan Duncan
Bridge of RAS Hercules

"ACTION STATIONS, all hands to action stations." Daryl's voice was barely audible over the bridge's klaxons.

Fifty-two to five.

How the hell was he going to do this?

Captain Duncan keyed in several commands. How would the enemy react? Once the Alliance ships fired their engines and pulled clear of the moon, the Legion vessels would have five to six minutes to react. The enemy fleet was still spread out and twenty of them, mainly cruisers, were powered down. What he couldn't tell was how well armed they were until either the drones got closer or those shit-heads opened fire.

He didn't have many ships to play with. They had to defend the landers as well as the *Hercules* once she was in low orbit.

The first thing he'd learned in training was to never engage a better-armed opponent from low orbit. The gravity of the planet boosted the kinetic energy of incoming ordnance, making them hit harder and nullifying defensive systems. The defenders weapons had to fight gravity, slowing them down and making them easier to deflect. As if that wasn't bad enough, every green cadet knew that a ship farther down in a planet's gravity bowl had a bear of a time maneuvering.

All-in-all, the low orbit needed to drop his payload was the worst place he could be in this kind of situation.

Duncan had no room for error. "Helm, flank speed. Launch fighters and drones."

He sent the commands through to the escorts, which began to

accelerate at a steep angle, the *Montalban* at the tip of a diamond formation. The *Hercules* was tucked in the center, allowing the faster, more maneuverable escorts to screen her.

The *Hercules* rocked as the Cerberus fighters and combat drones fired clear of her hull. Duncan watched the first enemy ships start to move, surging towards the tight Alliance formation. The *Tupu* and *Simcoe* began to fire at maximum range. The enemy ships broke formation, moving out of the way of the destroyers' barrage.

Duncan almost laughed. These idiots were more inexperienced than he thought. Completely uncoordinated, each acting independently. More than half were still not online. The more of these fucks he could kill while they were still dark, the easier it would be to disembark the troops.

Thank God for idiots.

Duncan used his finger to trace in attack trajectories for the drones on his console. He ordered the *Horizon* and *Montalban* to begin firing. If the nearest enemy ships just changed course, he'd have them dead to rights.

The two fleets were still several minutes out from reaching effective firing range, but the overexcited Legion ships were shooting full force, their shells detonating harmlessly as the defensive systems responded. Duncan angled his ships up slightly, exposing the formation's dorsal side.

The harmless fire from the *Horizon* and *Montalban* worked. The Legion forces broke to the side, avoiding the perceived threat. They angled upwards, chasing after the Alliance formation.

The combat drones shifted to fly downwards.

The incoming Legion ships increased speed.

Duncan issued the order for the other ships to steepen the climb. "Helmsman Gordo, slow us five percent. Let these fuckers close the gap."

He could feel Connelly's eyes on the back of his neck. He took a deep breath, running the numbers through his head quickly. He plugged in his calculations, letting Daryl run it through several simulations. This had to be timed perfectly before the dispersed enemy formed a single formation.

Duncan shifted in his chair.

The drones had cleared the trailing edge of the Legion's frantic mob. His eyes didn't waver from the timer icon, the seconds stretching one into another. For this maneuver to work they could't wait much longer.

The icon went green.

He sent the commands through to the other ships.

Fifty seconds.

The first of the drones turned sharply upwards. Their engines fired, hitting full power. They separated into five formations of twenty drones, each in columns of two. The first formation arched sharply, aiming directly at five of the nearest, cruisers, which were slowly powering up.

Fifteen seconds.

The drones opened fire at point-blank range. Their torpedoes and five-inch shells shredded the ships' thin armor. The drones tore past their targets, rotating for maximum time on target. One of the cruisers imploded while another buckled, flames pouring from cracks in its center. The final three took countless hits, vibrating as secondary explosions and chunks of armor plating flew into space.

Duncan smacked the arm of his chair.

Cheering filled the room.

Based on the readings the drones were transmitting, none of those ships would be capable of fighting. They were drifting, their partially heated power plants no longer functioning.

He tore his eyes from the drones. "Helm, initiate Maneuver 73-2."

The *Hercules* banked, metal straining as the engines fired, turning her mass away from the planet. The enemy tried to match their maneuvers, increasing speed to catch up. The Legion ships aimed right at the re-exposed dorsal sections of the Alliance formation.

At the last second, Duncan's ships reversed, rotating their main weapons towards the nearest enemy ships. The Legion destroyers tore by, weapons firing in front of the breaking Alliance warships.

Duncan hit his headset. "Fire at will."

Hercules shook several times as the main guns fired in rapid succession. Four Legion ships burst as shape charges ripped into their sides, several more taking serious damage as they ran full speed into the debris field.

Duncan's formation blasted back to full speed. His stomach turned, his body pressed into the chair as the *Hercules* swung back towards New Utica.

Eight more of the enemy ships were on fire from the drones' continued attacks. Two more vessels split apart, atmosphere dispersing in waves from their broken hulks. Unfortunately, the enemy's shock had worn off, and they had begun firing. Several drones were showing catastrophic damage, falling out of formation.

Combat drones were capable craft but relied on nearby friendly ships to draw enemy fire. The Royal Navy was built to fight defensive battles, draw the enemy to the waiting lasers of the capital ships.

A wave of surviving destroyers had come together, braking hard. They were banking, their trajectory indicating his detachment was their target. At these speeds, they had about five minutes before they would make contact again.

Assuming they held off the ships the drones hadn't shredded.

Duncan watched the first of the cruisers turn towards them, its guns actively tracking and firing at the shrinking drone formations. He plotted several courses, watching the simulations play out. The computer kept predicting the same result. That many cruisers would overpower them.

He couldn't trust the computer. His gut told him their inexperience would give him an edge the machine couldn't predict. The simulations were meant to give him an edge, but they assumed a tactically sound enemy. An enemy aware of their ships' capabilities.

An enemy like the Milipa.

This speed may give him an advantage. The destroyer captains had acted alone, failing to anticipate the actions of the Alliance formation. If the cruisers followed suit, Duncan would have a chance.

He began writing commands. "Connelly, make preparations for landing."

"Aye, sir."

Duncan pushed his orders through, overriding the warnings. "Execute first turn now."

The *Hercules* turned left, the *Tupu* and *Simcoe* following. They aimed directly at the nearest cruiser, accelerating again. The Cerberus fighters moved to the front of the formation, screening it from enemy fire.

The *Montalban* and *Horizon* made directly for the planet on a landing trajectory. The *Montalban* was almost as old as the *Hercules* and a good deal larger than a modern cruiser. He hoped they would think she was the second dropship.

The *Hercules*'s formation turned toward its slowly moving target, which was firing its thrusters, pushing itself to starboard. Its main guns swiveled around, firing accurate salvos towards the *Tupu*. The Cerberus fighters went to work, turrets firing on the incoming shells.

Detonations signaled their success.

Hercules's guns fired again. Shells struck the cruiser's sides, shape charges tearing deep into its armor. The Legion cruiser shook, spinning out of control. The *Simcoe*'s rounds followed. The cruiser vibrated momentarily before exploding, gasses and fire spitting into space.

Duncan pumped his fist. "Execute 73-3. Fire at will."

The *Hercules* turned again, aiming at two, now fully mobile, cruisers. The small number of remaining drones converged on the accelerating enemies. Some of the drones burst as the cruiser's weapons turned to engage them, but the others fired, slowing their target with the intensity of their barrage.

The *Tupu* and *Simcoe* fired simultaneously at the closest ship, the one to starboard, vaporizing it. The *Hercules* gunners clipped the remaining target's engines as it turned rapidly down toward the planet.

Damn.

The ship was delisting, but intact. Its cannons returned fire, the close range allowing the shells to slip past the *Tupu's* ordinance deflector. The *Tupu* shuddered, slowed as flames spurted from her engine mounts, though her armor absorbed most of the impact.

Duncan pulled up the *Tupu,* damage reports spilling across the screen. Based on how the enemy rounds had punched through the *Tupu's* armor, it was clear they had penetrator warheads. He hadn't expected that kind of firepower. The *Tupu's* landing and drone bays were damaged, but still functional, and her engine mounts were cracked, limiting her translight capabilities.

A lucky shot for amateurs.

How the fuck had these bastards built so many ships?

The *Hercules'* guns spun around, firing. The cruiser took another set of direct hits. armor failed, and the ship's power plant detonated, debris spraying out in a cloud from the explosion. The *Hercules* couldn't afford more hits like that before they entered orbit. Duncan would need as much firepower as possible to ensure his payload landed.

So far, the Legion was falling for his ploy. The majority of their ships were chasing straight after the *Montalban* and *Horizon,* while the remaining enemy ships were still several minutes behind. The Alliance ships had taken only superficial damage and were only moments from the planet's atmosphere.

Time to spring the trap.

Duncan checked his harness. "73-4 now. Connelly all guns move down full."

The *Hercules* turned sharply down, lining up behind the cluster of enemy vessels. The *Montalban* and *Horizon* entered New Utica's atmosphere, turning their landing bays to face the surface.

The mass of enemy ships seemed to go crazy, firing without any control or coordination, speeding in and out of each other's firing arcs. Duncan didn't know how they weren't hitting each other.

The taste of blood was in the water.

The atmosphere burned as the two Alliance ships' defensive weapons filled the air with flak. He didn't need a computer to tell him it wouldn't be long before his forces were overwhelmed. The enemy cruisers crossed onto the outer edges of the atmosphere, cutting their engines, turning to maximize their firing angle. They had taken the bait, assumed the *Montalban* would be dropping troops.

Duncan clapped. "Now. Get our ships out of there."

He heard the voice of Ensign Ricky relaying his orders to the escorts.

The Alliance ships fired their engines, blasting to full speed, bouncing out of the atmosphere, their main weapons firing across their now stationary targets.

The motionless enemy ships took devastating hits, shells crashing through their armor and engines, chunks of Legion ships igniting as they fell towards the planet's surface. The *Horizon* and *Montalban* settled into a high orbit at a 45-degree angle to Duncan's formation.

This would be messy.

The *Simcoe*, *Tupu*, and *Hercules* opened fire, guns searing the high atmosphere with combined volleys. They had to do the maximum amount of damage in a short time. The two Alliance formations had their shocked enemy in a crossfire. Engines were the key. If the Legions ships couldn't move, they would no longer be a threat. Duncan gripped his armrests, counting down to the next maneuver.

The *Hercules* shook, cannons firing as quickly as the crews could load them. The distance between him and his enemies was shrinking as quickly as the element of surprise was fading. The computer indicated thirteen of the enemy ships destroyed or disabled. The rest were breaking in all directions, engines straining against the atmosphere, only a few remembering to return fire on their Alliance attackers.

Duncan doubled-checked the final command before sending it through. The *Hercules* hit the top layer of the atmosphere, bouncing as she pulled her nose up. The violent vibrations spun Duncan's head as his ship approached the drop zone, her flight path flattening out.

He let go of the armrest, keying his microphone on. "Captain Duncan to drop bay. Launch all landers and drop pods."

It wouldn't take long before the enemy regrouped. His escort ships had settled in above him, turning their weapons to cover him. Duncan switched screens. He needed to get the ground team as much data as possible, then search for the best way to escape the system alive.

Duncan typed in additional commands, repositioning the sensor drones into lower orbit, directing their scanners towards the surface.

Duncan's forces had done their part, gotten the ground forces safely to the drop zone. He was determined to give Polis's force the best shot at doing theirs.

Showing these bastards what true soldiers did to traitors.

Captain Franklin Reed
Aboard Banshee 124
7ᵗʰ Ranger Battalion, First Company
Planet fall

CAPTAIN FRANKLIN REED closed his eyes, trading the cool grey of the Banshee's interior for blackness. He gripped his straphanger, forcing himself to breathe. The bay rumbled as the lander's engines finished powering up. This was the worst part of the service. Combat drops. He could handle hundred-degree heat, untold miles of trekking up hills — both ways — and even the blood-chilling horrors of combat.

Drops, however, scared the shit out of him.

He was helpless, stuck holding on for dear life as the pilots fought to reach the ground. He couldn't affect anything, couldn't fight back, couldn't maintain control. Even knowing these fuckers didn't have anti-aircraft weapons couldn't shake the tightening lump in his chest.

The floor shook violently. It wasn't the Banshee's engines this time. The *Hercules* was taking fire. His stomach pushed bile into his throat. He forced his hands to stay tightly locked onto the handhold.

The pilot's voice broke through the screaming engines. "Five seconds to launch."

Reed felt momentarily weightless before slamming backward, the big lander pulling free from the deck, her engines firing. He rocked forward, his torso growing heavier and heavier. The Banshee had breached the lower atmosphere. New Utica's gravity was beginning to grip him.

He opened his eyes. "Rangers, we need a quick dispersal. First Platoon, secure the immediate area. Second Platoon, unhook the Renards."

There was a chorus of 'yes sirs' from his lieutenants, Scot and Philis, who relayed the orders back to their platoons. He was glad to have these two with him. They were good soldiers. Lifers like himself.

Battle-tested.

Reed turned on his helmet's radio. He had to make sure everyone heard this. "Our job is to take the spaceport. There are likely combatants mixed in with civilians. Check your fire. Strict rules of engagement apply. Do not fire unless you are being fired on."

The ship dropped as they angled sharply towards the surface. Reed's stomach turned again.

Philis leaned in. "What the hell are we expecting down there, sir? What aren't they telling us?"

Reed closed his eyes again. "You know what I know."

He laughed. "So, nothing. We could be riding into a motherfucking mess."

The lander jolted, banking to left. Reed's heart dropped, and his eyes popped opened. He fought the bile back down from his throat, heart thundering in his chest.

Reed recognized that sensation.

He glanced out the window, saw black clouds appearing all around the lander.

These bastards had AA batteries.

A lot of them.

CHAPTER FOUR

Tim Fival
Cross Spaceport
Legion Anti-Aircraft Battery Number Four

Tim Fival took a deep breath. He pressed his eyes against his binoculars, fixed on the incoming landers. He'd grown up in a slum no more than ten miles from here, watched ships landing at this spaceport the entirety of his life, watched the heavy loaders bring in materials for that fucker Cross as he built his hi-tech plant. Never had he seen anything like this outside of news broadcasts.

For just a moment, he understood how the Milipa felt.

Debris from the battle above hit the atmosphere, filling the air with streaks of flame. He'd watched one of the Legion cruisers explode before his eyes, replaced with an Alliance ship twice its size. As a child, he'd have been thrilled to see that.

Not now.

Fival swallowed the lump in his throat. His heart was pounding, hands shaking. The Supervisor was right. The Alliance would protect that bastard Cross at all costs. They wouldn't let him face justice.

All the promises of the last election had passed. It was bullshit. Lies. Pandering from politicians who cared only about money and the people who provided it. Nothing ever changed. Nothing ever would. Unless they forced it.

Unless *he* forced it.

He watched the warship open eight sets of bays on her bottom side. He started a stopwatch, timing the hundreds of gray-blue specks spilling into the air.

They reminded him of the albatrosses he'd seen on the nature channel. The ships' long narrow cockpits widened towards the back. The wings were long with two large engines on each. He could also make out several small gun ports on their sides.

The craft turned their noses downwards, vapor trails following them. They broke into distinct formations. The largest headed towards him.

It wouldn't be long now.

Bursts of flame appeared. The warship was taking fire.

Fival's heart leaped. Some of the Legion ships were still fighting. The Alliance hadn't gained complete control of the skies.

Another set of vapor trails streaked from both sides of the massive ship. Marine drop pods.

Had to be.

Supervisor Kline had warned them to expect this. Special forces. Elite marines and rangers, trained killers. They wouldn't hesitate to kill another human being. Fival wouldn't either. The Alliance had slaughtered the Legion freedom fighters at Kensington, and they would slaughter his friends here.

He had to be strong.

Fival dropped his binoculars and held down his mike. "Alpha Team, pop smoke. All guns, prepare to go weapons free on my command. Set fire to maximum effective ceilings."

He looked back up at the incoming landing craft. He didn't know how many people those behemoths represented. How many husbands and wives, sons and daughters he was about to kill. There was a pang in his chest.

Fival looked back at his team. There was no time for this. They'd tried the peaceful path. He had attended the rallies and naively voted for change, only to be met with disappointment again and again.

It was time to try another way. "All guns, fire."

The ground under his feet shook, the air splitting like thunder as the anti-aircraft guns opened fire. Fival coughed, dust and smoke filling the air. These weapons were crude, ancient. Not the state-of-the-art killing machines he had built for Cross his whole life.

The sky above him blackened with detonating flak shells. He saw one of the lead albatrosses, for lack of a better term, break apart, fire and metal debris hitting other albatrosses in its formation.

Fival's mouth spread into a smile.

Crude, but effective.

He was nothing to Cross, less than nothing to the politicians, but it didn't matter. He was a leader in the Legion, and he would make sure these bastards paid the price for the government's neglect.

Colonel Fox Snider
Aboard Banshee 13
10th Recon Marines
Planet fall

ANOTHER BURST of anti-aircraft fire shook Banshee 13.

Colonel Snider lurched forward, barely maintaining his footing. Alarms wailed from the cockpit. The panicked voices of the lander's crew audible. The AA batteries confirmed one thing: the Legion presence was heavy in the drop area. They had either completely taken the spaceport or were fortified nearby with their own cannons.

He frowned.

Young had to have known what they were facing. New Utica had a formidable territorial army. They couldn't have been defeated so quickly. And if they had—

It raised the stakes on the operation.

The lander jolted, and Snider's stomach churned. Acrid smoke filled the cabin.

They were taking hits.

Snider pushed himself back up. "Harris, Belvin, check the goddamn coms vehicle. Make sure it's locked down. I want no surprises."

The rangers had volunteered to land with the tanks. He should have let them. He'd be in his pod right now, in control of his own descent, not escorting the coms vehicle and several Henshaws to the surface He hated these death traps.

If the Legion had AA guns, Lord knew what else they had. The spaceport teams would need all the Rangers they could get.

The banshee banked left. Snider lost his balance and fell to the ground. He rolled uncontrollably to the left, smacking into the bulkhead.

He could hear screaming from the cockpit. Snider tried to push himself up, his shoulder aching in protest.

The collision alarm sounded.

Snider looked up, eyes resting on the porthole across from him. The Banshee next to them was on fire, smoking billowing from its cockpit. It was falling directly towards them. The pilot had turned, pushing the lander's nose down, trying to pick up speed to avoid the impact.

But there was nowhere to go.

They were surrounded by other landers streaking towards the surface. All the pilot could do was bank, speed up, and avoid running themselves into another ship, pray the burning wreck missed them.

It wasn't going to work.

The sound of shouting rose above the klaxon as the pilot dipped the nose, banking hard left, still trying to avoid the spiraling craft.

Snider looked up. Marines hung from their handholds above him, dangling like fish on hooks. Others had fallen with bone-shattering force.

Snider dragged himself along the Banshee's wall towards the parachutes. Adrenaline surged through his system, dulling the pain in his arms.

It wasn't fast enough.

He braced his legs against one of window ledges and pushed. He managed another several feet. He looked around for his helmet and its radio.

He couldn't find it.

Snider cupped his hands, trying to yell over the chaos. "We have to bail out. Parachutes. Get the bay door open."

They couldn't have much more than twenty seconds left.

Several more marines lost their grip and fell, bodies smacking against the coms vehicle with the sickening sound of breaking bone. The com vehicle moved.

Fuck.

Snider's heart thundered in his chest. He looked back towards the parachutes, willing himself to move. He reached out, pulling himself forward. He stretched his fingers out as far as he could, his hand clasping around the strap of the nearest chute.

He pulled it towards himself.

There was a dull creaking and grinding sound from above him. Metal on metal. He looked up, the first of the chains holding down the coms vehicle had snapped.

It was starting to slide.

He worked the buckle, fumbling the latch. His fingers were numb, refusing to press down on the release button.

Snider yelled, urging his fingers to move. "Fucking, goddamn, mother-fucking piece of—"

The buckle snapped into place.

It was too late. The coms vehicle tumbled, flattening the colonel as it ripped out of the Banshee's side. It tumbled through the air, smashing both of the left engines as it went. Banshee 13 spun sideways into a barrel roll, debris and cargo spewing from her open wound.

It fell for several seconds before detonating, smoke and burning debris all that remained of its crew and cargo.

Lt. Derek Hiltabrand
10th Marine Recon
Two Miles North of Alena Bridge
72 hours from evacuation

LT. HILTABRAND FELL FORWARD OUT of his drop pod. He gasped, breaking his fall with his hands. He'd fucked that up, touched down harder than he'd intended.

He shook his head, trying to clear his vision. He turned, pulling loose his Heinlein submachine gun. He scrambled forward, lunging for the tree his pod had cut in half. He pressed his back against the trunk.

They hadn't expected flak.

There was a good chance the enemy was dug in all along these causeways. He signaled his troops to cover, catching the eye of Sergeant Oren.

Where the hell were they?

His platoon was spread out along the side of a narrow, sunken road lined with old-growth forest. He didn't recognize it from the recon photos.

Damn it.

This was a bad spot to land and a worse one to defend. Too low. Too easy to hit from the raised banks on both sides. They had to get moving. Alena Bridge was nowhere in sight, but they couldn't have overshot their landing zone by more than a few miles. They hadn't been in the air very long, and he'd seen its massive steel form on the way down.

He switched his wristwatch on, activating his locator. It searched for signal, trying to get a read on their location.

Nothing.

Either Polis' command vehicle hadn't touched down yet, they were out of range, or...

Or worse.

He'd seen a lot of Banshees on fire on the way down.

Hiltabrand flipped the compass on his watch open. If he was correct, they'd come down somewhere north of the bridge. This road was on a north-south trajectory. If they followed it, they'd run right into the bridge.

And God knew how many enemies.

He leaned out, peering down the road. No sign of activity beyond his own marines. Several more pods had touched down nearby, doors popping off. He could see members from at least three of his four squads, including Sergeants Oren and Franklin.

Hiltabrand looked back in the woods, a small flash catching his eye. For a moment, he wondered what it was. A gunshot answered his question.

He tossed himself flat, just as the edge of the woods exploded. Uncoordinated fire tore across the marine line. One of the newly arrived pods sparked and smoked as gunfire ripped into its struggling occupant.

The woman inside stopped moving, dangling from her harness.

Son of a bitch!

Hiltabrand racked the bolt of his weapon, leaned out. He fired a tight burst up at the tree line. His attackers yelled, ducking out of the way of his inaccurate fire.

He tapped his radio on. "Tiger Three-Seven, Tiger Three-Six Actual. Move to the left. Keep in cover. Find us a way up that bank. Take Able and Baker Squads."

A second later, Oren's voice replied. "Tiger Three-Six, copy."

Fire rained down at Hiltabrand, kicked up dirt that sprinkled down on his pressure fatigues and helmet like rain. Their aim was worse than his.

Hiltabrand took a deep breath, pushing down his panic. This wasn't the Milipa or even the Frontin. These idiots were reacting to each burst of Alliance fire. They hadn't realized how strong their position was. He peered over his tree, searching the dark edge of the wood.

There.

A muzzle flash.

He fixed his gaze on that spot, aimed just below where he'd seen the flash. He squeezed the trigger. It barked once. Twice. Three times. Bursts of .45 rounds tore into the woods. A scream and the body of his enemy tumbling down the incline told him he'd hit.

Hiltabrand ducked back into cover, looking down his line. Most of his platoon was tucked in behind their pods. Bullets were striking everywhere, ricocheting off the pods, blasting holes into the dirt. Dust and debris shot up around each impact, filling the air.

One of his marines pitched backward, blood dripping from a gaping hole in the top of his helmet.

The enemy weren't accurate, but there were a fuck ton of them.

He tapped his radio again. "Warren, Monforte, frags. Kilwan, smoke on my orders. Where the hell is my machine gun?"

His radio crackled, and Corporal Gomez's voice responded. "About twenty feet to your right. I can't get to the RAR. Davidson's dead."

Hiltabrand turned. Sure enough, Davidson's body was lying in the open, his legs still moving. The RAR lay in the dust several feet from him. Gomez was tucked in behind a small pile of earth, huddling with her ammo drums, her rifle slung.

He growled. "Gomez, Scotts, Barllet, Dalair grenades now. Everyone else, covering fire."

Hiltabrand never took his eyes from the machine gun. Several explosions roared behind him. The distinct crack of his team's

Enfield rail rifles picked up. He jumped to his feet, stumbling as he got his balance. He ran crouched over, trying to keep himself low. Human voices whooping and hollering accompanied the sounds of the enemy rifles.

The buzzing and whining of bullets surrounded him. Hiltabrand reached down and grabbed the RAR with his right hand before sliding into cover next to Corporal Gomez, dragging the heavy weapon behind him. Gomez pulled open the ammo can and started feeding it into the weapon. Hiltabrand rolled over, pushing out the gun's bipod. He rested it just on top of the earthen rise Gomez had used for cover.

Hiltabrand could hear screaming, though he couldn't tell where it was coming from. The smoke was dissipating. Even with the machine gun, this wouldn't be easy.

He caught Gomez's eyes, she nodded. Hiltabrand pushed himself up onto the dirt, leveling the barrel at the woods in front of him. He fired short, controlled bursts. The woods erupted as he raked his weapon back and forth, branches and chunks of bark becoming shrapnel. He saw three, maybe four more bodies slide down the hill.

The drum ran dry.

The enemy fired at his position. Gomez screamed, falling backwards as a bullet caught the top of her shoulder. Hiltabrand grabbed her leg, pulling her back behind the embankment.

Oran's voice filled his helmet. "Tiger Three-Six, Tiger Three-Seven. In position. I picked up some of Third Platoon, too. We're coming in from the left rear. Check your fire."

Perfect.

Hiltabrand fed a fresh ammo drum and charged the bolt. "Tiger Three-Seven, move forward. I'll hit them with the RAR again. Get in behind them, and we'll get them in a crossfire. Franklin, eyes on me."

The sergeant looked over. Hiltabrand switched off his radio, using his hands to signal bayonets. The line drew their blades and fixed them to their rifles.

Hiltabrand saw Monforte and Warren pull two more grenades.

They yanked the pins and tossed them towards the top of the rise, in front of the Recon Marine position. The grenades detonated, flinging flame and debris in all directions. Two charred corpses collapsed, moving in an unnatural way as they rolled down the slope.

Hiltabrand opened fire. The machine gun shredded the trees and brush. The shadowy figures at the edge of the woods dropped backward.

Franklin stood, pulling a pistol from his belt. He waved, moving up the rise. The rest of Hiltabrand's platoon followed, disappearing deeper into the woods. Yelling, grunting, and screaming echoed from the woods. Hiltabrand dropped the RAR, reaching for his Heinlein. It wasn't there. He must have dropped it

Idiot.

Hiltabrand dashed towards his marines, drawing his pistol. He used his hand to help push himself up the slope faster. His heart pounded. Even with his pressure fatigues depressurized and his visor up, he was sweating. He pressed through the first set of trees, picking his way past the bodies littering the ground.

Something slammed into him, toppling him sideways. He rolled, kicking his opponent in the chest. A large, dark-haired woman, knife in hand, fell backward. Hiltabrand grabbed his pistol from the dirt, evened it at the woman, who was back on her feet.

She lunged again.

He fired, two rounds blasting her chest open.

The Legion was breaking. Despite the tenacity of their opponents, the cold steel of the recon marines' bayonets had turned the tide. Scores of enemy troops were dropping their rifles and running.

Hiltabrand got to his feet, picking another target. A shorter man with a torn shirt knocked a marine down, slamming his rifle into the marine's face. Hiltabrand squeezed his trigger. The rounds went wide, hitting a tree instead. The man whipped around, firing from the hip, sending bullets whistling past Hiltabrand.

Hiltabrand corrected his aim, emptying his magazine. The man stopped moving, dropping to his knees gasping, blood oozing from his open mouth.

Oren's squads slammed into the sides of retreating soldiers. The few enemies who still had their wits turned, firing at the oncoming marines. Several of Oren's group tumbled to the ground, screams of pain rising above the gunfire.

Hiltabrand ejected his magazine and slammed in a full one, his weapon's magnetic rails whining as the fresh battery charge hit them. He fired as fast as he could find targets. Another group of Legion assholes dropped. As fast as the fighting started, it ended. Hiltabrand's pistol slide locked open for the second time. He reloaded and holstered his weapon, breathing hard.

If this was the best the Legion could throw against them, they would take Alena Bridge in no time.

Lieutenant Melissa Jade
7ᵗʰ Ranger Battalion
East Platform, Cross Spaceport

"FIFTEEN SECONDS!"

The tension and fear in the pilot's voice made Jade's pulse quicken.

The Banshee's sides clanged with the sounds of bullet impacts. Jade racked her rifle's bolt, stepping to the front of the lander, just beside the lead Renard. Her knuckles turned white as she gripped her weapon. Her job was to clear and hold the east platform until reinforcements could arrive.

The radio had been going wild since the first teams had hit the planet. Ranger units were meeting heavier resistance than anticipated. The spaceport was crawling, and the AA guns had complicated the landing.

Those guns needed to be silenced.

The Renard revved its engines, a pair of rangers waiting by each strap. They needed its guns and the guns of the Jackson behind it if they were going to hold that platform.

She closed her eyes, momentarily letting her mind return to holding her twins, Holly and Jean, for the first time. That's where she would be right now if it wasn't for the fucking Legion. It had been six months since she's held them to her. Six months since she'd seen their smiles, heard their laughter.

Videos weren't enough.

Watching her children walk for the first time on shaky handheld recorder had sucked. She was missing so much.

If she died in this shithole, she'd be pissed.

The ship jolted as it touched down.

Jade opened her eyes. "Keep tight and right. Check your targets. Watch for civilians, fire if fired upon."

The ramp dropped.

Gunfire poured through the opening. Rangers screamed, falling as the enemy fire ricocheted around in the confined space.

Jade shouldered her rifle. "Free the damn tank."

The Renard began to fire, the intensity the enemy attack lessening as its twin .30-caliber machine guns raked the barely visible courtyard.

Jade hoped there were no civilians in this mess.

She fired several rounds, using movement as her guide through the smoke rising from in front of the lander. The Renard's engines roared, treads creaking as it tipped down, exiting the lander down its steep ramp. The tankette was drawing fire from all directions.

This was their best chance.

Jade signaled her squads forward, using the tank as cover. The Banshee needed to lift off, let additional landers touch down.

They had no time to waste.

Renards were the perfect vehicle for this kind of assault. The driver began turning the turretless vehicle side to side, raking the edge of the platform with intense, nonstop fire.

Jade moved forward directly behind the Renard. She ran her eyes around the platform. The pad itself was square and open to the air. She could see several other pads, standing fifty to sixty feet in the air above the main facility. On either side of this platform was a single set of stairs leading down towards the customs area. Behind the Alliance forces, partially hidden by the Banshee, was a large freight elevator. A set of sandbags covered the opening, its doors shut and chained.

The walkway leading to the pad was fortified, two bunkers guarding the stairs. Sandbag defenses were erected every five or six feet on the pad's edge, hiding at least fifty soldiers, their helmets and weapons peeking out of cover.

They needed those positions.

There was no cover for her troops beyond the tanks. Somewhere nearby there were at least two AA-guns. She could hear their rhythmic firing. Those guns had to be silenced to protect the strike force still in the air.

Jade darted out from behind the tank, firing at the nearest bunker. The rounds left small pits in the cement. She pulled a grenade and tossed it at the base of the structure. It exploded, pock-marking the bunker but causing no other damage. This structure was well built. Reinforced concrete pillboxes, complete with gun ports and a radar dish.

How the hell had these fuckers prepared such thorough defenses?

Jade could hear the Jackson engine throttling up behind her.

The rangers were running forward on both sides of the tank. A Legion machine gun nest was firing at the turning Renard. Eight rangers fell dead, the machine gun sweeping the area between the lander and the tankette.

The cement bunker fired a poorly aimed rocket at the Renard. It roared passed exploding just to the side of the Banshee.

She tapped her headset. "Cannibal, Zulu Three-Six."

Milo, the Jackson's commander, responded. "Zulu Three-Six, Cannibal, go."

She tossed a red smoke can towards the bunker. "Fire on marked target. Burn it down."

Cannibal turned its turret towards the cement bunker, machine gun fire bouncing off its forward armor. Another rocket launched from the bunker and skipped off *Cannibal's* forward armor, detonating in between one of the ranger RAR teams, killing them instantly. *Cannibal's* cannon roared, its shell going straight through one of the gun ports. The pillbox burst apart. Cement fragments, dust, and twisted rebar rained down across the platform. Black smoke filled the air from the bunker's smoldering remains.

The Renard turned towards the Legion's sandbags, and its guns barked. The enemy machine gun nest disintegrated in a storm of bullets, the combatants disappearing in a mist of blood and sinew.

Jade signaled her rangers forward, dashing to the front of the walkway. *Cannibal's* .30-caliber hull-mounted gun tore into the position in front of her. Jade signaled Baker and Dog Squads to the left. She turned right, firing several well-aimed shots at the nearest herd of enemies. One Legion soldier grabbed his shoulder, falling to his knees. Another stumbled, tumbling over the edge of the landing pad.

Jade squeezed the trigger again, hitting the wounded man square in the chest. Blood splattered the deck as his body crumpled. The Legion forces fired back, bullets sparking on the metal floor. A soldier behind her screamed. Another man stumbled past her, clutching his stomach, falling back onto the landing pad.

The enemies ducked behind one of their barricades to avoid the Renard's weapons. They fired blind, toppling over another ranger, dead.

Jade pulled a grenade from her belt, yanked the pin, and rolled it towards the barricade. It detonated, blowing four more defenders to hell.

Cannibal's gun barked again, obliterating the second concrete bunker.

The enemy scattered as the Renard's guns came back around, their bodies piling up as they tried to reach the stairs. With their defenses gone, the enemy broke, falling over each other in a hell-bent attempt to escape.

Jade reached the closest set of stairs. They were open, narrow, and filled with panicked enemy soldiers. Sargent Marquez fired his Heinlein down the steps, its .45-caliber rounds knocking people down. Jade looked over the edge.

Just below them on the roof of the central building were the AA guns, three quad-barreled monsters, each tracking and firing at different targets.

Jade hit her radio again. "Cannibal, Zulu Two-Six. Got another tasty treat for ya."

Johnathan Gram
Gram Family Home
Remagen Township

JOHNATHAN GRAM TIGHTENED his grip on his father's rifle. The house shook again, the sound of combat growing closer and closer. He peered outside. Remagen Bridge looked like it was burning, along with most of the horizon. It wasn't fully dark, but the sunlight was disappearing fast. The figures moving outside had taken on the eerie look of shadows.

Gram closed the window as another explosion vibrated the pictures off his walls. They smashed against the stone floor, shards of glass scattering in all directions. Gram dropped down, moving back to his huddled family.

Marty was sobbing. "Daddy, what dat?"

His wife Elsie hugged her close. "It's nothing, sweetness. Just a storm."

Elsie met his eyes. He tried to force a reassuring look on his face, but it didn't help. They both knew they wouldn't be able to stay here much longer.

He touched his daughter's shoulder. "Shush. Daddy's here, you're safe."

Gram felt helpless. He had stood up at that Legion meeting and told everyone that this Kline character was full of shit. The government would get word of what Cross Industries was doing, they would stop this. Prime Minister Brittain was a good man. He wouldn't allow an industrialist to put money over people.

He had stood before all of his angry neighbors and called for reason, for peace. This was a time to come together as a people and work for change without all the hate-filled political rhetoric. It was time to show the quality of the Alliance. Violence was an unacceptable means to effect a political end. It was everyone's job to prevent an environment that nurtures hate. If their tolerance did not extend to those with whom they disagreed, killing wouldn't solve it. If their compassion didn't include their political opponents, it was wanting.

He could still see Kline leaning his head back, laughing. The room following suit. At the time, Gram had ignored them, dismissing them as closed-minded fools.

The ground shook, and the window glowed red for a moment.

Marty reached for him, whining quietly. Gram let his rifle drop, picking her up. She was shaking, sweat pouring from her. He held her tightly, letting her bury her face in his chest.

Elsie mouthed at him. "We have to go."

Gram nodded, rocking Marty slowly back and forth.

How had he been so wrong?

Kline, as intolerable an ass as he was, had been right. Brittain didn't care. Parliament didn't care. According to the Supervisor, the Legion had only prevented a few shipments from leaving. A peaceful blockage to get the governor's attention. Sure, they had formed some militia units, called out the territorial guards and governor. Nothing harmful or dangerous. For the central military to show up, guns blazing, over a few shipments of ammunition...

The back wall of the house burst inward, wood shards and bits of metal landing everywhere. Marty and Elsie were screaming. Grams' muscles were locked in place. The home in which his grandfather and father had grown up was burning. The house in which his daughter had been born swayed and creaked in the smoke-filled air.

Elsie grabbed his arm. "John, we have to go."

He snapped out of it, swallowing the bile in his throat. He handed Marty to his wife. Gram tore his eyes from her shaking form.

He couldn't bear it.

Ignoring the goosebumps erupting over his skin, he grabbed his rifle. He scurried to the window on his hands and knees, dragging his weapon with him, the glass slicing his knuckles. He eased his back against the wall and pushed up with his legs.

He used the rifle to push back the drapes peering outside. The street was full of people, several other houses were burning. None of them looked like Alliance soldiers.

Gram dropped back down. "Baby. I am going first. If it's safe, I'll signal. Stay behind me, we are going to head towards the town hall."

Elsie nodded, her lower lip trembling.

He stood, forcing his muscles to move, the rifle heavy in his arms. He hadn't fired it since he'd been a much younger man. Hopefully, muscle memory would be enough.

Gram eased open the door, his heart hammering in his ears. He stepped through, eyes sweeping the crowd in the low light. No one noticed him. He took a few steps, moving down the steps, gun held out in front of him.

He turned around, waving his hand. Gram forced a fresh smile onto his face, trying to look reassuring. Elsie moved out from under the table, still holding Marty tightly to her breast.

He met Elsie's gaze.

The air filled with a loud whistling sound. A shell crashed into his home. Flames engulfed his wife and daughter. His family home incinerated in a ball of flame and debris. A wave of heat hit him, tossing him backward, his eyes and face burning. He landed on his back, his head whipped back. Pain lanced through the back of his skull.

He fought to keep his heavy eyelids open, to remain conscious. He couldn't focus, couldn't remember what was happening.

"Elsie? Martha? Where are you?"

Gram faded into unconsciousness, his throat desperately trying to form the names of his family.

CHAPTER FIVE

General Herman Polis
4th Infantry Division
One mile from Remagen Bridge
71 hours until evacuation

General Polis leaned forward, the low light straining his eyes. They had four or five minutes before the last daylight faded. Without the *Hercules's* drones, he had a poor overview of the current situation. At first, the lack of intelligence hadn't affected him. He'd studied the initial readouts, memorizing as many of the details as he could. It had given them an initial edge.

Not anymore.

The data coming from the rest of the armored unit, his Harkler Command Vehicle's own drones, and communications from ground troops was limited, sporadic at best. Even with his advisors using the holotable, it was hard to get a useful view of the chaos outside.

The attack wasn't going well, that much was clear. The Legion's AA guns had managed to take out more than fifteen percent of the Alliance Banshees, including the ones carrying the communications vehicle, Colonel Snider's command squad, and all of their Henshaw AA tankettes.

Major Marshall's lander had crashed, leaving him embedded with one of the marine platoons going after the bridges. Anderson had complete command at the spaceport. Hopefully, he had enough experience leading infantry to handle the situation.

The majority of the bridges were fortified, full of tenacious, if inexperienced, defenders. At this point, all of the bridges were untaken. Alena Bridge wasn't even under attack. There were reports of handheld anti-tank rounds and mortars overshooting the Alliance positions into local towns. The last thing he wanted was civilian casualties, even if they were at the hands of the enemy.

It was a waste.

Plus, explaining their deaths to Parliament would be a bitch.

So far, his only blessing was the Legion's lack of fighters or rotary aircraft. Some reports suggested the defenders at the spaceport were breaking.

He tried to raise the governor or any of the territorial military units. No one answered. Either the Legion had blocked communication or—

He shuddered.

Polis had expected resistance, but nothing of this magnitude. Anti-aircraft batteries, anti-tank weapons, and tens of thousands of troops. If they weren't so poorly organized, this fight would already be over. The Alliance forces would have been slaughtered on the landing pad.

That bastard Young had to have known what was here.

The Harkler rocked as it sped up, moving down the road towards Remagen bridge. The driver was shouting coordinates to the secondary driver. The rhythmic sound of the sponsons' machine guns filled the armored vehicle's interior.

Polis keyed in several commands. "Conner, get on the horn to the Bloodhound. I want her out of the mess at the spaceport and on the way up to Remagen. Have Anderson divert the closest Renards and a Jackson if he can spare one."

Anderson had correctly placed the majority of his armor at the spaceport because of the larger landing zones. Projections had suggested more of the enemy would concentrate there. The rangers and infantry units had needed the backup. The McGees would have been enough fire support for the marines if the Legion didn't have anti-tank weaponry, but now...

If they couldn't take the bridges, the mission was over.

It looked like most of the Banshees carrying the McGees hadn't made it. Polis had initially made contact with the column, but he'd lost them. Either the McGees were toast or out of range. Either way, they wouldn't be part of the solution. Without their firepower, the Marines were moving slowly. They had to push through position after position, with a serious expenditure of ammunition. The assault on the spaceport had more than enough support with *Big Dawg*, the two Whitmans, and the remaining tankettes.

Polis had his eyes on the prize.

It was time to change the pulse of the battle. Polis couldn't let the Legion control the tone of this fight. His best bet was to use the *Bloodhound* like a hammer, punch through the enemy's defenses at Remagen Bridge. Report after report from various elements of his strike teams indicated Legion units falling back when faced with determined, organized assaults.

Bloodhound would be the force to scatter the defenders on the bridge.

Every image his observation drones sent back showed well-fortified structures. At best estimate, the Legion had landed less than three weeks ago. No one could fortify this well, that quickly. Cross or the territorial armies had to have expected an attack and prepared these defenses.

Polis's money was on Cross. The man was a manipulative, paranoid fuck. He'd probably built these bunkers to protect himself from his workers. During their last altercation, Cross had talked about angry workers, dogs who would bite the hand that feeds them.

Polis had dismissed his blather as political rhetoric.

Apparently, it had been more than that.

Polis activated his final sensor drones, ordering them to higher altitudes, hoping for a better view of the battlefield.

He shifted in his seat again. "Let Marshall know help is on the way."

Tim Fival
Cross Spaceport
Legion Anti-Aircraft Battery Number Four

FIVAL'S HAND SHOOK.

This wasn't going well. The time spent drilling had been useless. The first few moments had looked promising, landers bursting and falling all around them. The Alliances ships had spread out, returning fire. They had begun getting through.

Too many had landed.

There were explosions and gunfire coming from all the nearby platforms. Fival had watched people and debris falling past him.

His teams had sustained their rate of fire but were struggling to maintain the proper altitude settings. The landers and pods constantly changed speed and direction.

He wanted to scream.

It shouldn't matter. He should have been prepared. He'd promised Kline he was ready. Had he really expected the surprise to stop their enemy?

No surprise attack was a surprise forever.

Goddamn it.

Fival would die before allowing the Alliance to take this spaceport. This was his home. The government had to learn a lesson. The territorials and politicians who had already died had done so because of their refusal to see reason. They had chosen not to listen. These bastards would get that same chance.

You can't force someone to be a slave for a company's profits, Milipa or no Milipa. What was the point of fighting to defend democracy and freedom if you had to give up that freedom to win?

He had one option. Turn his AA guns on the platforms. Blast the first man or woman who dared approach his position. His guns would be just as good at harvesting flesh as aircraft.

They'd regret setting foot on his roof.

Fival heard a pop. A wave of heat hit him. An explosion ripped apart one of his flak cannons. Its barrels warped and cracked and it smashed to the ground, flattening several of his crew. The smell of burning flesh and blood hit Fival's nostrils.

His stomach turned, bile flooding his esophagus.

The ground rippled, shaking him from his feet. His back protested as he hit the shingles of the stone roof. He rolled onto his stomach, shaking his head. His vision cleared. The gun crew was gone, a massive hole in the roof revealing their fate.

What the hell had happened?

He looked upwards. On the edge of the nearest platform sat a tank, its long barrel angled down at him.

He scrambled to his feet, ignoring the pain in his back. "Swing right, swing right. Target Marvin platform."

Several of his troops looked up, their eyes widening, color draining from their faces. He looked back up, the tank rocked backward, its muzzle flashed.

The ground beneath Fival gave way. He was falling. He pumped his arms, his hands scraping along the stone wall, fingers breaking and bleeding. He had to grab hold of something, anything.

But nothing was within reach.

Major Jeff Marshall
Embedded in the 10th Recon Marines
Remagen Bridge, Two Miles from Cross Port
70 hours until evacuation

"FUCKING BASTARDS."

Major Marshall dropped back into cover, releasing his empty magazine. Remagen Bridge was fifteen feet from his troops' position, but they were stuck cowering behind these boulders. His first three attacks had failed miserably. The enemy defenses were formidable.

He needed something that hit harder.

He needed one of the mortars or rockets the Legion had been lobbing at them. Granted, if he had known his lander was going to crash, he would have grabbed heavy weapons. He tried not to think about his rangers fighting without him at the port.

He had to trust that Anderson was taking care of them.

Another mortar whistled past, missing their position. The jackasses didn't know what the fuck they were doing. Only a handful of rounds had struck anywhere nearby. The fire in the distance suggested they'd hit the nearby town.

The Legion had added murdering civilians to their repertoire.

The two pillboxes sitting on either side of the entrance of the bridge were undamaged. In addition, there was a makeshift tower right on the top of the bridge. The Legion had a perfect vantage point over the entire engagement zone. The Alliance forces couldn't get close enough to use explosives, and their portable anti-armor weaponry had been lost in the backs of the missing McGees. The enemy wasn't worried about wasting ammunition.

Marshall's attacks had nowhere to go. The area was too flat and open. The bodies of his troops littered the courtyard.

To complicate matters, his teams kept beating back assaults from both sides. They'd found at least fifteen concealed tunnel openings. Marshall had walked directly over one without noticing it. The whole valley was crawling with Legion soldiers. Each time the enemy had attacked, they had maintained complete surprise, hitting the Alliance position and falling back before the marines could react.

Marshall's troops had blown the openings of each tunnel they'd found, but without going in and clearing the entire system, they could be sure the tunnels snaking beyond them weren't intact. Marshall didn't have the manpower for that. Flamethrowers would change this game, but he didn't have any. Regardless, it did no good to dwell on the things he couldn't control.

Marshall pulled out a flare, tossing it over his shoulders. The enemy machine gun fire picked up, as the inexperienced soldiers went after the light. He leaned out, examining the terrain again.

No situation was unwinnable.

The bank on either side of the bridge sloped downward. The right side was rocky, covered in some sort of old stone ruins, but it was directly under the guns. In daylight, it offered no cover. The bank nearest his position was worse, grassy and barren of anything to use as cover. It wasn't directly under the pillboxes but easily targeted from that damn tower or any soldier on the bridge.

Neither option appealed to him. He could wait. Polis was bringing armor up from the rear to crack this nut.

Fuck that.

In twenty years, Marshall had never needed anyone to bail him out, and he wasn't about to sit on his hands and wait. The cavalry could ride to someone else's rescue.

Besides, the setting sun presented an opportunity. A team could crawl through the ruins without being noticed. Especially if the enemy was distracted by a diversionary attack from the grass. They could get close enough to use their explosives.

The three platoons at his disposal should be enough. Two platoons under the command of Captain David Paxton were tucked in just behind the ruins, inside a patch of trees. What was left of his own command platoon was spread out along a small group of boulders fifty yards from the grassy rise.

Marshall slapped a fresh magazine home. "Henry, get your ass over here."

His communications operator, Henry Oligar, crawled over. Several machine gun rounds whizzed overhead, chipping the top of the rocks.

Oligar sat up, resting on his hands and knees. "Sir?"

Marshall leaned in. "Get me Paxton. I want him to sneak up to the defenses through the ruins. Blow that goddamn cement fucker to hell. We will distract them. Go in five."

Oligar shook his head, relaying the command on his radio pack. "Paxton acknowledges."

Marshall searched for Sergeant Nieman in the dying light, found him pointing his rifle around a cluster of rocks. "Sergeant?"

Nieman looked over. Marshall repeated his orders. He would take three squads and go straight at the bridge. The remainder of the Platoon, including all three machine gun teams, would stay with Nieman and provide cover fire.

Marshall holstered his pistol.

He crawled to the edge of the boulders, pulling his rifle from his back. He closed his eyes for a moment, steadying his breathing.

This wouldn't be fun.

He could feel the tension coming off the troops stacking up behind him.

Marshall pressed the rifle into his shoulder. He nodded. A flare shot into the air, slowly falling towards the river. The machine guns from the Legion positioned opened fire. Clumps of grass and dirt sprayed into the air as they swung back and forth over the empty field.

Nieman's teams returned fire, the RAR gunners focusing their fire on the tower. The enemy faltered under the intensity of the volley. Marshall stood, running towards the bridge entrance. The soldiers behind him were yelling, the distinct crack of their Enfield rifles contrasting with the rhythmic chugging of the machine guns.

He fired from the hip, his rounds chipping the cement of the pillbox in front of him. Marshall's legs burned as he struggled to keep his footing on the blood-soaked grass.

His foot caught on something. He fell. A bullet whistled over-head. A woman's scream, the clank of armor, and a thud followed.

The screaming grew louder as the Legion positions poured on the fire. The small area was bottlenecking his forces, ranger after ranger cut down by the tower and line of defenders along the bridge's railing.

Marshall pushed himself to his knees, bringing his rifle up.

He aimed at the bridge. He could just make out movement along Remagen's railing.

Marshall squeezed the trigger, putting several clusters of bullets in that direction. At least one body toppled into the river below.

The flare went out.

He was plunged into near darkness, muzzle flashes and tracers providing the only real light in the cloudy sky. It was time to fall back. He wouldn't trade any more lives for more time.

The clunk of the Legion's mortars cut off his thought process. The bright burst of their explosions lit the ground, exposing the mangled remains of his troops. Marshall turned, movement catching his eye. Another trap door right on the edge of the river was opening. If those insurgents reached the surface, he'd be caught in a crossfire.

Fuck.

Marshall clicked his radio. "All troops, Berserker Six. Enemies coming from the river, 2 o'clock."

He waited, trying to ignore the chugging sound of the tower's guns. The first head crept from the opening. He fired one clean shot, bursting his enemy's skull. Several more Alliance troops had joined him, their quick bursts of fire keeping the Legion in their hole.

Two more explosions lit the courtyard and tossed Marshall to the ground. One of the Legion weapons had found its mark. Three people to his left were flung toward the sky, a bloody mist filling the air. He ignored the bodies falling next to him, locking his eyes on the tunnel.

The area was brighter, fires burning throughout the tortured courtyard.

One of the Legion soldiers had made it clear in the confusion. She was firing back, moving towards his position. Her bullets zipped over his head.

They had to plug this fucking tunnel.

Marshall felt his belt. Nothing. "Damn it!" He keyed his radio. "Someone grenade that rat hole!"

Two grenades sailed past his head. The first was knocked down by the Legion woman. The other rolled past her into the entrance she was defending. Both exploded, the woman and the tunnel opening disappearing in a wave of blood and dirt.

Several of the rangers cheered.

Marshall stood. "Shut it. This fight isn't done."

He looked back. Paxton's force had blown a small hole in the first pillbox. His men had already charged through, many already visible on the other side. The tower's machine guns had left his team, trying to plug the leak. Even with the covering fire of Nieman's troops, the tower's tracers were cutting down marine after marine just before the opening.

The second pillbox was undamaged, assisting the tower in suppressing Paxton's attack. They were ignoring him, clearly unaware that Marshall's group had stopped the assault from the trap door.

This was Marshall's chance.

He ran, reloading as he went. His rangers followed. In another ten feet, they would be out of the line of fire.

The Seventh Rangers had bled for this bridge.

It was time to return the favor.

Captain Kevin Beliard
5th Armored Corp, McGee Detachment

Two Mile North of Alena Bridge
68 hours until evacuation

SMALL-ARMS ROUNDS BOUNCED off the McGee's bullet-proof window.

Captain Kevin Beliard jumped. Enemy fire was intensifying. The .50-caliber gunner spun. His weapon barked in bursts.

Beliard shifted in his seat, trying again to connect to the communications vehicle. His laser link searched for an active signal node.

Nothing.

This whole operation was fucked.

He had spent all his luck making it to the ground alive. Beliard's Banshee had taken fire, narrowly missing the island's edge as it crashed down. Most of the occupants were dead, and the Henshaw tank was scrap. His two McGees had survived, but their radios hadn't.

It had taken hours to get the McGees loose. Without communications, he could only guess at his exact location. At first, things had gone smoothly. Based on his compass readings and the distance they'd covered, he guessed they had to be near Alena Bridge.

Until they'd hit this goddamn road.

Narrow and winding, trees and a surprising number of skillfully hidden machine gun bunkers lined its sides.

They started around a bend, eyes peeled for movement in the trees. The sounds of gunfire increased. The driver, Melvin, slammed the brakes. Beliard lurched forward, bullets hitting the vehicle's armor from all sides.

Blocking the road were two of his McGees. One was burning on its side, its surviving crew tucked in behind the wreckage. The second vehicle was firing wildly, its machine gun spinning side to side, ripping up the edge of the woods.

A rocket sped out the trees, narrowly missing the lone McGee's turret. It burst in the trees, raining chunks of wood onto the hood of Beliard's vehicle.

They couldn't maneuver around the ruined vehicle. They'd have to move it to keep going.

Assuming they survived this attack.

Beliard picked up his SMG. "Melvin, cover the left flank, Hank keep the fifty hot. Give 'em hell. The rest of you into the woods."

He opened his door, the wall of hot air from the burning McGee hitting his face. Beliard crouched low, sprinting into the trees as Melvin drove forward. The crew of the vehicle behind them had followed suit. Its commander, Lieutenant Martinez, was coming up behind him, his rifle clutched to his chest.

Martinez and his four soldiers halted just behind him. "What's the move, Captain?"

Beliard brought his gun up. "We are going to flank them. Catch them in a crossfire."

The two McGee engines roared, their big .50-caliber guns barking as they rolled forward, supporting the beleaguered defenders. Beliard, Martinez, and their eight troops slithered towards the enemy gunfire. With any luck, this would be a machine gun nest, maybe a stray patrol. Not a full bunker. Their only chance if it was a bunker was the portable rockets they carried that were meant for Snider's marines.

Even if none of his soldiers had ever fired one.

He pushed a branch out of the way, handing it to the man behind him. A twig snapped. His throat caught. It was too dark to see the ground well.

They needed to be silent.

Gunfire flashed through the darkness directly in front of him, firing out at the road. Another ten feet and they'd have stumbled right on top of the enemy.

Beliard couldn't make anything out. He should have brought his night vision visor. Why hadn't he thought of that? Snider had made him load extra. Marines always drop in with them.

He raised his hand, stopping their advance.

Martinez pulled a flare, meeting his eyes.

Beliard nodded, signaling his people to cover.

The flare shot into the air, illuminating the enemy position. Beliard's neck erupted with goosebumps. There was at least a platoon, maybe two spread out in a trench along the edge of the trees. The McGee's fire was too high, hitting just over their heads.

He picked a grenade off his belt, pulled the pin, and tossed it. It exploded, clearing the edge of the trench. The enemy fired back towards Martinez's position.

Martinez tried to get back. He stumbled, grabbing his leg. His chest and side burst as the Legion soldiers hit their mark.

Beliard opened fire. The Legion soldiers were trapped like fish in a barrel, falling easily to his gun. Jean and Potter were just ahead of him, their steady aim picking apart the enemy. Rhoads, Toffer, Smith, and White were spread out behind him. Beliard pumped his trigger, his submachine gun taking out several traitors at a time. As soon as the flare went out, they would need to retreat. The surprise wouldn't last long, and he didn't have enough troops to hold this position.

At least he could correct the fire from the .50-calibers.

A grenade landed just behind Potter. Beliard tried to yell, but it was too late. Its detonation rippled through the trees, and he was tossed from his feet, his SMG disappearing into the brush. The smell of burning flesh from Jean's and Potter's smoldering bodies choked him.

He reached for his pistol. Legion soldiers were crashing through the underbrush. Rhoads and his remaining team met them head-on with bayonets. Toffer stabbed the lead opponent, kicking the body clear. He fired two rounds at another man in front of him.

Rhoads impaled the man in front of him. A tall legion woman next to him kicked him in the side, brandishing a long silver knife. Rhoads swung his rifle butt at her but missed. The woman didn't, slamming the back of his head. She lowered herself for the kill.

Beliard got his pistol free and fired several quick shots from the ground. The woman collapsed, a bloody hole in her side.

He looked for another target. Toffer was dead, blood trickling through his mouth. A pile of dead enemies at his feet. It hadn't been enough. One man had him by the throat, another had driven a knife into his chest.

Beliard swallowed.

He fired the last of his magazine into Toffer's attackers.

A few of the Legion soldiers came towards him. Beliard fumbled with his new magazine, heart beating painfully in his chest.

This was it.

He was going to die here.

His attackers raised their rifles. They stopped moving, blood spraying onto Beliard's armor. They fell, large holes in their chests.

The woods erupted with fire — accurate rifle fire. The Legion troops around Beliard fell. The enemies in the trench panicked, jumping out of their fortifications, trying to escape the onslaught. They ran headlong into the McGee's guns, dying in a wave of blood and bone.

The woods fell silent.

Beliard didn't move, fixed to his spot. He tried to put together what had happened, his hands still frozen onto his half-loaded pistol.

A young marine lieutenant appeared beside him and held out his hand. "Lieutenant Derek Hiltabrand, Tenth Recon Marines."

Beliard slapped the magazine into place. "Captain Kevin Beliard. Thanks for the assist."

Hiltabrand pulled him up. "Maybe you can return the favor. We landed in the wrong place. We are headed for Alena Bridge. Can you confirm we are headed in the right direction?"

Beliard dusted himself off. "Not really. We're headed that way. As near as I can tell, this road leads to a small town. The bridge should be on the other side."

Hiltabrand beamed, slinging his Enfield over his shoulder. "Perfect. Matches my own estimates. Mount up, sir. Time's wasting."

Beliard holstered his pistol, walking back towards the McGee. He would be happy to be inside its protective armor again.

And even happier to get the damn bridge secured.

He'd had enough of this shithole.

Corporal Dean Harper
7th Ranger Battalion
Cross Spaceport Promenade
68 hours until evacuation

CORPORAL DEAN HARPER threw himself behind a group of metal crates. Avril, Tennyson, and Leonard were right behind him.

He pushed his back against the wall. "Gentleman, try to keep up. There's killing to be done."

Tennyson laughed. "Killing or not, my feet are killing me."

The stone floor vibrated, the sound of a big motor reverberating through the room.

Big Dawg slammed through a wall, its .30 caliber machine guns turning the opposite side of the promenade into a death trap. Harper watched as its main cannon fired, the shell blasting apart the position and the enemies he had been firing at.

Harper glanced around the courtyard. The facility's main gate was directly across from him. Two, eight-foot-high passageways led downward to the parking structure. The promenade had at least 14 other doors to various parts of the facility.

There was a large fountain in the middle of the walkway shaped like an angry eagle. On the far side of the walk, streaming towards the exit, were the remaining Legion defenders.

Harper reloaded. "Let's go, boys."

The Ramsey tank moved towards the facility's main gates, followed closely by *Lead Slinger*, one of the two Whitman infantry tanks. Their guns were turning the entire courtyard into a blood-soaked mess, the enemy soldiers unable to hide in the confined space.

Harper moved forward, hopping into the fountain. The water

splashed as he made his way to the other side, soaking him. He knelt down, firing at the retreating enemy.

He almost felt bad for these assholes. They stood no chance against the monstrous tanks. Harper thought of Alisha's face, fighting the urge to smile. If he couldn't be home for his own wedding, at least he could fuck up these idiots. The Legion's attack on Kensington had cost him a few friends.

Two more tanks screamed out of the parking tunnels, guns blazing. Bullets whizzed around him, his whole team dead before he'd realized it.

They were Legion tanks.

Fifty more enemy combatants followed the tanks, yelling as they charged.

Harper tripped, falling out of the fountain and onto the tile floor. He had never seen a tank like that. They were smaller and flatter than the Alliance models, and the size of their main guns suggested they were tank hunters. They were well-armed for their size. He scrambled along the tiles, rolling out of harm's way.

The closer tank fired, and its round hit the *Lead Slinger* head-on. The Alliance tank shuddered, its front armor holding. It turned sharply, guns turning to meet the new attackers. Harper pushed himself back up, adding his fire to that of the other Alliance troops tucked in nearby.

Big Dawg's main turret swung round and fired. The shell missed, scraping the enemy tank's armor and detonating in a mass of infantry. The blast threw their bodies, which bounced off the walls in the confined space. Two more of the squat Legion tanks thundered out of the other tunnel, firing together. Their rounds struck *Big Dawg's* turret, detonating harmlessly on its thick armor.

Harper turned to meet the enemy infantry pouring from the second parking tunnel. He dropped into a prone position and fired off aimed shots, each one killing several people at once. From the corner of his eye, he could see the Legion soldiers who, moments ago, had been running for their lives rallying and returning to the fight.

He threw himself back into the fountain, the water and blood soaking through his uniform. He gagged as he pushed bits of his friends aside, scrambling towards the Alliance position. Tracer rounds from an RAR whistled overhead as he reached the edge of the fountain and pushed himself up.

His head spun, bile building in his throat.

A tank round hit the eagle fountain, masonry flying in all directions. A sharp pain tore through his leg.

Harper cried out. He reached behind him, found a jagged piece of shrapnel in his thigh. He wrapped his fingers around it, pulling it free. Pain laced through his body, white spots darting in front of his eyes. He pushed his back against his fountain's tile wall and forced himself to breathe.

He pulled his pistol with one hand, keeping pressure on his wound with his other.

Lead Slinger was directly in front of the fountain now, its quad fifties roaring, blasting at the righthand hallway entrance. What Legion infantry were still alive had either ducked into cover or behind the crates and small garden wall.

The four flat tanks were moving around *Big Dawg*, like wolves around a moose. *Big Dawg* backed up, running into two of the tanks. They spun to the side, rocking backward on one track, almost tipping over. *Big Dawg* fired again. Its target exploded, its turret ripped from its hull, deep red flames spewing from its shattered frame.

The Legion tank that was still moving ran directly at *Lead Slinger*. The smaller infantry tank backed up through the front of the fountain.

Harper ignored the pain in his thigh, throwing his body over the fountain wall. He crashed into the stone floor. He was numb, his body heavy.

He refused to die here.

For a moment, he could see his fiancé standing in front of him in her wedding dress, her smile lighting up her eyes. He reached for her.

His hand hit the cold stone floor. He snapped back to the present, pulling himself forward. The ground was wet and slippery. The RAR was still firing. If he could get behind its position, behind the crates, he'd rest.

The pain in his shoulder was growing, he turned onto his back, pushing himself with his good arm and leg. *Big Dawg* had taken out another one of the Legion's tanks, spreading its burning wreckage across the left tunnel opening. The final two Legion tanks were retreating towards the entrance, lobbing shells back at the Alliance tanks.

Lead Slinger moved forward, blocking the enemy's line of fire, its turret turning to fire on the remaining enemy infantry. The flat tanks hit *Lead Slinger* with everything they had. Multiple shells struck its side armor. One shell skipped off its turret, ripping open the ceiling.

Big Dawg fired, tearing the treads off one of the flat tanks. Unable to move, the flat tank fired again. *Lead Slinger's* armor finally gave in, a burning hole appearing in its side.

The tank shuddered, flames bursting from the split in its armor. The top hatch opened and the tank's commander scrambled out, screaming and thrashing. He fell from the tank, his uniform and skin burning. Harper looked for his pistol, the man's screams tearing at his nerves. He wanted to shoot the tank commander himself.

End his suffering.

Damn it.

He couldn't find his sidearm anywhere.

Another roar split the air. *Big Dawg's* round missed, hitting the side of the entrance. The front of the building toppled, leaving the whole front of the spaceport open to the night. The final enemy tank left the building, its treads breaking an additional piece from the wall.

The room was shaking, cracks spreading out in waves across the ceiling. Blocks broke loose, tumbling onto the promenade.

Big Dawg fired again, finishing the damaged tank. A wave of heat and flame raced toward the ceiling. More jagged pieces of debris broke loose, raining onto the stone floor and fracturing it.

Harper had to make it out of here. He wouldn't leave Alisha this way. He reached back again pulling himself over the floor. The pain in his shoulder had lessened. The sound of gunfire had stopped. *Big Dawg's* engine sounded faint, far away. The rumbling from the ceiling filled his ears.

Harper looked up.

The block directly above him was falling.

CHAPTER SIX

Lieutenant Derek Hiltabrand
10th Recon Marine Division
Alena Village
67 hours until evacuation

Hiltabrand pressed himself against a small building at the edge of town. He'd finally caught sight of the bridge as they'd descended into this valley. It had been a good damn thing they had run across the column of McGees. Their big fifties had sped up their advance.

Not to mention he'd been going in the wrong direction, even if he hadn't admitted it to Beliard.

Hiltabrand flipped down his night vision visor and activated it.

He leaned out, the green of the night vision making the town look eerie. There was uncoordinated movement everywhere, unusual for this time of night. It looked like the majority of civilians were trying to evacuate, avoid the fighting.

Hopefully, this meant the Legion hadn't spread as deeply into the planet as it had seemed.

Hiltabrand couldn't see any weapons or defensive structures. No AA units or other heavy equipment. Just small, wooden multi-storey buildings crammed tightly together and a surprising number of hastily built roadblocks on most of the major entry points into town.

He heard footsteps and turned to see Sergeant Oren and Captain Beliard walking up beside him.

Oren lowered his own night vision visor. "Shouldn't be too difficult an approach."

Hiltabrand nodded. "Nope. Lots of movement though."

Beliard pointed. "Let's not jump the gun. How much are we talking?"

Hiltabrand lifted his night vision device, popped it off, and handed it to Beliard. He was glad he had remembered to bring his own visor. He'd be going in blind if he'd left it behind as Snider had suggested.

Beliard raised the visor. "Those buildings have me worried. Flat, long roofs, lots of cover. They could hit us from all over."

Oren adjusted his helmet. "I'd feel better if we had backup, or at least a radio operator and medic. We won't ever be able to call for help if we step into shit."

Hiltabrand nodded. "We don't have a ton of ammo left either. Last thing I want is a drawn-out firefight. I don't think the bridge will take itself."

This was the downside of bringing the night vision. He could have taken two more magazines in its place. He also should have collected ammo from his fallen comrades or even from the Alliance-issued weaponry the Legion was using. Failing to restock from the dead and wounded was a rookie move. One he'd expect an asshole fresh from boot to make. No wonder Paxton had his own company.

Idiot.

Oren traced the town's edge with his finger. "We could use the woods. Probably have to leave the McGees, though."

Beliard's face tightened.

Hiltabrand shook his head. "No, we need those guns. If we take that side road, we can skirt around the majority of the activity."

Beliard's gaze followed the road. "I'm in. Mount up?"

Hiltabrand lifted up his rifle. "Your call, boss."

Beliard laughed. "Alright. Let's rock and roll. My vehicle will take the lead. The other two will take up the rear. I'll leave the marching orders in your capable hands."

Hiltabrand nodded, keying his mike. "Charlie and Delta Squads, move up front. Charlie, right, Delta left. Able Squad, rear guard. Look sharp. Do not fire unless you are fired upon. I want no civilian casualties, clear?"

Beliard's McGee pulled up in front of him.

Beliard opened the door, pulling himself up. "See you on the other side, Lieutenant."

Hiltabrand nodded, then followed behind the armored vehicle.

The first street was quiet, empty, the dull thrumming of the McGees' engines thunderous in the night air. Charlie Squad was tucked in along a wall to the left, Corporal Vern in the lead. The corporal stopped at the edge of a building, aiming down the next street. Several of his troops hopped past him, continuing down the street.

Nothing was moving. Hiltabrand felt his heart slowing, his grip loosening on his rifle. Why was he so nervous? Compared to a drop, this was easy.

Several minutes later, they reached the edge of a large square with a wide archway for an entrance. Corporal Higgens raised his hand. Delta Squad lined up behind Higgens. Charlie Squad followed suit on the opposite side of the street.

Beliard's McGee slowed. Its gunner swiveled around, watching the roofline

Both corporals looked back at Hiltabrand. He gave them the signal to move forward. Both squads sprinted through the archway, checking corners as they moved. The McGees and Hiltabrand's group started towards the courtyard's center.

Hiltabrand's gaze studied the layout. From the looks of it, this had been one of the so-called "company markets" he'd always heard about on the news. The bane of the lower class, if he believed liberal politicians. Each establishment had the same style of dull gold lettering. Each read Cross something or another. Cross Hardware, Cross Foods and Pharmacy, Cross Liquors.

It reminded him of the PX.

There were some restaurants, brightly colored with more ornate decorations, their patios still set for service. Delta Squad climbed over the wall of the nearest building, clearing the first floor.

Beliard's gunner yelled, his weapon barking.

Corporal Vern twitched, crashing through a glass table as he fell.

The whole block exploded. The night sky lit up, gunfire coming at them from all directions. Private Hays collapsed next to Hiltabrand.

Hiltabrand took a knee, firing at the swirls of people pouring in from the opposite side of the courtyard. Even in the dark, he could tell these weren't all combatants. Some had mining gear on, others rifles that looked like museum pieces.

It was like the whole town had turned up to kill them.

This was insane.

He only had twenty-three marines left — they didn't stand a chance against so many. The RARs had run dry hours ago.

Sergeant Oren was thrown backward, a round hitting him from above, his rifle skidding away. The sergeant grabbed the wound, moving towards cover.

Hiltabrand glanced upwards. He fired at the flashing from the buildings' roofs. He had no way of knowing how many enemies had gotten up there, no way of calling in an air strike.

They'd have to fall back.

Beliard's vehicle looked like a Christmas tree. Bullets impacts threw sparks, their light disappearing in wisps of smoke. Hiltabrand's nostrils stung with the smell of burning metal and blood.

The McGees in the rear screamed past, tires kicking up dirt, the three big guns throwing a jet of rounds at the other side of the court-yard. The wooden structures disintegrated. Stone walls chipped and burst under the intensity of the vehicle's .50-caliber guns.

Hiltabrand got to his feet, signaling his team to pull back. He turned, saw a fresh group of attackers approaching from behind them.

They were surrounded.

Exposed.

He had to get them dug into the buildings. It was their only hope.

He activated his radio. "Enemies from the rear. Fall back into structures. Able Squad, Baker Squad engage the rear."

The nearest McGee backed up, turning into the oncoming troops. The enemy faltered under the machine gun fire, the lead wave of combatants retreating behind the arch, bodies covering the ground.

Hiltabrand sprinted and threw himself into cover. He dropped his magazine, slapping in a fresh one. If the McGees ran out of ammo, this fight would be over real quick.

Major Jeff Marshall
Embedded in 10th Recon Marines
Just outside Alena Village
Sixty-one hours until extraction

MAJOR MARSHALL WAVED his men forward. "Pick it up. Move it."

They had just reached the edge of a shitty-looking town. The flat roofs, tightly clumped, rundown wooden houses, and dusty streets reminded him too much of home.

Polis had radioed minutes after they had finished off the Legion resistance at Remagen. Alena Bridge was still untouched. The three platoons assigned to the job were missing. Polis' drones had only found one of the platoons, along with several of the missing McGees.

From the best images Polis had, they were being torn apart in a city square about half a mile from the bridge. They were surrounded by a thousand or more combatants on the ground and rooftops. It didn't look good.

Marshall turned a corner. The street they were on was narrowing, funneling them towards the square. His troops were spread out in clumps, running towards the sound of fighting. If Polis's intel was wrong and the Legion wasn't concentrated in the square, Marshall risked being caught off guard, out of position. If all the enemy truly was focused on the trapped platoon, then it didn't matter how spread out he was now.

Speed was the vital factor.

When the call had come in, Marshall had left one platoon to secure the bridge and high-tailed it towards the trapped marines. Polis had sent several updates, indicating the McGees' guns were holding the enemy off. If Marshall could reach them before the ammunition ran out, his team might be able to break them out.

The tanks were finally coming down the road, but were still twenty or more minutes from Alena Bridge, assuming they didn't meet resistance. The damn road was choked with dead soldiers from both sides. The three platoons assigned to take Alena Bridge had landed on top of a staging ground, right onto anti-aircraft turrets and bunkers. The reports from the few survivors said they'd met tanks.

Most had died in the air or trapped in their pods. Recon marines had a nickname for their landing pods — coffins. This was a brutal reminder that name didn't come from their size and shape alone. To die like that...

It was unthinkable.

Marines knew the risks, but that didn't make the sight of their bodies easier for Marshall to see — or lessen his sense of guilt. Losing people was an element of leadership that would never get easier. He would bear that burden until he died. Hopefully, at home in bed. Years from now.

He had no wish to be the burden on some other leader's mind.

The Alliance troops turned another corner, the flames and tracers now easily visible over the building tops. Marshall raised his hand, bringing his winded formation to a halt.

Oligar moved to his side. "I'm not picking anything up from the McGees. Looks like Hiltabrand's platoon. From what we've picked up, he is ordering a charge against the arch. They are trying to break out."

Marshall pulled up his wrist display, zooming in on the combat area. The overhead image showed a large arch or a group of several small arches almost directly in front of his approach. If they cut across the next side street, they'd run right into the enemy line.

Marshall closed his display. "Captain Paxton. Get up here."

Paxton bounded up on his left, red-faced. "Yes, sir."

Marshall pointed to a group of nearby fire escapes. "Take your platoons onto those roofs. Cover our approach and engage anyone you encounter. I'll proceed down this side road and hit the enemy from behind."

Paxton nodded. "The images the general sent showed activity all over the rooftops. We may not be able to offer much help if those bastards see us first."

"True, but they will be too busy shooting at you to notice me."

Paxton laughed. "Bait it is."

Marshall gave Paxton what he hoped was a reassuring smile. "Be careful. This is a rescue. I don't want any more marine blood spilled in this fucking village."

Paxton turned away, waving his troops to his position.

Oligar leaned in. "Sir, I can't get a clear signal through to either Polis or Hiltabrand. The enemy is jamming us."

Marshall checked rifle. "Doesn't matter, Corporal. We can worry about radio issues later. We've got to move. Those marines' lives are on the line."

Johnathan Gram
Anaheim Woods
Seven Miles from Cross Port

GRAM'S HEAD and neck throbbed. Anaheim woods were full of the sounds of screaming. The Legion had saved him, moved him to the safety of this makeshift hospital. Their doctor had cleared him, reassured him that he was fine. Bumps and bruises.

Nothing serious.

It was a miracle, the graying doctor had said. An explosion like that should have popped his eardrums and shattered his skull. A few days' rest, and he'd be back to normal.

Back to normal?

A miracle?

This was anything but a miracle. It was a nightmare.

Gram wasn't even sure that normal existed anymore. The image of his wife and daughter's charred bodies were burned into his mind. The smell of their cooked and smoldering skin lingered in his nostrils.

He was trapped, his heart locked into that single moment.

Gram wanted to cry, but he couldn't. He was numb. He took a deep breath, digging his fingers into the damp, cold peat under him. The trees swayed in the breeze, the sound of the fighting still audible. He couldn't see the burning buildings anymore, but the smell of smoke was still heavy in the air.

Gram had heard rumors of fighting in the capital. He had been warned to evacuate because of the pending Alliance aggression. He had ignored the warnings.

Now it had cost him his soul.

The Supervisor had been right. He had allowed his idealism to blind him.

Hoping that a politician countless light years away could understand or care about a few workers on New Utica was idiotic.

In less than a second, he'd lost everything that mattered to him. He tightened his grip on the peat until his fingers hurt.

The Alliance would pay for every life they'd taken.

Two women walked by him. The shorter of the two, with black hair, was helping the second walk on a badly mangled leg.

The injured woman was shaking. "This is over. We are dead. Fucked. We never stood a chance. Did you see what happened when that monstrosity came up the road?"

The black-haired woman glanced at Gram as they passed. "I don't think anyone walked away. I've never seen so much blood, so many mangled bodies. The smell of it."

The injured woman stopped. "Our rockets bounced. We are fucked. So fucking fucked."

"We'd need something massive to crack those things. Kline said nothing about this."

Gram had heard the sound of vehicles passing by on the road below. They'd been loud, their engines roaring above the distant fighting.

The Alliance had brought battle tanks in. His family at Cross Industries had worked their hands to the bone assembling the shells for those tanks — only for the Alliance to bring them here to murder them. Gram had worked as a chemical engineer for Cross, creating explosives for shells and ammunition. He knew what an impossible task it was to kill a Ramsey tank.

The image of Marty's face crossed his mind again. The way she had clung to him. Shaking. Sobbing. Gram pushed himself up, his legs cold and shaky.

He *did* know what it took to kill one of those monsters. That was his chance at revenge. His chance to show them once and for all that the force of arms can't win obedience, or intimidate and murder people into submission

No army could erase the will to be free, to be treated equally, with respect. That was the bedrock principle of the Alliance. They military had forgotten that.

It was time they relearned the lesson.

CHAPTER SEVEN

Lieutenant Derek Hiltabrand
10th Recon Marine Division
Alena Village
61 hours until evacuation

Hiltabrand ducked down behind the wall, bits of stone and mortar following close behind him as a bullet struck where his head had been. His heart pounded as he slapped his last magazine into place. This was insane. It was like being in a tornado, debris and bullets swirling around the square. He wasn't even sure how many people he had killed.

Humans.

Alliance citizens.

He took a deep breath. There wasn't time for reflection. If his platoon stayed here much longer, they'd all be dead. He popped out from cover. The nearest McGee had backed up near the wall, screening the remaining marines from the enemy. At least fifty combatants were picking their way through the bodies of their comrades.

One large man was crawling on his stomach, his dented helmet glinting in the rising sun. Hiltabrand aimed, squeezing the trigger. The round hit on target, splitting the man's head open.

Hiltabrand ducked back into cover. The best bet was to go for the arch. He had marines positioned on both sides of the street, though he wasn't sure how many of them he had left. They could hit the enemy on both sides, drive them back up the street, then make a goddamn bee-line to the trees. They would only get one shot at this.

Hiltabrand hit his mike. "Tiger Three-Seven, Tiger Three-Six, comeback."

Oren's voice sounded strained. "Tiger Three-Seven. We're down to the last ammo. If we keep at this much longer, they will be able to take my position with a feather and a rubber band."

Hiltabrand couldn't help but chuckle. Even wounded, Oren's sense of humor came through. Hiltabrand had been sure the man had died. He had seen him take a bullet, seen him grab his shoulder.

He hadn't seen him reach Able Squad's location.

Hiltabrand shifted his grip on his weapon. "We'll be right there with ya. We need to get the fuck out of Dodge. Go for the arches, then the woods. Regroup on the ridge."

"We'll need to get word to Beliard. They can't be much better off."

Hiltabrand peered out. "That's gonna be hard. Nearest McGee is fifteen feet away. Give me cover in sixty seconds."

Oren's voice was barely a whisper over the crackle of the radio. "We'll give you our best."

Hiltabrand turned around. "Bobby, front and center."

A lanky private scrambled down the line towards him. "Yes, sir?"

He pulled the man close. "I need a runner. Get to that McGee. We are going to try a breakout. When we go, we'll need their help. Go in five. We will rally on the ridge."

Bobby nodded, his face ashen.

Hiltabrand gave what he hoped was a reassuring smile. "Don't worry, we've got your back. Now go!"

The fire from Oren's side picked up. Hiltabrand took a deep breath, then raised himself up. He picked a target and fired, watching Bobby sprint towards the McGees out of the corner of his eye. The ground behind him popped, dust and pebbles flung into the air as bullets struck the earth.

Fuck.

The enemy was shooting from the roof above them.

The nearest vehicle shot backward, its tires squealing. It spun around, aiming its front at Bobby. The distance between them disappeared, its door opened.

Bobby reached for a hand.

There was shouting from the rooftop. Hiltabrand looked up. A half dozen satchels were flying towards the McGee. The first few landed short, another bounced off the roof, the last one landed just in front of the turret.

The satchels detonated. The McGee's turret was ripped from its frame. The front glass cracked, the vehicle's armor ripped open at the seams, its fuel cell bursting into flames that engulfed the vehicle. Two burning men ran from the wreckage screaming.

Hiltabrand didn't hesitate, but fired two rounds, killing them both.

Cheering rose up from all around, drowning out the sounds of battle. Hiltabrand emptied his rifle, knocking down his exuberant enemies. The Alliance troops would have to make their move now. Before their enemy's jubilation subsided. He'd have to hope Beliard followed what he was doing. The fucking damaged radio was taking a toll.

Hiltabrand set down his empty rifle and clicked on his radio. "Third Platoon, fix bayonets. Charge on my order. If you can get clear, get clear. Do not wait for anyone."

Oren's voice came back fast. "We're ready."

He drew his pistol. "Hargood, Ozwald, keep as much fire as you can on those rooftops."

Hiltabrand closed this eyes for a moment, drew his pistol, and clicked its safety off.

Opening his eyes, he activated his mike "Go!"

He jumped to his feet, hopping over the wall. He dashed back towards the arch. His team opened up on the Legion troops in front of him as Oren's men charged from cover and ran towards their comrades.

Several enemies stumbled backward, surprise written on their faces. The first of Oren's marines slammed into the oncoming enemy. A tall private skewered a Legion officer, while another marine shot his opponent at point blank range, before silencing him with a bayonet to the chest.

The engines of the two McGees roared, their tires squealing. Hiltabrand looked back, saw attackers pouring from the buildings in pursuit of the vehicles.

His throat went dry. This was like holding back a tide. The fifties would cut through a group of enemies, blood, and gore falling like rain. Then the stream of bullets would move on only for more enemy combatants to appear.

Hiltabrand swallowed.

He turned back towards the arches, sprinting across the blood-soaked mud, stopping only to fire. He picked his targets carefully. Each round had to kill.

The shock of Oren's breakout was wearing off. The enemy had stopped running, turning back towards the meager Alliance platoon. The marines had made progress. Oren's team had taken the majority of the arch, Hiltabrand's own group mere feet from it.

The street beyond was still filled with attackers, but once the marines had the arch, the McGees could come about and blast a hole through the crowd.

This would work.

A short, round Legion woman bolted at him from the side. Hiltabrand squeezed off a round, toppling her backward. A second man came at him from just under the arch, brandishing a knife, his eyes bloodshot, crazed. Hiltabrand fired again, but his shot went wide.

Fuck.

He refocused, his heart pounding. He squeezed the trigger.

Nothing.

He glanced over the top of his pistol, saw his slide was locked open.

Out of ammo.

The wild-eyed man was almost on top of him. Hiltabrand waited until the last second. The man stabbed at him. Hiltabrand pivoted out of the way, grabbing the man's forearm.

He slammed his elbow into the man's throat, throwing his attacker to the ground. The man coughed and sputtered, trying to stand. Hiltabrand slammed his pistol into his opponent's skull with a dull crack. He whipped back around, reaching for another magazine.

The pouch was empty, a small hole in the bottom.

Cold sweat erupted on his skin, trickling down his spine. His hands shook, adrenaline filling his system. Hiltabrand fumbled with his bayonet, pulling it free.

Two Legion soldiers were firing at him, another charging at him.

A couple of marines slid in beside him and opened fire, the crack of their rifles ringing in Hiltabrand's ears. The three Legion soldiers dropped, along with several more he hadn't noticed.

Before Hiltabrand could ask the marines for a spare pistol magazine, something tossed him forwards, his hands barely breaking his fall. His ears rang, his head and stomach swimming. Someone was grabbing his shoulders, pulling him forward. He pushed them off, rolling onto his back.

His vision cleared. Another McGee had been smashed, flames pouring from the turret's opening. It looked like a grenade had gotten inside of it.

Oh, God.

Beliard's gunner swiveled the turret from side to side. Its rate of fire had slowed, picking targets carefully. Its ammunition must be low. Without that gun, they would all die here. Hiltabrand wouldn't allow that. Someday, he'd have a last stand, but this wasn't it.

Period.

Hiltabrand scrambled back to his feet. "Anyone have a spare pistol mag?"

Private Hargood swiveled on his knee, his face taut and white. He tossed Hiltabrand a magazine. Hiltabrand caught it and slammed it home.

He clicked his radio. "Tiger Three-Seven, Tiger Three-Six. Start pushing forward. Baker Squad, with me. Cover Beliard. Marines don't quit. Oorah."

Hiltabrand released his slide, then fired towards the tidal wave of oncoming enemies. Beliard's driver noticed, backing through Hiltabrand's team. The vehicle spun one hundred and eighty degrees around, moving through the archway.

Hiltabrand fired several more shots, waving the retreat. The few remaining marines turned, running after the McGee. The sun was now fully visible on the horizon.

Hiltabrand sprinted under the arches, nearly running into the McGee. Oren and his troops were tucked in along the walls, firing down the street. Beliard's fifty had increased its rate of fire again. The street was teeming so thickly with enemies that it reminded Hiltabrand of a parade or political rally. Crowds of people who wanted to kill him.

Gunfire from the roof peppered the Beliard's windows and armor. Hiltabrand turned around, facing the way he'd just come. The attacking enemy was almost on top of him.

Hiltabrand raised his pistol to fire. He'd been wrong. Today *was* going to be his last stand.

Time to make it count.

Commander Barbara Crichton

5th Armored Crop
1 mile from Alena Bridge
61 hours until evacuation

COMMANDER BARBARA CRICHTON bounced in her seat as *Bloodhound* sped up the road. Her periscope was clear. They had a mile to go to reach the bridge. The drones showed heavy fighting in the town below and the woods crawling with movement. So far, no one had wanted to tangle with her.

Unfortunately.

She would have preferred a straight-up fight, and this would be anything but. Crichton had never taken a bridge without infantry support, but she didn't have much choice. Marshall's forces were still moving into the town below. The army was securing the city entrance. The only other marines nearby were on their way down from Pegasus Bridge, under Captain Rayland. Crichton could wait. Maybe she should. But it would take at least another hour for any infantry to get to her.

Well past dawn.

Besides the enemy's lack of marksmanship, the low light was the Alliance force's strongest advantage. She looked to her right, double-checking the status of her column. All four tanks read green, except *Cannibal,* the lone Jackson. It was down to forty-six percent ammunition.

Crichton tightened her grip on the periscope, watching the data stream across her console. The drones were reading about one hundred and twenty-five heat signatures spread out on either side of the bridge. There was no indication of anti-tank weapons.

Isn't that what intelligence said, too?

Crichton pressed her eyes to the periscope. She could make out the line of reinforced bunkers and towers that characterized the Legion's defenses. Alena had three forward bunkers, one on either side of the bridge, and a third in a fork about fifteen feet in front of the bridge. A large tower was right behind the bunker on the bridge's left-hand side.

Crichton was going to go straight in, light up the bunkers while *Cannibal* dined on the tower. The smaller Renards could run down the barbed wire and do what they did best.

Tear up infantry.

Crichton typed in her commands, relaying them to her column. The small acknowledgment light beside each tank popped up quickly.

Her gunner, Corporal Tyrone Mae, laughed. "Look at them move. Fuckers can hear us coming. Bet they scurry away like shit-smeared rats when we clear our throat."

Sergeant Kroner, *Bloodhound's* driver, came over the intercom. "Time to get some."

The green of the periscope's night vision illuminated the many scurrying defenders. Mae must also be watching. Crichton could feel the man's excitement. He was a gifted lead slinger. Best gunner in the Corps. When Mae finally got his own tank, Crichton would be up shit's creek. She had never met anyone who could manually operate the sponsons while still getting the main cannon on target as well as Mae.

Automation was fantastic, but it never really worked as advertised. In theory, the gunner could select targets and the computer could use triangulation from drones or other tanks to lock onto it. The gunner could then select the rate of fire, have the computer manage firing, or pull the trigger himself. In practice, *Bloodhound* lacked the space for big, complex AI. The automation was always twitchy.

Not to mention that Crichton had lost count of the number of times their drones had been shot down, or some kind of interference had prevented target locks. Combine that with a tank's ability to pick up good, old-fashioned battle damage, and it meant manual control was the norm for most tankers.

Crichton swiveled in her chair, lowering her periscope directly onto the first bunker. "Column, this is *Bloodhound*. Break and engage. Full speed. Good hunting."

Crichton slammed back into her chair, the noise of the engine drowning out the electrical hum of her instruments. She could feel the movement of the turret, but kept her eye on her target. She picked one of the two gun ports, locking the target into the firing computer.

Before she even ordered it, Mae had fired. The tank rocked as the high-explosive round sped from its barrel. Crichton blinked instinctively, avoiding the flash of the explosion.

She surveyed the damage. Cement debris was spread out on the slope. The building was on fire, but intact. Tracers spat from the bunker, bullets peppering *Bloodhound's* front armor.

She locked on. "Hit it again."

Bloodhound vibrated as its treads ate into the ground, pulling its weight up the hill. Crichton felt the barrel recoil back as the shell streaked towards the bunker. Another bright flash and the bunker's concrete and steel frame opened to the sky. Burning people ran out of the wreckage. A quick burst of machine gun fire from the nearest Renard finished them.

The smaller vehicle was already passing Crichton's lumbering tank. Two of the three Renards slid into view, their guns flashing every few seconds as they sent short bursts of hot lead into the enemy lines. The Legion had already begun to break, falling back towards the bridge from the slag heap that had been the center of their defenses.

Crichton could hear the tell-tale buzzing of the sponsons coming to life, their double-stacked .30-caliber machine guns joining the volley of the Renards. Crichton felt a momentary twinge in her chest as she watched her enemies collapse.

She forced her focus onto the second bunker, gauging range. She locked in the coordinates. The turret spun, the moaning of its hydraulics filling the compartment. The first of the Renards crossed the barbed wired, turning its forward armor to face the machine gun nest in front of the bridge.

There was a flash from the tower.

Fuck.

Anti-tank round. It hit the Renard's side armor, just above the tracks. The small tank burst, flames and secondary explosions ripping across the barricade. The tank's broken corpse rolled back for several feet before coming to a stop.

Crichton keyed her radio, ignoring the flashing red of the command screen. "AT, AT! From the tower. Hit that cocksucker. All tanks, break. Kroner, get us moving."

Cannibal had fired, its shell smacking into one of the tower's braces. The building swayed but remained standing, its other three legs holding firm.

Bloodhound's autoloader snapped shut on a fresh round. Mae fired immediately, the heat from the round momentarily overpowering the air-conditioning. The shell hit high, exploding on the tower's roof, shingles and bits of steel armor falling into the river below.

Another rocket shot from the tower, smacking into *Bloodhound's* forward armor with a dull thud. A damage alarm wailed.

Without looking, Crichton disabled it, refocusing her eyes on the tower. She aimed her scope just under the top of the tower, waiting for the sound of the breach to close.

The tower exploded, collapsing in a fiery heap onto the Legion troops below. *Cannibal* had fired first.

Mae and Kroner were whooping and hollering, their attention on the droves Legion soldiers fleeing from their position. The Renards had advanced past the final bunkers, cutting holes into the lines of running soldiers.

Crichton pulled her eyes away from the scope. "Skip a shell, shrapnel shot. Hit those fuckers."

Mae nodded. "Yes, ma'am."

He flipped a switch, turning his hands downward. The turret rotated quickly, the gun lowering towards the ground. The autoloader moved, swopping the penetrator shell for the anti-infantry round.

Crichton watched the enemy firing uselessly against the tanks. The main cannon fired again. The shell skipped off the ground and detonated in the air just above the fleeing troops. Thousands of shrapnel fragments and smaller explosives rained on dozens of enemy combatants while Mae kept the sponsons firing, adding to his kill count.

Cannibal whipped round, firing on the nearest enemy bunker.

It took only a few minutes for *Cannibal* and *Bloodhound* to level the remaining bunkers. Kroner had turned towards the bridge, crossing the body-strewn ground at full speed.

Mae had joined the Renards, pouring machine gun fire into the retreating enemy. Sparks spit from Alena Bridge's trusses as bullets hit along its length. The intensity of the column's fire broke the remaining defenders, their inexperience and fear overcoming them in the face of the oncoming Alliance tanks.

Bloodhound started across the bridge, its treads picking up speed on the metal surface. Crichton fixed her eyes on the far side of the bridge. It stood to reason if the enemy wasn't stupid, they had built similar defenses on the river's far side.

She didn't notice the low ammunition light turn on as she zeroed in on her next kill. The alarm system still was overridden, its warnings silent.

General Herman Polis
4th Infantry Division
Outside of Cross Spaceport
59 hours until evacuation

GENERAL POLIS WALKED to the front of his command vehicle and leaned down by the driver. He watched through the windscreen as the convoy left the city. The three APCs were tucked in between the Whitman and two Jacksons with three Renards taking up the rear. The infantry was still tied up, both in the port and all along the length of the route.

Tramo's intelligence was worse than poor. It would take a large, dedicated force with space superiority to tear these islands away from the Legion. More if the territorials were bottled up or had already surrendered. Territorial units weren't known for their resolve. It wouldn't surprise him if some of the infantry he was facing had territorial backgrounds.

He walked back towards his chair, uncrossing his arms as he sat down. He pulled up his command screen, shifting uncomfortably in his seat. Nothing had changed. *Bloodhound's* column was crossing the bridge, Marshall's forces were still in Alena Village, and his own troops were finishing off the resistance directly around the spaceport.

Polis stood again, crossed his arms again.

He studied the holotable, hoping for something different. At their current speed, barring any attacks, they would reach Alena Bridge in an hour. His various advisors and intelligence officers were beaming, chattering in ecstatic voices.

Victory. Revenge.

Polis wanted to share that optimism, but he couldn't. They were blind to the danger. He wasn't So many things had already gone sideways. He reached down and typed in the command to zoom in on the bridge. Crichton's group certainly seemed to be on top of it. When the infantry platoon trailing the convoy in the truck got boots on the ground, they'd secure the bridge. The mission was still on time.

He hoped.

With the enemy fleeing and all the bridges in his hands, they could easily reach the Cross Facility by early evening and get back to the spaceport by morning. Then they could dig in and wait for retrieval.

He stared down at the slowly updating data, willing whatever he was missing to show itself.

Nothing changed.

Bloodhound's column kept advancing. Marshall's team had begun assaulting a huge mass of combatants, and Polis' own convoy was still snaking up the road. All Polis could do was focus on his mission — retrieve Cross and get him back to the port. The only way to truly know what traps were still ahead, unseen, was to spring them, face them head-on. He fell back into his chair, pulling up a casualty report. Too many dead. Too much equipment destroyed.

The mathematics of war.

CHAPTER EIGHT

Lieutenant Derek Hiltabrand
10th Recon Marine Division
Alena Villa
58 hours until evacuation

Hiltabrand's slide locked back. He turned, deflecting the blow of a charging man. He slammed his pistol down onto the back of his attacker's neck. The combatant crumpled to the ground with a grunt. He squared his body towards the oncoming Legion soldiers. He tossed his pistol at his next opponent's head, causing him to duck. In one motion, Hiltabrand pulled his knife and lunged at the ducking man.

They toppled to the ground together as Hiltabrand drove his knife into the man's chest. He pulled the knife free and stabbed it down several more times until the man stopped struggling. Something moved in the corner of Hiltabrand's vision, and he rolled sideways, knocking another enemy to his knees. Hiltabrand killed him with a single thrust to the back of the neck. Another attacker appeared beside him, swinging her rifle butt down at him. He tried to get out of the way, but couldn't move fast enough. The metal buttplate slammed into him, knocking his helmet loose. He fell backward, his vision momentarily white. He kicked blindly, his feet connecting with what he hoped was his assailant's knees.

He tightened his grip on the knife and rolled to the side, vision clearing. His attacker was on her back, not moving, head resting on a chunk of jagged debris. Hiltabrand ensured she was dead with a quick thrust to her heart.

Bullets whizzed overhead, drawing his attention. He glanced backward at the gunner on Beliard's McGee, who had turned to fire into the charging mass in front of Hiltabrand. The enemy fell back towards the buildings on the other side of the square.

Thank God Beliard was alive and kicking.

Gunfire from the roof peppered the ground in front of the arch, covering the enemy from counter-attack. Not that Hiltabrand had any intention of attacking. The arch was the marines' only cover from those guns. They had to get to the woods, assuming they had enough ammunition to outlast the tsunami of attackers flowing down the streets.

Hiltabrand looked over at his dead opponent's rifle. He wiped his blade on his pants and sheathed it. He fumbled with the rifle before yanking it from the dead woman's grip. He pulled it into his shoulder, the feel of it calming his racing heart. He aimed towards the horde of retreating combatants, picking his first target.

He squeezed the trigger.

The enemy soldiers were so thick, they nearly fell over each other as they scrambled away from the McGee's gun, unaware of the fire coming from the marines. Each round from the Alliance guns passed through the clumped enemies, knocking down multiple people at once.

His eyes caught an officer moving in front of the others, waving a short sword around.

Asshole.

Hiltabrand fired. The man collapsed into the wave of his comrades.

Hiltabrand's chest tightened. So many of his platoon dead...

He had to focus, had to trust his fellow marines to do their jobs. Oren and Beliard knew what they had to do — there were no more orders to give, nothing to organize. Hiltabrand's job now was to take down as many fuckers as possible.

He picked another target and fired. His training took over, his hand working the weapon steadily. He concentrated on making each round count.

The crack of gunfire from behind him had increased. The tracers from the McGee's turret disappeared, though the roar of it guns was still audible. It must have turned back to deal with the mess facing Oren.

"Son of a bitch!" Hiltabrand tossed aside the now empty rifle. Trying to ignore the surging enemy in front of him, his hands scrambled for a weapon among the dead. He found a small pistol and pulled it from the ankle holster of a dead Legion soldier.

Wasn't much to look at, an old thirty-two naval pistol. Probably a family heirloom from the Empire Period. He clicked the safety off as he got to his feet. The enemy hadn't charged. They were still holding back just outside the buildings, their poorly aimed salvos hitting in front of the Alliance position. The gunfire behind him had been replaced with cheers.

Hiltabrand looked around. It was as if someone had flipped a switch. The whole area was quieter, and the gunfire from the roof had stopped. Beliard's McGee was moving forward, blocking his view of the street. Without his helmet, he had no access to the radio.

He almost laughed.

It didn't matter what the fuck was going on. It was time to go. He caught sight of the few marines still with him, signaling them to follow Beliard. He started backing up, his eyes scanning for his Colt or his helmet. Impossible to find amid the jumble of bodies, debris, and equipment.

Damn.

Hiltabrand spun around and sprinted towards the arches onto the street beyond. His heart leaped. Oren's men were celebrating, slapping the backs of at least two platoons of marines. He caught sight of a Major in ranger attire.

He must be the head of the ranger detachment.

The major made eye contact with him, still breathing hard. "I heard you needed a hand. Major Jeff Marshall."

Hiltabrand tried to force a smile. "Yes, sir. Lieutenant Hiltabrand. Thank you, sir."

Captain Beliard came up behind him. "Too damn close. Those shits were thick as flies on a dung heap. Glad to see you in one piece, LT."

Marshall pointed at Hiltabrand's forehead. "Better get that cut looked at before we move. I believe we have a bridge to take."

Hiltabrand nodded, touching his head. A sharp pain lanced through his body. He looked down at his fingers, saw they were bloody. He stared at the blood for a moment. He hadn't felt the injury happen. He looked up. "I'm fine. My marines deserve the attention. We all need ammunition, assuming you have any to spare."

Marshall laughed. "And helmets, it seems."

Hiltabrand couldn't force a laugh. His command was all but wiped out, and they hadn't even reached the bridge. He had been trusted with an entire bridge, and he'd got caught by a rabble.

He'd failed.

Nothing would change that. Nothing would change the men and women he'd let die. This mission was supposed to be the mission that would let him show his worth.

He'd been wrong about that.

Instead, it had taught him the taste of defeat.

Marshall continued. "We'll get your team sorted out. I want to get moving. The radios are too fucked to reach anyone outside of this valley. I don't want to get caught with our pants down if there are more of those fuckers out there. Their defenses aren't what we were led to believe."

Hiltabrand nodded. This wasn't the time to dwell on failure. There was a lot of work to be done.

Lieutenant Colonel Anderson
5th Armored Corp
Cross Spaceport
58 hours until evacuation

LIEUTENANT COLONEL ANDERSON waited patiently as the door of his command vehicle opened. Early morning sun burned his eyes from the hole in the port's entrance wall. The dull humming of the two Renards stationed nearby drowned out the cheerful talking and laughter of the soldiers outside.

The ramp made a dull thump against the tile floor as it touched down. Anderson stepped out, fixing a smile on his face. Polis's reports and the sighting of tanks, even shitty ones, had him worried, but he refused to let it show around the grunts.

The soldiers nearby were mainly rangers. Many were asleep, huddling in small groups in the dark corners. Anderson yawned, his own eyes heavy. The few army soldiers were from his own unit — tank drivers, medics, and engineers.

His eyes rested on the burnt-out wreck of *Lead Slinger,* and the wreckage of the Legion tanks. *Big Dog* had reported sighting at least three more of these thin monstrosities.

A ranger Lieutenant, a fairly attractive one, came up from the side. "Colonel, Lieutenant Melissa Jade. Did you need something?"

Anderson met her gaze. "This your lot, Lieutenant?"

She blushed, her eyes flicking over the rangers. "Yes, sir. I saw no harm in some rack time. Could get nasty later."

Anderson raised a hand. "No explanation needed. I've been in the trenches. You've gotta sleep when time allows."

She held his gaze. "The area is secure. Elements of the Sixth Regiment went to patrol for whatever of the enemy is left nearby. We haven't been able to raise them in about an hour."

Anderson could see bodies piled in the rubble outside the gate. "Still struggling with the radio?"

Jade nodded. "We haven't been able to raise anyone outside this port. Some of the tanks have gotten sporadic signals from the bridges. We can't get any signal from drones to look for any sign of 'em. Either these fuckers have a jammer up nearby, or we have the wrong goddamn transmitters for this marshy shithole."

He pulled off his helmet, letting the sun hit his face. "Could be either or both. Drones are working here, so if it is a jammer, it's not very strong."

Jade shrugged. "I'll take your word for it, sir. I've never encountered jammers before."

Anderson surveyed the gate "Defending this gate is top priority. These guys are inexperienced, but they aren't idiots. If it were me, I'd hit this point hard before my opponent could solidify their position."

Jade nodded. "The shit bricks have made several runs at the gate. Nothing serious, just infantry. Our armor put 'em down." She adjusted the rifle on her shoulder. "But what happens when they roll up with more of their own armor? If those beast are tough enough to take down Whitman, then—"

He cut her off. "Agreed. The Renards won't offer much resistance, and the Jackson's armor won't hold up."

Jade's brow furrowed. "That's what I was worried about. I asked for a heavy weapons team. The army's spread out still. One of the marine units is supposedly nearby. No word from them yet."

Anderson looked back towards his command vehicle, catching sight of his adjutant. "Bob, get out here."

The small, bald, flimsy looking man trotted down the ramp. "Sir?"

"Get hold of the First. I want three pack howitzers up here, along with their heavy weapons team. Also get Big Dawg back up here."

Bob turned and walked back without a reaction. The man was a good adjutant, but had no decorum. If they were being jammed...

Anderson put his helmet back on. "Get your rangers to their feet, and be ready to move out in twenty."

Jade's face tightened. "Sir?"

He put on a reassuring smile. "I want those last tanks. One of the drones followed them. We lost contact, so we'll have to go out and find them. I won't leave them out there to prey on the territorials, whenever those guys get off the couch. Besides, we have soldiers overdue out there. Let's get them back."

The lieutenant nodded. "Yes, sir."

She turned on her heels, heading towards one of the groups of congregating rangers. Anderson normally preferred a marine unit or one of his regular army units backing him up. Rangers were good at what they did, but he didn't trust them outside the hilly, wooded areas that were their specialty.

This was the opposite. Tight corridors where the volume of fire was often more important than making slow, accurate shots. That being said, Anderson had been pleasantly surprised by how well Jade had functioned with *Cannibal* and his other vehicle. She had gotten farther faster than any other unit.

He had been looking for someone to replace his infantry liaison officer, someone he could embed with his infantry and act as a go-between with other branches. It had never been his specialty. From what he had seen so far, Jade was perfect — as long as she could perform as well in a situation outside her wheelhouse. This outing would be the perfect audition.

Even if she didn't know it.

Major Jeff Marshall

7ᵗʰ Ranger Battalion
Alena Bridge, 11 Miles from Cross Port.
58 hours until evacuation

"ALL UNITS, Berserker Six. Alliance forces approaching, north-north-west from the woods." Major Marshall clicked off his radio as he moved down the final slope towards the Alliance position. Spread out at the bottom of the hill were several tanks and Polis's command vehicle. Smoke was still rising from burnt-out wrecks — Renards, based on their size. All of the bridge's defenses were smashed, the gentle rise in front of it covered with debris.

Marshall wiped his forehead. Barely three hours past dawn, and it was already scorching hot. The humidity from the bay and connecting rivers made his armor stick to his skin. If these woods weren't crawling with enemies, he'd tie the armor to his pack.

But the enemy was everywhere.

Since leaving that shithole town, the Alliance force had been attacked almost every twenty-five minutes. Beliard's McGee kept drawing most of the fire, the Legion combatants sacrificing themselves in an attempt to eliminate the combat vehicle's bone-dry fifty-caliber guns.

It was ludicrous.

Wasting so many people to take out a single combat vehicle made no sense. Marshall dropped his magazine and checked the witness holes and charge indicator in its side. Three rounds, and the battery had just enough power left to shoot them off. The enemy's tactic did have one benefit — it ate up ammunition, trading Legion soldiers for Alliance bullets. Most of Hiltabrand's team were completely out. Had Marshall's team arrived fifteen minutes later, he doubted any of them would be alive.

Marshall reached the bottom of the hill and signaled his group to rest. He walked towards a small, huddled group of officers, Paxton and Hiltabrand just behind him. A young lieutenant on the far side of the gathering looked up and pointed at him. General Polis and

Major Stone, Snider's second-in-command, turned. Both men looked worried.

Not a good sign.

Marshall hadn't had any news from the other sectors since his lander had gone down. If other units had struggled the way Hiltabrand and Paxton had, the Alliance force risked being trapped — or worse. He hoped his rangers hadn't let Anderson down.

Or vice versa.

He nodded a greeting, catching his breath as he stopped in front of the holotable in the center of the group.

Polis smiled. "Morning, Major. Bob, get this man some water. We were discussing the next phase of our operation. Got some uphill left to climb."

The lieutenant Polis had pointed at walked away.

Marshall popped the clasp on his chest plate. "Where's Snider? Did my rangers take the port?"

Stone frowned. "Communication's down?"

Marshall nodded. "I haven't had a clear idea of what's going on since we landed."

Bob returned and handed him a canteen of cold water. Marshall took a deep drink, the icy water making the heat more bearable.

Bob pointed to the map. "If you will look here, Major, Anderson, the army, and your rangers have secured the port with fairly minimal losses. Unfortunately, the poor intelligence, flak defenses, and mines have caused issues along the road."

Marshall finished the water with a gulp. "They had mines, too? Tramo really dropped the ball."

Bob raised his eyebrows. "Indeed. The loss of the Henshaws, all but Captain Beliard's McGee, and several Renards can be attributed to poor intelligence. Not to mention the Whitman."

Goosebumps erupted on Marshall's arms. "How the fuck did they do that?"

Polis pointed to the holoimage of the spaceport. "Armor. They have tanks spread out at the spaceport's main gates. Anderson is going after a missing army unit and any remaining enemy tanks."

Bob nodded. "Communication issues haven't helped. Most of the squad-level transmitters and headsets are not working much past a mile. The drones and command vehicles seem to be functioning fine. Since the blackout areas and affected equipment are not consistent, we surmise we are dealing with poorly employed jammers."

Marshall pulled his chest plate off. "But we have the bridges and the port?"

Stone pursed his lips. "Yes. Once we get Cross, and Anderson has eliminated the armor, we should be in good shape. It's about speed now. Attacks have continued along the length of the line here."

Marshall couldn't help but smile. "I noticed. My team's ammo almost ran dry."

Polis crossed his arms. "You hit the nail on the head, Major. The issues we are facing are two-fold. First, everyone is struggling with ammunition. Even when we can secure additional stores of physical rounds from the enemy, we're not in one place long enough to set up stations to replenish our magazine batteries. We need to get the marines resupplied and recharged. Second, we need to assign sectors to specific officers. With Snider and his command staff dead, we can't risk confusion in the chain of command."

Bob continued. "Exactly. Our units in two sectors, which include three bridges and the approach to the spaceport, lack officers in charge. We also lack an escort for the supply caravan. It will be undefended as it moves between bridges."

Stone grinned. "I think the major here solved that issue. If he is willing, Captain Beliard can escort the trucks."

Beliard, who had just walked up, nodded. "Easy peasy. As long as I can get some belts for the fifty-cal."

Polis motioned his head to the supply truck. "Bob will see to your needs. That just leaves the final bridge sectors. Major, I want you with me. Captain Paxton, you can take over Remagen. We still need a commanding officer for this center sector, Alena and Nijmegen Bridges."

Marshall pointed. "Give it to Hiltabrand. That son-of-a-bitch is tough. Kept his cool in there, did a great job keeping his team together. He's not a captain, but if you have Rayland in charge of Zone Three and Stone goes with you to Four, he'll do. The kid can handle himself."

Polis sized him up. "Lieutenant, can you handle that?"

Hiltabrand's face went red, his voice soft. "Yeah — I mean, yes I can. Yes, sir."

Polis laughed. "Alright. Bob, list *Captain* Hiltabrand in command of Zone Two and get him up to speed on his command."

Hiltabrand's face turned a deeper shade of red, a small smile spreading over his face.

Bob nodded, pointing to the trucks. "Let me see to your ammunition needs as well. If you'll follow me."

The pair walked away, followed by Beliard and Stone.

Polis leaned over to him. "You sure the kid can handle it?"

Marshall nodded. "Yeah. That town was hell. He did a good job. What other option do we have?"

Polis stared at him, but said nothing.

CHAPTER NINE

Captain Ursa Blomb
6ᵗʰ Infantry Regiment
Cross City – Eighteen Miles from Cross Spaceport
57 hours until evacuation

Captain Ursa Blomb glanced around the corner of yet another building. This block looked the same as the last. Tall, sand-colored adobe buildings lining each side of the street. Small carts with produce and other goods clumped at either end. He looked down at his armband. The map was still blank.

He cursed under his breath.

"We are so fucking lost." Corporal Wes Montgomery fell into cover beside him.

Oliva Dunn, his lieutenant, snapped back. "We are not lost. I grew up on a shithole like this. Another few blocks till the marker."

Montgomery made an exasperated sound. "What fucking marker? Our equipment is being jammed. Radio's out."

Blomb looked around at the line of rangers behind him. "Shut it. We have to be close. Let's get the damn intel and get the fuck out."

Sergeant Riggs put up his hand. "Grunts, get going. End of the street. Move. Wes, your butt has the rear."

Montgomery rolled his eyes, nodding.

Blomb and his squad stood and ran, crossing the square. They tucked in behind the carts, eyeing the next intersection. Nothing, like the street before. They had seen a few terrified citizens, a few windows closing, but otherwise, the streets were devoid of everything but litter and dust.

His company's four platoons were spread out across three blocks, moving steadily towards the target the drones had identified. He wished he could be as confident as Dunn that they were still moving in the right direction. Blomb had grown up in a small agricultural community surrounded by tall mountains and large open spaces. His sense of direction was crap in this maze. He'd felt lost the moment he had entered the drab, cookie-cutter landscape.

Blomb raised his head over the cart, watching for any signs of movement. This whole region couldn't be under Legion control, could it? Could the majority of citizens here have evacuated already?

What the fuck was going on?

The street beyond sloped downward, ending with a large triangular building in the center of a forked road. The left fork looked like it turned down into another residential street. The right opened onto a small grassy park.

Dunn tapped Blomb on the shoulder, pointing.

Tank tracks.

She had been right. They were on the right path. Judging by the depth of the treads, the vehicles hadn't been moving fast. The enemy's base of operations had to be nearby.

He turned to Dunn and Riggs, signaling them to bring up the Howler rocket launchers. If those tanks were still about, he wanted to have them for breakfast.

Blomb turned back to the field, lowering his visor into position. He zoomed in on the field. Once he and his troops crossed into that opening, they would be exposed. There were buildings on either side of the park and a small stone wall was on the far end.

If there were shit-for-brains Legion troops on the field's far side, the wall would give them excellent cover. If they were in those buildings—

He tapped on his radio, crossing his fingers. "Cobra One-Seven, Cobra One-Six."

There was a cracking on the other side. "Go ahead."

Blomb pulled his visor up. "Are you still on my right flank? Near the small three story building, just before a park?"

Garvin sounded far away. "Yes, sir. I believe so. It all looks the same, aside from the park. Green is new."

"Take your troops into that building and clear it out. I don't want anything nasty catching us from the side."

"Copy. We'll have it cleared in no time."

Blomb clicked off his radio and waved his troops forward. They moved quickly, crossing into the field. Dunn was in the lead, followed closely by several others. Montgomery and Riggs were just behind Blomb as he made a bee-line towards the wall.

Dunn stopped and fell backward, her face missing. The sound of gunfire split the air. Blomb's muscles locked for a moment as he fought to understand what had happened.

They were under attack.

Machine gun fire ripped across the field, catching his troops in the open. Blomb turned, waving his force back.

Popping and whistling sounds filled the air.

Blomb was thrown from his feet, something searing his back. He rolled over, trying to orient himself. Montgomery was dead, his broken body sitting in the bottom of a crater.

The tanks were nearby, even if he couldn't see them.

Another set of high explosive shells exploded in front of him. He stood and fired off a few rounds in the direction of the machine gun fire. He couldn't tell how many were out there or even exactly where they were coming from.

He took several steps before a soft electric hum filled the air.

Before he had time to worry about it, another massive rumbling explosion hit him. The building into which he had just sent Garvin's team collapsed, dust and shards of brick shooting in all directions.

Blomb threw himself flat, covering his head.

He opened his eyes, locking his rifle into his shoulder. A line of combatants had appeared behind the wall, rifles resting on the stone. Their barrels were jerking quickly, firing without aiming. Blomb aligned his sights and squeezed the trigger, hitting an enemy in the head.

The remainder of his platoon had also gone prone. He couldn't make out who was still alive, their faces blocked by their own rifles.

They couldn't stay here. Every time a mortar or tank fired, it was right on target. This whole area must have been pre-sighted. Their only hope was to fall back and force the Legion soldiers to come to them. The Alliance troops could use the streets as funnels and exploit the Legion's inexperience.

Even now, the enemy struggled to hold their position against the accurate suppressive fire from Blomb's company. Several RARs had begun firing from somewhere behind him.

It was now or never.

He keyed his radio. "Suppressive fire. All platoons, fall back to the next street. Jordan, get your heavy weapons platoon into position."

Another tank's shell tore up the ground less than twenty feet in front of him. Flames engulfed more of his soldiers, dirt and hot metal filling the air. Blomb stood and took a step backward. He registered the small popping noise too late.

The newly activated mine detonated, killing him instantly.

Blomb never saw the Legion reinforcements slamming into the rear of his company, didn't see his command's last stand come to a swift and brutal end.

General Herman Polis
4th Infantry Division
Cross Industry Island
52 hours until evacuation

POLIS POPPED OPEN the top of his command tank as it passed under the first gate into Cross's facility. He had been an active voice against facilities like this for his entire career. No company needed such a massive gate far behind the Milipa frontier. No patriot should be so afraid of his fellow citizens. No one should have so many secrets that they needed to lock them away behind steel parapets.

Seeing the Cross facility's defenses in person only strengthened his beliefs. The front gates were massive, more than 35 feet tall and bristling with gun ports. Cameras were clearly visible along the top parapet. There was a guard house with heavily armored sentries visible inside.

How anyone could come to work here and still feel free...

That was the problem. These kinds of fortresses, for lack of a better word, had created the Legion. These businessmen were no better than robber barons, putting profits before people, pushing the legal bounds to line their pockets, hiding behind the public's fear of the Milipa.

Fuckers.

Young was an idiot. Polis hated men like Cross. If Young wanted to win points with Cross, he had sent the wrong person. Polis would make sure that Cross paid for this.

Somehow.

If the Legion caught and gutted the industrialist, it was his own fucking fault. Supporting Cross with the lives of servicemembers because he managed to bribe his way to popularity was a crime. Polis couldn't believe Parliament would support this kind of man.

This kind of situation.

All these cities were hovels, huddling in the shadow of this massive facility. It was medieval, and the whole Alliance would know about it. Polis' command vehicle was recording everything. The drones were taking millions of pictures.

Polis would finally have some teeth in the debate. No sane person could see this and not realize something was wrong. Even the Milipa wouldn't do this to their own.

And they were nasty.

Polis' tank came to a halt in front of a spiral staircase leading up a tower at the facility's center. He pushed himself up and walked along the top of the vehicle towards its forward section. He gripped the side ladder and slid down.

Four big men wearing jet-black armor with the logo of Cross Industries approached him. They all were brandishing military-grade Heinlein sub-machine guns.

Polis did his best to hide his disgust. If Cross needed firepower like that to guard his factory, what kind of business was he running?

They kept looking around, aiming their weapons carelessly. They looked... *twitchy* was the term. Whatever was going on in the capital, it had these mercenaries freaked out.

Marshall spoke from behind him. "These guys look ready for a fight, no? The Legion must be knocking at the door already."

Polis turned around. "If Cross resists, there is no telling how they will react."

Marshall rubbed his chin. "Wouldn't shock me if they shot first and asked questions later. I'll stay on my guard."

Polis shook his head. "No, I'll go. If something happens, you'll need to deal with it. Bob has the communication and command codes if you need them. Cross won't recognize your authority."

Marshall frowned. "Sir—"

"No arguments. My personal guards are better equipped to deal with this than the marine detachment. End of discussion."

Marshall didn't move, eying Polis's guards. "Yes, sir."

Polis turned back to the Cross guards and signaled his soldiers to follow.

The shortest guard spoke first. "Do you have an appointment?"

Polis laughed. "No. Tell Cross that General Polis is calling."

"No appointment, no entry." Two of the Cross guards raised their weapons.

Polis could hear his own guards click the safeties off their weapons. The hydraulic squeal of his command vehicle's machine gun sponsons caused all four of the Cross guards to look up.

Polis smiled. "Gentleman, I am here with the authority of the Admiralty to rescue your boss. You can take me to him now, or we can duke it out and I'll go through you. Your choice. We don't have time to play games."

The short man's face went a blotchy purple color. "Follow me." He turned and tapped a code into the tower's entrance pad. The bars slid up, allowing the guard to start up the stairs.

Polis glanced at Marshall, before following the short man up into Cross Tower.

Colonel Bradly Anderson
5th Armored Corps
Cross Spaceport
52 hours until evacuation

ANDERSON CHECKED HIS PISTOL, clicking off the safety. He put the pistol back into his holster. Lieutenant Jade and her platoon were spread out in front of his tanks, joined by a company from the Sixth Infantry Regiment. Including the Harkler command vehicle, he had six vehicles. Two Jacksons, one Renard, *Howler*, and *Big Dawg*.

He knocked the top of the Harkler three times. Its engine came to life, the sound of its revving engine like a massive animal clearing its throat. The other vehicles followed suit.

The spotter on the roof had seen smoke rising fifteen or twenty miles south of the gate. No one had missed the gunfire and explosions. It was a good chance the missing company from the Sixth Regiment had stumbled into some shit.

Anderson caught Jade's eye, nodded.

She turned, waving her hand forward. The infantry moved past the Renards guarding the gate into the street beyond.

The Harkler crept forward, rocking as it picked up speed. Anderson climbed down, pulling the hatch shut and locking it into place.

If that was the missing company, it was time to bail them out.

Johnathan Gram
Legion Weapons Depot

GRAM KEPT HIS WRIST LOCKED. This wasn't something he normally did without protective gear. Pouring this form of liquid hydroglycerin was dangerous. Beyond its instability, it was highly acidic. In all his years working as a chemical engineer for Cross, he had never attempted anything like this. He was the careful one, the by-the-book technician.

The last drops of liquid poured in the binding solution. He swirled the two liquids together, carefully placing the beaker over the flame.

He let out a breath.

Even though this was the hundredth time he'd done this today, he still felt nervous.

Gram's head spun. The six beakers he had boiling down filled the room with the caustic smells of the chemicals. He longed for a mask or rebreather.

The room was small and hot, the lack of windows and poor lighting adding to the danger of his task. This wasn't the proper facility for this.

He wiped his forehead.

Nothing mattered now beyond revenge. If he was going to get back at these murderous pigs, there wasn't time to be picky. If something went wrong, he'd just be joining his family a little bit sooner than intended.

Gram swiveled in his chair, moving to another table. He picked up one of the metal tubes the smug-looking colonel had brought him. He rolled it over in his hands. The metal was rough, bits of rusted flakes coming off in his palm as it turned.

He didn't care for the colonel — the man was more of a politician than a patriot. He was clean-cut, arrogant, selfish, and stupid. Gram doubted he was involved with the Legion for anything more than personal gain, a symptom of the disease that had infected the cure.

Men like the colonel were inevitable.

Men like the colonel weren't his problem.

His problem was the unthinking masses who followed people like the colonel, the mass-murderers rampaging through his home town. The butchers who had slaughtered his family without thinking or remorse.

Gram closed his eyes, trying to drive the image of his burning house from his mind. He opened his eyes, saw his white knuckles against the dusty red pipe in his hands.

This was his chance.

He uncurled his hands from the pipe and placed it on the stand in front of him. Gram placed a funnel on the open end and scooped a mass of finished explosive gel from an early batch. He dropped the green, pus-like gel into the funnel.

He watched the liquid bubble down into the pipe. To think something so small would be the means of his revenge, show so many his resolve. Gram glanced over at the pile of finished bombs.

Twenty cylinders per vest.

More than enough power to smash those metal monstrosities to dust.

CHAPTER TEN

General Herman Polis
4ᵗʰ Infantry Division
Cross Tower
51 hours until evacuation

When did I get so damn old?
    Polis took a deep breath as he entered a reception area. The sound of his racing heart filled his ears. He fought the urge to snap at the Cross facility guards in front of entrance. The march up to Cross's office had only reinforced his ire. Eighteen claustrophobic flights, with guard posts and paintings spread throughout. If he had to see one more portrait of Cross, he'd vomit.

Or shoot the fucker.

The only actual rooms he'd seen were the reception area on the first floor and Cross's office at the top. As long as he'd served in the military, the army and navy had clashed over resources. They wouldn't need to if men like this didn't waste resources for vanity, if they were true patriots.

The reception area he'd just entered was just as ostentatious. All the walls were covered in murals depicting what he could only guess was the Cross family story. The propaganda version at least. The small reception desk was immaculately clean and looked like some sort of very old hardwood polished to a high shine.

Cross should have just put a sign outside the man's office reading, *I'm compensating.*

Jackass.

Polis couldn't imagine being called up here as a worker. He remembered how terrifying it had been the first time he'd been called to Whitehall. It was all he'd been able to do to keep his hands from shaking. He remembered sweating through his uniform jacket.

Whitehall had nothing on this tower.

Polis took another deep breath. He couldn't let his emotions take control. If he met Cross this wound-up—

Cross's secretary, a short woman who looked like she hadn't eaten in a year, looked up. "Do you have an appointment?"

The guard in front took off his helmet. "Gene, boss is expecting the General."

Gene looked up, sneering. "Sure thing. Go ahead."

Polis and his guards, along with two of Cross's men, entered the office. The room was massive, far larger than Polis would have needed as a headquarters for his entire division. The ceilings were vaulted, with paintings matching the ones in the entryway.

The wall opposite the door had been replaced with stained glass windows.

Cross was sitting, legs up on his desk, one hand on his knee, the other tucked into his perfectly tousled hair. His lips curled into a greasy politician's smile beneath a thin mustache and goatee.

Cross sat up. "General Polis. It's been what, a year?"

Polis put up his hand. "Not long enough, I'm afraid. You know why I'm here."

The man shifted, letting his feet fall. "Of course. Do you?"

He ignored the man's comment. "New Utica is under attack. The

Admiralty has put the whole planet under martial law. I am removing you on their authority."

Cross's smile fell. "None of the trash you're playing with is a threat to me here. Utica is mine, and I will give it up for no one. Especially you."

Cross's guards raised their weapons, aiming at him. A surge of adrenaline hit Polis' system. He uncrossed his arms, letting his right hand fall onto his holster. He hoped his own escorts had followed suit.

Polis kept his voice steady. "Mr. Cross. I am ordering you under the Articles of Alliance to have your men stand down. Refusal would be considered an act of treason. You're to come with me for evacuation."

Cross turned and picked up a cup he'd left on the window sill. He tapped a ring against the glass, sipping the deep brown liquor. He looked up at Polis. "Are you deaf or just an asshole? I am going nowhere."

Polis popped the clasp on his pistol. "I don't have time to argue with you. Last warning."

Cross spun on the spot, his face purple and red "You don't have the stones for this. I'll make—"

Polis didn't wait to hear the threat. He drew his pistol and squeezed off two shots, dropping the nearest Cross guard. The sergeant of Polis' guard fired immediately, killing Cross's other bodyguard.

Polis pointed at Cross. "Ready to go?"

Cross was rigid, his knuckles white on his glass. "This isn't over."

Polis nodded towards the door. "Yes, it is. After you."

The industrialist hissed through his teeth. "Bastard. You'll pay. My friends will make you pay for your attitude. I *promise* you."

Polis said nothing, indicating with his pistol where he wanted Cross to go.

Cross moved slowly around his desk, a venomous look on his face. A large vein on his forehead throbbed. Polis turned to his troops, pushing a confident smile onto his face. Cross's guards would have fired, he was sure of it. That meant their trip back down the tower wouldn't be any safer.

He popped out his magazine, trading it for a fresh one. "Sergeant, Cross and I will go first. Keep us covered. Don't miss the corners. Slow and steady. Let the Harkler crew know we may be coming in hot. Secure and hold the square."

The sergeant nodded, tapping her headset, and repeating Polis' orders softly into it.

Polis grabbed Cross and pressed the pistol into the small of his back. "Shall we?"

He was sure he heard Cross muttering more insults, but he didn't care. If this did go south, he'd personally make sure the fucker got what he deserved.

Captain Derek Hiltabrand
10th Recon Marines
Alena Bridge
48 hours until evacuation

HILTABRAND FORCED HIS EYES OPEN. He shook off the heaviness on his eyelids as the blast of a truck horn echoed through the trees.

It was late. The sun had dropped past midday, starting to melt into the horizon. The heat was beating down on his face. His mouth and throat were dry. Sweat ran down his back under his armor as waves of heat rose from the asphalt.

When had he fallen asleep?

Another horn blared.

He pushed himself off the tree trunk into a sitting position, glancing in the direction of the sound. Three olive-drab Hydra transports and Beliard's McGee had stopped in front of the command tent. A line of marines were flocking to it.

Hiltabrand stood, his whole body protesting as he forced weight onto his legs. He rolled his shoulders, picking up the replacement rifle Major Stone had lent him.

Stone.

Hiltabrand's stomach turned. The look Stone had given him when he'd asked for a weapon could melt rock. Hiltabrand knew the failure in town had proved he wasn't ready for this command. Stone knew it.

Marshall was a ranger. He'd viewed Hiltabrand's attempt to survive that shit storm as heroic. As leadership. Any idiot would have done the same. He knew the moment Stone had made eye-contact him that the major disagreed with Marshall.

Why Stone had remained silent, he didn't know.

Hiltabrand crossed the yard towards the command tent. He pointed at the nearest lieutenant, Flay, who nodded and waved his troops to their feet.

Hiltabrand pushed aside the flap to the command tent. The climate-controlled air hit his face, sending shivers across his skin. The building wasn't complete and most of the equipment was still sitting outside. They had thrown it up mostly for the stronger radio equipment.

And the AC.

Hiltabrand caught Sergeant Oren's attention. "Trucks are here. Lieutenant Flay's team is starting to unload."

Oren turned, his arm in a sling. "Okay, sir. We'll get 'er done."

The grizzled sergeant hadn't stopped working since they hit the ground. Hiltabrand swallowed away a pang of guilt. Another great example of his leadership. He had slept while his subordinate worked.

Injured.

There were still more than twenty-four hours before any hope of evacuation. He needed Oren's experience, but not at the expense of the sergeant's health.

Hiltabrand put on a smile. "Oren, have you slept?"

Oren cocked his head to the side. "No, sir. Had to get my arm looked at, and trucks don't unload themselves."

Hiltabrand pointed at the sling. "Noncoms with broken wings don't offload crates. Take a nap. Flay and I can handle it."

Oren frowned.

Hiltabrand walked over to the radio and picked up a spare hand mike. He wanted to check in with Major Stone, see how his defensive zone was faring. He turned the nob to match the radio frequency for Stone's area, then depressed the button. "Predator Six, this is Tiger Three-Six Actual."

He waited.

The seconds stretched on without a response. He tried again, but no one answered. He met the radio operator's gaze. The man shrugged.

Hiltabrand set down the hand mike. "We live, Corporal?"

The corporal rolled his eyes. "Heard from them ten minutes ago. Dude on the other end was bitchin' 'bout those trucks."

Hiltabrand ignored him. He waited as the corporal tried one more time. Just what he needed, more communication issues. There were too many other things to do to waste time with this. The Legion was active. They weren't going to hide forever, and if they figured out what was going on, they wouldn't let Cross go. The last thing Hiltabrand wanted was to end up in a mess without coms.

Nothing.

The corporal looked back over his shoulder. "Keep trying?"

Hiltabrand nodded. "Until you get something. I want to know as soon as you do reach someone."

Hiltabrand left the tent, making his way towards the trucks. His gaze rested on the communication tower they had put up. It should be enough to cut through the interference they had experienced.

Either the enemy had something bigger or—

Hiltabrand looked at the edge of the woods. The hairs on the back of his neck stood up. There was movement. Figures. Shadows creeping forward, towards the light.

Fucker

Hiltabrand shouted, pointing. "Woods. The god damn woods. Fire!"

Several of the men around the truck turned their heads. The RAR team swiveled around, pointing their weapon towards the woods. Several of Flay's men looked up and turned their heads towards the trees. Hiltabrand pulled his rifle into his shoulder.

The tree line erupted. Bullets tore through the leaves, killing a handful of marines instantly. The Hydras lurched as machine gun fire peppered their frames.

Hiltabrand squeezed the trigger, emptying his magazine as he moved for cover. Flay had managed to reach a small ditch in front of the woods. Three more of his platoon were trapped beside him, pressed against the side of the ditch.

They were trapped. Unarmed. If the Legion advanced, Flay and his men would be dead. The rest of the platoon was spread unevenly across the field. Beliard's McGee turned, the bark of its .50-cal comforting.

Fuck.

If Hiltabrand hadn't fallen asleep, he would have control of the situation. At least he'd be sure how many marines he had on hand. He had two companies at his disposal between the two bridges, but he wasn't sure how many were there versus the southern bridge.

He loaded a new magazine, the electric hum of the rifle's recharged rails lost in the din of battle.

He couldn't worry about the other bridge. The trucks had stopped there before coming here without incident. All he could do was focus on the here and now. He'd have to trust his section commanders. His job was to hold this area and push these fuckers back.

Hiltabrand sighted another target and knocked him down with a single shot. From the trees directly in front of him, a large group of Legion soldiers burst out. Twelve, maybe more. They looked like unarmed men. Hiltabrand held his fire, his gun following the lead man. They were running right at the trucks.

Right at Beliard.

Fire from the RAR cut across the charging men, the McGee's fifty adding its own hail of bullets. The enemy collapsed one after another under the whirlwind of enfilading fire — Except for the first man, the one in Hiltabrand's sights. He squeezed the trigger, missed.

Fuck.

He corrected his aim. The man bucked sideways, stumbling, but kept his footing. Hiltabrand fired again.

The man threw himself down, escaping Hiltabrand's round. He landed out of sight somewhere near the McGee's front tire.

Hiltabrand stood. He'd have to go after that fucker.

The vehicle exploded. Liquid flame and shrapnel fell in ribbons across the marine position. The explosion rang in his ears.

Beliard...

He blinked, trying to process what had happened. He hadn't heard a big gun or mortar. No vapor trail. The biggest thing the enemy seemed to have were machine guns.

Nothing strong enough to breach a McGee's armor.

What the hell had hit it?

He focused on the enemy. Another set of men broke from the woods, running past Flay towards the remaining trucks. Bile filled his throat and his stomach turned.

The Legion soldier, the one who had thrown himself under the truck.

He must have had a bomb.

Another set of attackers were coming at him. The fire from his team was sporadic, his marines in shock. The explosion had dropped people into cover.

Only the RAR team seemed to have their heads on straight, their steady fire ripping up the leaves and enemy in equal portions.

A fresh surge of adrenaline hit Hiltabrand in the gut. If the Legion destroyed the remaining supplies, they'd rob the other positions of ammunition. He couldn't let that happen. He keyed his radio. "All units, Tiger Three-Six. They have explosives. Protect the trucks. Marines, focus. Stay in this fight."

General Herman Polis
4th Infantry Division
Cross-Industry Island
48 hours until evacuation

POLIS LET GO of Cross's collar and tossed him to the ground. The two officers in front of the Eagle personnel carrier looked tense, guns pointed behind Polis and toward the tower.

He hadn't looked, but from the sound of the shouting behind him, Cross's personal guard had pursued him down from the guard rooms.

Polis worked the stiffness from his hand. "Private, load our VIP and get ready to move out."

The soldier nodded, knelt down, and pulled Cross to his feet. Cross didn't resist,but yelled a string of incoherent insults.

Polis turned back to his command vehicle. "Load up, let's get out of this shithole."

Marshall was standing beside the Ramsey, a bemused look on his face. "That took forever. Trouble?"

"Not terribly. A few guards who thought they were big damn heroes and an industrialist who thinks he's more than a spreadsheet."

Marshall laughed. "I missed all the fun, General."

Polis felt the corners of his mouth turn up. "Really? Then next time, I'll let you retrieve the brat and I'll watch the rides."

Marshall nodded. "May have trouble up ahead. Stone's forces are under attack from the woods. There's a lot of confusion. Whatever these shit stains are using to fuck up communication is getting stronger. We are barely getting anything from other positions now."

"The faster we get back to the port, the better." Polis nodded to the Ramsey. "Let's get this old girl's guns back in it."

Marshall crossed his arms. "If these weren't the acts of desperate, unorganized wastes of skin, I'd be suspicious of how they always seem to be in the right place."

Polis looked away. "Hard to imagine they would have so many soldiers lined up, ready to counter-attack in the middle of nowhere."

Marshall started towards the transport. "Especially if they have forces assaulting the capital."

Polis turned and followed the major. "If they weren't, we'd have run across territorials. Only an idiot would leave that port unguarded, unless there was fighting somewhere more crucial."

Marshall nodded as they entered the Harkler. "Maybe they were after Cross, but it still smells fishy."

The hatch snapped shut behind them. Polis's stomach turned. If the Legion really had these kinds of resources, they had spread far beyond industrial worlds and backwater outposts. If they had intel on where to be, it meant only one thing.

The parasites had infested Whitehall.

The Harkler started moving. Whichever dickheads had sold them out had fucked up, shown their hand. The minute Polis got off this rock, he'd report Cross and this damn situation to Parliament and get an investigation started. Be the fox in the henhouse. What Cross and his kind did was disgusting, but the Legion were murderous traitors. Polis sat down at his console, flipping the switch to the communication hub.

Nothing.

He activated the drone camera feeds.

The fizzling on the screen wavered, but continued. He'd hoped Marshall had been wrong, but if the drones were down, the enemy had specialized equipment. Probably permanent structures with cyber warfare equipment to muck things up this badly. Even the infrared imager wasn't responding.

Those kinds of materials were classified, compartmentalized, top secret. How had these laborers built equipment like that without being noticed?

Polis tried a few more combinations of commands, cursing himself for not having activated the cyber defenses sooner.

He drummed his fingers on his armrest. "Do we have any communication capabilities left?"

The driver's answer was barely audible over the noise of the engine. "Only short-range laser link."

Polis let out a sigh, pulling down his periscope. He looked out over the terrain moving past the Harkler. Cross was an egotistical maniac, but he had an eye for beauty.

The grass was even and green, spreading out as far as he could see under the fading evening light. The only structure visible was a tall lighthouse, its red and black stripes contrasting with the blue edge of the horizon.

The Harkler picked up speed, following the gradually narrowing road. Polis bounced in his seat, his hands gripping tighter to the periscope's handles.

Grassy, open fields gave way to the dense forests, the trees' long shadows spreading over the road.

Polis watched for signs of enemy activity, but there were none. The time ticked by as they sped towards Arnhem Bridge.

The driver slammed the brakes.

Polis lurched forward. His breath caught in his chest. He turned the periscope forward. In Front of *Cannibal* and the remaining *Renard* was a line of Legion soldiers. Their uniforms were a mess, faces covered in grit and grime. Many were visibly wounded. Only a handful had weapons.

The leader clutched a white flag to his chest.

Polis hit his mike. "Major, check these people out. Keep them in front of us."

The Legion soldiers didn't move. *Bloodhound* pulled even with *Cannibal*. The massive tank's guns swiveled towards the enemy.

Marshall left the Harkler through a side hatch, joining a band of his soldiers.

Polis zoomed in on the huddled mass, straining to see anything out of place. The enemies were following Marshall with their eyes as he stopped several strides short of the front of the column.

The lead enemy dropped the flag and crossed the distance between them in two long-legged strides. He reached a hand out to Marshall.

Smiling.

CHAPTER ELEVEN

Lieutenant Melissa Jade
7ᵗʰ Ranger Battalion
Cross City – 15 Miles from Cross Spaceport
47 hours until evacuation

L ieutenant Jade fought down the bile burning her throat. She gagged, coughing. Her nose and eyes stung, the smell of burnt skin and gunpowder heavy in the air. The laughter of the last hour was gone, the feeling of victory disintegrated.

Reality had reared its head.

Dead Sixth Infantry soldiers filled the street and the field beyond. Broken bodies, separated limbs, and burnt bits of Alliance troops were everywhere she looked. The pockmarked landscape, falling ash, and tread marks laid out the events. Mines, mortars, and incendiary shells had done their job, eradicated the soldiers she had come to save.

This wasn't the first time she had seen death, but she'd never encountered anything like this. Frontin raiders and Milipa pirate incursions, but nothing like this. The violence of it.

How could the Legion be this strong?

She swallowed, pressing back another wave of nausea.

Jade's platoon moved up the street, sticking close to the walls. She picked her way through the shattered buildings, forcing her eyes to stay up and open.

The enemy had to be right here.

They had heard gunfire as they approached. Several fires still burned openly among the ruined buildings, the tread marks in the street crisp and fresh despite the falling ash.

She strained her ears, trying to pick out sounds above the rumbling of Anderson's vehicles. Only the soft clank of body armor and the thud of combat boots.

Jade looked down the last leg of the decimated street. Three doors, the largest of which was a rolling dock door, were still standing on one of the charbroiled buildings. They would have to clear the structure before moving on.

The Legion had planned this ambush in great detail, luring the Sixth into a kill zone. It was a professional, well-planned maneuver. The first she had witnessed from these ragtag traitors. She wasn't going to be their second.

She held up her hand, thumbing her radio. "Checkmate Six, Zulu Two-Six. Permission to clear the building. End of the street, left side."

Anderson's voice came back quickly. "Zulu Two-Six, Checkmate Six. Permission granted. We have lost drone imaging. Be careful."

Jade stumbled on the mangled body of a man in front of her. The man's tags were wrapped around what was left of his neck. Her breath caught in her chest. The faces of her husband and twins swam into vision. They were crying, a letter of condolence in hand. Nobody, no belongings. Just a tan envelope, with red lettering informing them she was missing in action.

Sergeant Marquez's voice sounded from just behind her. "You okay, Lieutenant?"

Jade bent down, picked up the tags, and slid them into her pocket "Fine. Sergeant, we are going to clear the buildings."

These soldiers had died for the Alliance. She could at least make sure as many of their families knew their fate as possible.

Without body tags, the army only had missing. She wouldn't wish that uncertainty on anyone.

Marquez hurried past, several rangers in tow. They stopped on either side of the door. Marquez nodded and a man in front of her turned and smashed open the door. The team disappeared inside.

She stood. The remainder of her unit were tucked into cover in the damaged building, their faces gaunt and pale. The building was small — it wouldn't take Marquez long.

Jade tapped her radio again. "Rangers, fan out. Collect tags."

The tanks kept moving, the army unit trudging along behind them. One of the Jacksons had lowered a minesweeping attachment, making its way onto the field.

The boom of detonating mines filled the air. She ignored it, focusing on grabbing as many tags as she could find.

A gunshot rang across the road. She turned towards it, falling to her knee, aiming in the direction of the sound.

Another shot sounded, more clearly than the first. Her eyes scanned the area.

Anderson's voice sounded tense. "Lieutenant, confirm shooter?"

She charged her bolt. "Don't see shit. Sounds like it's coming from the building."

Marquez burst from the door, firing his pistol wildly over his shoulder. Legion soldiers followed a second later, their guns raised. They were firing from the hip, bullets spitting off the ground around the sergeant.

Jade aimed her Heinlein for the doorway and held the trigger down. "Confirmed. Legion soldiers coming from the building. Engaging."

Many of the nearby rangers followed her lead, knocking down

enemy combatants as quickly as they appeared on the street, the enemy running headlong into the concentrated fire of Jade's team.

The flow stopped, but the incoming fire didn't. The ranger next to her shook violently and collapsed to the ground. Another of her troops near the door fell. She looked up, muzzle flashes giving away the shooter's position on what was left of the building's upper levels.

Jade clicked her radio. "Striker, fire support. Upper windows. Blast these fuckers."

The nearest Jackson turned on the spot, its massive barrel angling upwards.

Jade was tossed backward. Her shoulder broke her fall, pain pulsing across her nerves. She looked around, saw a jagged piece of burning debris right next to where she'd fallen. She coughed, her ears ringing. She could hear screaming from somewhere. Her radio had gone crazy, a jumble of voices filling her ears.

She shook her head, pushing herself up from the shattered ground, her eyes trying to focus.

The world came back into focus. She was on her knees, several feet from where she had been. *Striker* was on fire, its turret lying on the ground. Two flat Legion tanks charged out of the garage door. They were moving quickly, firing freely at the stunned Alliance armor.

A shell skipped off of the Harkler's rear armor and detonated in the rubble. The air sounded like it was full of angry hornets as rifle and machine-gun fire tore into the ground all around her.

Jade got to her feet, waving her troops towards the ample cover supplied by the shattered buildings. She threw herself safely in between bits of a foundation. She dropped her magazine and slapped in a fresh one.

She looked out. The Renards were scrap, burning heaps of metal. *Big Dawg* had turned, its turret following the nearest of the flat tanks.

It fired, narrowly missing its target.

Jade picked a window and fired at it. She couldn't tell if she hit anything. As long as those windows were occupied, the Alliance forces were pinned down. Legion troops were still spilling from the doorway, but Jade's rangers had managed to keep the enemy bottled up so far.

Until their ammunition ran out.

She hit her radio, cutting through the panic calls. "Checkmate Six, Zulu Two-Six. I need fire on the windows."

"Busy, Lieutenant. Let me clear the road."

Jade tried again. "AA guns, sir. Heat 'em up. They can hit the windows."

Big Dawg was moving, using its treads to rotate more quickly than the hydraulics. The Harkler had come about, it massive front gun searching for a target.

Big Dawg and the Harkler fired simultaneously. The flat tank shuddered as its front armor gave way to the 178-mm cannon of *Big Dawg*.

Anderson laughed. "You're on, LT. Keep your heads down."

The Harkler's turret-mounted AA guns turned and opened fire on the building. Bursts of flak fire detonated in the windows. The wall of the building collapsed in a wave of dirt and blood, exposing the panicking enemy soldiers within.

Jade's rangers opened up on the surviving targets, their accurate fire dropping the enemy quickly.

The second flat tank came back into view as it turned sharply around a corner. Its gun fired, smoke streaming from its barrel. *Big Dawg's* rounds were going wide or hitting right in front of the smaller tank. The flat tank returned fire, its speed keeping it just ahead of *Big Dawg's* gunners. A shell from the Legion tank detonated on *Big Dawg's* forward armor, but failed to stop the massive tank.

The Legion tank turned again and whipped its barrel around.

Right at her.

A surge of adrenaline hit Jade's bloodstream. She threw herself out of the way. An explosion ripped through the foundation.

Shrapnel balls bounced around the enclosed space. Screams filled her ears. Pain shot through her shoulder.

She grabbed the wound, blood flowing freely through her fingers. She let out a breath. The armor had caught the majority of the shrapnel.

Shot.

These fuckers had shot.

She pushed herself up. Ignoring the pain, she slung her rifle on her back. The flat tank roared up and over the edge of the ruins, right into the middle of the foundation. It fired another round, killing a dozen of the soldiers around her.

The enemy infantry was still cowering in the rubble on the other side of the street, the Alliance command vehicle's machines guns suppressing their courage.

Jade had to move. The flat tank was ripping them apart. She'd take her chances against the infantry.

She caught Marquez, making the signal to fix bayonets. He nodded, passing the order to the next man.

Big Dawg's barrel finally found its target. The flat tank split down the center, its armor black and burnt.

Perfect.

The enemy infantry would break when they realized their surprise had been spoiled. She stood, letting her wounded arm stay limp on her side.

There was yelling from behind her and the radio exploded with overlapping voices again. *Big Dawg* started to turn, but stopped, shuddered as explosion after explosion ripped into its side. The tank's armor gave in, its turret bursting flame, its side open and smoking.

Jade blinked, her mind blank. She looked in the direction of the incoming fire. Six helicopters were flying low on the horizon, machine gun fire and rockets filling the air between them. The command vehicle's AA guns had destroyed the first chopper before its rear armor split and internal explosions ran along its hull.

The helicopters turned towards the infantry.

Jade tried to fall back into cover, but the helicopters' machine guns won the race. Jade was dead before her body hit the ground.

General Herman Polis
4th Infantry Division
12 Miles North of Arnhem Bridge
46 hours until evacuation

GENERAL POLIS ACTIVATED HIS HEADSET. "Marshall, back off. Fire teams spread out. Guns up. Keep our guys covered."

He watched the huge mass of attackers inching away from the woods. Judging from the information Marshall had obtained, the Legion was alive and well. If they had enough forces left to attack Stone twelve miles up the road, why would they surrender here?

It didn't make sense.

It was contrary to everything Polis had experienced with the traitors. They'd refused to surrender in each one of the engagements so far. Even after each bridge had been surrounded, most of the enemy had chosen to jump into the rivers rather than surrender.

Why give up now?

Polis zoomed in on the periscope. "Cannibal, cover our rear. Bloodhound, up front. Be ready."

Cannibal, along with Marshall and most of the army personnel, turned and rumbled past outside of the periscope's line of sight. The few soldiers Polis could see were stationary, their guns raised.

Polis activated the intercom. "Legion soldiers, hands on your head. Single file. Move slowly towards the APC."

The wounded enemies pushed into a single-file line that snaked down the road. The Alliance troops formed up between the command vehicle and the enemy. Four of Marshall's troops went forward, inspecting the first of the Legion prisoners. After several seconds, the lieutenant at the front of the line nodded.

The man passed through.

Polis let out a breath he hadn't realized he was holding. He loosened his grip on his periscope, searching the tree line for movement, any sign of activity.

This could still be a ploy.

He squinted. The sun was almost gone. If the Legion had troops more than fifteen feet back, he couldn't see them. What he wouldn't give for one operational drone.

He turned back to the procession of prisoners. The first man was approaching the APC, arms on his head. The officer in front of him bent down to handcuff his ankles.

The Legion soldier rammed his knee into the officer's chin and pulled his pistol free in one motion. The officer crumpled to the ground.

The crowd went crazy. Some prisoners ran towards the army soldiers while others sprinted toward the woods. The enemy with the pistol fired point blank on Marshall's other guards, who toppled backward.

Bloodhound opened fire, supporting the scrambling Alliance marines. Its machine guns put down as many attackers as they could reach, but the enemy was right on top of them, fighting hand-to-hand for the Alliance soldier's weapons.

The Legion was outnumbered and dying quickly. Polis watched one of his troops drive forward, using his bayonet to kill his opponents.

Polis turned his scope. The Legion soldiers who had gone into the woods had emerged, running towards the troop trucks and APC.

A shot of adrenaline hit him.

The aggressive attack was the distraction. He hit his intercom seconds too late. The first of the Legion attackers reached Cross's APC.

The vehicle detonated, a heap of smoking scrap metal all that was left of the man Polis had been sent to rescue.

Johnathan Gram
12 miles south of Arnhem Bridge

MARTY WAS BURNING, clinging to her mother. Their flesh blackened, hair evaporated in flame. They were screaming. Screaming for him. Begging for help. He couldn't move, his limbs heavy. He forced his arm up, but his hand were charred, crumbling as heat disintegrated his flesh.

Gram pushed the nightmare images from his mind.

His chest tightened as he ran, his wounds screaming and lungs burning with the exertion. He locked his eyes on the command vehicle, focused on moving his feet. His revenge was so close at hand.

He couldn't give into the pain.

The man who'd led the assault on his home was protected in the belly of the metal behemoth's armor. The bastard that had killed his girls was slaughtering the men and women he'd grown up with, worked with his entire life.

Gram would get his revenge.

The command vehicle's gun's roared. Bullets zipped past him. He could hear yelling, screaming, as Legion believers gave their lives to kill this monstrosity. Their sacrifice had worked. The military fuckers had attempted to stop them, ignoring those fleeing to the woods.

Those who had the real power.

The first vehicle had been destroyed before the soldiers could react.

He heard the crack of a rifle behind him. His shoulder exploded with pain. He stumbled slightly, clutching his wound. He barely kept his feet. The bark of the rifles behind him increased their tempo, the command vehicle's engines thrumming as its treads turned.

Gram's target began to move.

He didn't have much time. He forced his legs to pump faster, his muscles aching with each step.

Another stab of pain shot through his leg. He screamed, collapsing forward. He slammed into the ground, driving the breath from his lungs.

Gram rolled onto his back, gasping for air. His leg and shoulder were on fire, his chest heavy. He looked down, saw his knee was shattered, blood running down his shin. Someone nearby was screaming. He realized it was his own voice.

He was screaming.

He shivered, sweat pouring down his forehead. He tried to lift his arms, but couldn't make them budge, his hands were boulders. His heart raced.

Am I in shock?

The smell of blood and burning oil stung his nostrils. The screaming and noise around him had subsided. His vision was blurring.

He shook his head, trying to see.

The image of his wife's face floated across his vision. Her smile. The way she laughed at his dumb jokes. The way she had looked in the moonlight the first time they'd made love. He could almost feel her skin against his.

He blinked. The image melted, replaced with the wide-eyed look of fear she'd worn at her death. Her arms wrapped around their child.

Focus.

He'd be with them soon.

Gram forced his eyes open. The command vehicle was almost on top of him. He didn't have to move, didn't have to do anything but hold on.

He forced his fingers to wrap around the makeshift cylindrical trigger. Gram took a deep breath, letting his mind fall back to his family.

His finger pressed down on the trigger.

The neatly stacked explosive vest detonated against the vulnerable underbelly of the Harkler. The war machine filled with a wave of deadly flames. The Alliance crew died quickly in the inferno. The reserve fuel tank detonated moments later, blasting the vehicle apart from the inside.

Gram had his revenge.

CHAPTER TWELVE

Lieutenant Harlan Landro
3ʳᵈ Infantry Regiment, 5th Company
Cross City, 1 mile south of Cross Spaceport
43 hours until evacuation

L andro waved his troops towards the spaceport. This was no
place to stop these bastards. It was too open, and the Alliance
troops were too outnumbered. The Legion helicopters strafed the
ground methodically, forcing his troops from position to position.
They needed somewhere safe from air attack, well back of the enemy
advance.

Landro needed to draw his opponents to a place of his choosing.

The street they were on was long, narrowing as it stretched away
from the spaceport. The buildings were old, rundown, and empty.
Landro and his troops had been lucky — if they'd gotten any farther,
the Legion would have had them trapped.

Fuck.

He should have known better.

The only reason people left their home this suddenly or

completely was an emergency. No one wanted to be stuck in the path of a storm.

Except for nuts.

A rocket roared past him and detonated against the building behind him. He covered his head as the second story disintegrated in a wave of jagged adobe.

He stood up and grabbed Corporal Ogden, his coms officer. "Move it, O! Get me the marine heavy weapons team on the line. We need to clip these whirlybirds' wings."

Another rocket burst nearby, showering his company in dirt and pebbles. These bastards were hitting too close.

Landro pulled Ogden around the back side of the smoking building. He tossed the woman into cover and pressed himself against the wall. He pulled his pistol free, firing at the mass of Legion troops pressing toward them.

His eyes stung, the smell of smoke burning his nostrils. Visibility was low. The enemy fired in uncoordinated inaccurate bursts, their rounds skipping off the ground and walls. A nearby officer caught a bullet in the back, dropping silently to the ground. Another screamed, his arm and shoulder thrashing with multiple hits.

Landro pulled his magazine and pressed in a new one. He stepped away from the wall, rounds hitting all around him. He backed up, firing as he slid into cover.

He let out a breath, looking toward Cross spaceport. They were maybe a mile away from the gate and the protection of the tanks and heavy weapons.

Ogden stood up. "I got hold of Erga's heavy weapons. They can be in range in ten, two more companies in tow."

He rubbed his eyes. "Tell them to stay back and dig in. We'll be coming in hot. There's a shit-load more than two companies out there. Not to mention those goddamn copters."

Ogden nodded, her face white.

Landro put his hand on her shoulder. "We got this, stay cold."

She smiled. "Ice cold."

Landro couldn't help but grin. "Fifth Company for life. Fivers. Ice for blood. We've gotten this far with these fuckers on our asses. We'll make it. Now, get going!"

She nodded, moving away along the wall towards the end of the street. He caught the eyes of his RAR team, pointing to a hole in the bottom of the fractured wall. The two men moved, squeezing into the broken building.

He waved the rest of his fire team inside. His company couldn't run if someone didn't stay behind and delay the Legion infantry. He wouldn't shirk that responsibility. His fire team had the best shot. He wouldn't risk more than that.

Landro tapped his own radio. "Fivers, Pharaoh Two-Six. We are making a run for the port. Don't stop. Just keep your heads down and move. Able Squad will provide cover fire."

He heard the RAR team open fire as he squeezed into the small room. The roof and second floor were gone, but the first floor was only fractured, its once smooth surface covered in perfectly round holes. The building jutted out into the street, making it a natural choke point on the narrow approach.

As long as the helicopters didn't blast the building down around their ears.

His soldiers looked scared, hands visibly shaking as they fired their Enfields in an even rhythm. Landro ignored the sound of the helicopters buzzing overhead.

Don't worry about things you can't kill.

He found a fist-sized hole in the wall and peered out. The mass of Legion soldiers were flooding down the street after his retreating platoons. Large swaths of people collapsed each time the RAR swept the enemy positions, the attackers in the rear falling over the bodies of their allies.

Landro aimed his pistol into the center of the crowd, firing each time he identified a target. They couldn't let up. They needed to buy time, give the rest of the platoon a chance to get clear. At the rate the enemy were replacing their fallen, minutes might be all they could afford.

The machine gun's steady stream of death barely slowed the Legion's advance. The dead clogged the narrow street, their blood filling the gutters, but it didn't deter the enemy from advancing. It strengthened their resolved, agitated them into a frenzy.

He looked away, sweat pouring down his face as he reloaded. The confined space was scorching hot. He wiped his forehead. A fresh wave of enemy fire hit the building, and Corporal Tyber slumped forward, then slid down the wall.

Bullets blasted through the wall everywhere, peppering the furniture, shredding the building, brick by brick.

Private Savio made a horrible choking sound, and collapsed, gripping his throat. Two other soldiers cried out and clutched at minor wounds. The foundation groaned, the building's walls bowing outward.

It was time to go.

If the enemy got much closer, Landro's troops wouldn't stand any chance of escape. He fired again, burning through his ammunition in less time than it had taken him to load.

Landro waved toward the exit. "Let's get the fuck out of here. Stay close to the walls. Don't look back! Keep your damn heads down. Don't stop until you reach the port."

The sound of the machine gun stopped. Its operators leaving the empty weapon on the ground and running through the exit.

He loaded his final magazine and sprinted out of the building. He ran full speed towards the next block. Landro couldn't see anyone — there was too much dust in the air. His muscles tightened as he turned the first corner.

The helicopter's mini-guns opened fire behind him. A fresh wave of adrenaline hit his system as bullets blasted all around him.

Pain ripped through his abdomen.

Landro looked down, saw a trickle of blood seeping from a crack in his armor. His legs weren't moving. He collapsed. He pressed his hands to his stomach, trying to stop the bleeding. He rested his entire weight on the wound and rolled himself against the wall. He lay still.

Everything was spinning. And... what was that sound?

Maria

His wife was singing nearby. He could smell bacon and eggs. She was cooking breakfast like she did every morning. The pain was gone. His skin was warm, his eyelids heavy.

They drifted closed.

Major Jeff Marshall
4th Infantry Division
12 Miles North of Arnhem Bridge
44 hours until evacuation

MARSHALL PUSHED HIMSELF UP, the ground spinning beneath him. His stomach turned, eyes burned, the smell of smoke and burning fuel stinging his nostrils. He blinked, trying to focus.

The world came back to him all at once. The thunder of machine guns and the crack of rifles surrounded him, broken only by the sounds of the injured and dying.

Oh no.

Another wave of nausea hit him. Polis's command vehicle was gone. Cross was dead. The transports were on fire or slag.

Suicide bombers.

Madness.

The Alliance forces were surrounded. Marshall grabbed his pistol as he stood. He ran his gaze around the chaos. The Legion soldiers swarmed over the edge of the woods. The remainder of the general's troops, three platoons at the most, were falling back down the road towards the Cross facility. *Cannibal* and *Bloodhound* pressed forward, firing on the woods.

He hit his radio. "Bloodhound, Cannibal pull back! They are using suicide bombs."

On cue, five more enemies sprinted out of the woods. The machine guns on *Bloodhound's* sponsons caught three, and *Cannibal's* smaller forward gun only killed one.

The last man lit off his vest against *Cannibal's* side armor.

The tank rocked to the side, its treads and wheels flying apart. The vehicle crashed back to the ground, smoke pouring from its cracked armor. The top hatch opened, and a woman pulled herself up, coughing. She tried to climb, but rifle fire from the woods caught her. She jerked, falling back into the remains of the tank.

Son of a bitch.

Marshall pulled a smoke grenade and tossed it towards the trees. "Bloodhound, pull back. Hit the woods at green smoke. Marines, Fourth Division, push forward to me."

Marshall activated his night-vision locator strobe and hoped the other troops were still wearing their visors. He sprinted into cover behind the burning wreck of Polis's command vehicle.

Between the smoke and the gathering night, he could barely see. They had to break out, get to Stone's position.

Before it fell.

Bloodhound fired its main gun. Dirt and bodies flew into the air, the fire from the Legion's main position lessening.

Two fire teams of Alliance troops had already reached him, the light from burning woods dancing across their terrified faces. He nodded, forcing a reassuring smile onto his lips.

If these were his own rangers, he'd go for the woods behind them. Very little fire was coming from that direction, and they'd have more cover.

But these weren't his rangers, and *Bloodhound* was too loud and too big to hide in the forest. The road was the only option, even if it wasn't safe.

He lowered his visor and zoomed in on the road ahead. He activated his night vision. There was a blockade just ahead, fifteen to twenty Legion soldiers visible behind piles of wood. The enemies weren't firing, only watching, their figures ghostly and green through his night vision.

He pulled another smoke grenade off his webbing and threw it.

He turned to the soldiers and marines around him. "Fix bayonets."

The Alliance troops complied without a word, the singing of steel blades drawing from scabbards barely audible through the noise of battle.

Marshall tapped his radio. "Bloodhound, Berserker Six. I've got another bone for you. Once you take it out, move to the rear. Keep us covered. Stay clear of the woods."

The radio crackled. "Bloodhound copies."

Marshall could hear the mechanical whir of the hydraulic turret turning. He held up his hand, waiting. *Bloodhound's* gun barked, the shell bursting the barricade into kindling, illuminating the position for a split second. Marshall squinted, examining *Bloodhound's* handiwork. The enemy combatants were gone, replaced by a deep crater.

Marshall waved to get the attention of the troops around him. "Move, people!"

He ran and didn't look back. The sound of whooping and hollering carried from the woods over the sporadic gunfire. Marshall didn't look, imagined the wave of enemies breaking cover, surging after them. A man in front of him collapsed.

He leaped over the body.

If someone had told Marshall he'd leave his own dead behind, he'd have punched them.

Until today.

Sacrificing the living for the dead would only create more corpses. Marshall wouldn't ask anyone to make that kind of sacrifice.

The road curved to the right. The sound of gunfire grew quieter, beyond the barking of *Bloodhound's* guns. A lieutenant he didn't recognize ran in front of him, waving a group of Alliance troops forward. Marshall's muscles tightened, his lungs burning with the effort of running in armor.

To be eighteen again.

Marshall was about to order the young lieutenant to follow him when the man turned, raised his rifle, and fired twice off into the trees to the left. A group of Legion soldiers broke from the woods. The lieutenant's fire team met their enemies with steel, their bayonets flashing in Marshall's night vision.

The lieutenant stabbed one man, kicked his body away. He turned, slamming his rifle butt into the head of another.

Marshall fired, the soldiers and marines around him adding to his volley. The edge of the woods tore apart, leaves, branches, and bodies toppling to the ground.

Panic gripped the enemy. Legion assholes faltered, then scrambled backward, falling over each other as they moved back into the protection of the woods.

Marshall lowered his weapon. "Move it, people. We have a long road ahead of us."

Captain Derek Hiltabrand
10th Recon Marines
Alena Bridge
40 hours until evacuation

HILTABRAND EASED open his bolt for the fifth time in as many minutes. The same round, its silver finish glinting in the dark, unchanged.

Waiting.

He hated waiting.

Legion forces had hit them every few hours since the assault that had killed Beliard. The enemy was close, lurking out of sight and range of his guns. Hiltabrand wanted to leave this ditch and run them down but knew he couldn't.

Intelligence was a fucking sham. The Legion forces on the planet were overwhelming. Major Stone was dead, his sector in shambles, Pegasus and Arnhem Bridges in the hands of the Legion. The demoralized survivors from the Alliance positions had trickled in between attacks, the same hopeless look on all their faces.

Survivors from Remagen Bridge had reinforced Hiltabrand's position as well. Captains Paxton and Rayland were dead. None of their teams had seen them since the first attack. The only thing that was clear was his bridges were the last ones under Alliance control. It was blind luck. He'd seen the Legion soldiers fast enough to halt their surprise attack. It had allowed them to fight the enemy off and save an ammo truck.

Luck had spared him. He'd always thought Paxton was the lucky one.

Paxton, dead. Hiltabrand cursed under his breath. They were rivals. They were friends. He never imaged Paxton would have bought it on this rock. An image of the man's family flashed in front of his eyes. Paxton's wife opening the manila letter from the Admiralty, crumpling to her knees. The tears streaming from her eyes as she realized she would never see her husband again. His young daughter's panic as she tried to figure out what was wrong.

Hiltabrand swallowed, forcing his mind back to the moment. Sargent Oren had gotten the radio working just long enough to get hold of Lieutenant Baxter's detachment at Nijmegen Bridge. The disorganization of the Legion had given Baxter enough time to dig in and hold his position.

Better to be lucky than good.

Altogether, he had almost 350 marines defending the two bridges. Two days ago, he would have given anything for this opportunity, the chance to lead in a high-stakes battle.

Not now.

Hiltabrand looked down the line. His marines were dug into

small fox holes running the length of the road on both sides of the bridge. He had one platoon on the bridge itself, positioned to leverage the marksmanship of his marines.

He slid his bolt closed.

Now he had the lives of 350 men and women in his hands — 350 marines versus God knew how many of these bastards.

It wouldn't be enough.

He felt a hand on his back.

Hiltabrand fought the urge to jump, looked back over his shoulder.

Oren slid down beside him. "Easy, sir."

Hiltabrand cheeks burned. "What's the word?"

Oren shifted his wounded shoulder. "Fucked. I can't raise anyone beyond Nijmegen Bridge. Baxter doesn't have much information, but he is sure the spaceport is under attack."

Beads of sweat erupted on Hiltabrand's neck. "One problem at a time. We better fall back to Nijmegen."

Oren nodded. "Or they need to fall back to us."

Hiltabrand laughed. "Sarge, you just told me the spaceport's being roasted. Unless you want to put up a fucking cottage with a picket fence and retire, we'd better get going."

But where? As far as Hiltabrand could tell, there were only two options: move to the Cross Facility and hope to use its fortifications, or head for the spaceport. Either choice had its risks—

"Without the port, we'll all be staying put." Oren unknowingly finished Hiltabrand's thought, his face passive. "But Cross's main facility may be our best bet until a rescue can be mounted."

He rubbed his chin. "Assuming they send anyone."

"This thing won't last forever."

Hiltabrand thought back to the briefing. "Neither will we. Do we have the manpower to get anywhere? There could be an awful lot of assholes between us and the spaceport. The Cross facility's is closer than the port and would be better cover than the woods, give us a base of operations to strike from."

Oren moved back to the edge of the foxhole. "The port's also half the distance from here, so unless you are sure we can get off planet—"

"No." Hiltabrand looked back towards the woods, his temper flaring. "These islands are small, isolated. If the bridges are destroyed we'll be trapped with no supplies and nowhere to run."

Oren nodded. "It's definitely a risk either way. The Legion are probably expecting us to run for it. No matter where we go, we'll have to fight our way there. Kind of a pick-your-poison moment."

Hiltabrand rubbed his neck. "I'd rather take my chances on the spaceport. Get ready to blow the bridge. At least that'll cut down on the number of fuckers nipping at our heels."

Oran response was soft. "Yes, sir."

Hiltabrand knew what he was thinking. Blowing the bridge would leave any Alliance survivors trapped and surrounded.

He swallowed, watching Oren hurry away. The port was their best bet. If they were trapped on New Utica, no high wall would keep these bastards out forever.

He'd rather die on his feet than cower behind a wall. If they could reach the spaceport, they could at least go down swinging.

CHAPTER THIRTEEN

Commander Barbara Crichton
5ᵗʰ Armored Corps
Pegasus Bridge
35 hours until evacuation

"Thirty seconds."

Major Marshall's tense voice filled *Bloodhound's* compartment. Crichton wiped the sweat from her brow, peering through the periscope at the ghostly form of Pegasus Bridge, illuminated by *Bloodhound's* night vision.

There was no movement, smoke still rising lazily from the wreckage of the hastily constructed Alliance defenses. Only the bridge's two roads and small pedestrian walkway were intact. She could make out a few barricades, but not many.

The bridge was short, just wide enough for *Bloodhound* to squeak through without ripping off her sponsons. The bastards must be hiding in plain sight, cowering in the wreckage. More than two hundred Legion soldiers had been slaughtered defending it the first time. More had bled to retake it.

They wouldn't just cut and run.

Crichton glanced at her command HUD. Fuel and ammunition were under twenty percent. The sponsons had already run dry. Her stomach turned, bubbling.

Marshall was crazy.

Even with all her guns full, the idea of trying to cross a bridge like this with just forty-five exhausted grunts for support would have made her feel uneasy. Granted, they had taken Alena with no Infantry, but they'd had multiple tanks then. There just wasn't any other choice. The river was too deep for *Bloodhound* to cross, the current too strong to swim.

Their best bet was to book it, get across the bridge and keep moving. So far, the Legion hadn't been organized enough to pursue them. They'd have to hope that trend continued.

"Fifteen seconds."

Crichton took a deep breath. "Smoke. Both barrels. Fire on my command."

The hydraulics of the autoloader wined. She punched in the target for the main gun, then the hull-mounted 105-mm cannon. Both guns tilted upwards, matching their angles.

She watched the time tick down. "Fire."

Both barrels roared. One smoke canister landed just in front of the bridge, while the other landed in the center of the bridge. Smoke poured out of the devices, clouding her view.

"Both shells on target." Mae's excited voice broke Crichton's concentration.

"Stay on task, Mae." Crichton's heart pounded in her ears. It was hard not to get pumped up when *Bloodhound* cleared its throat.

She zoomed in the periscope, trying to stay focused. "Hit 'em again. Then load shrapnel. Mae, keep 'em going. Don't let up."

Mae grunted a response.

Crichton keyed her radio, listening for the autoloader to finish. "Berseker Six, Bloodhound is hungry and ready to roll, sir."

Marshall responded. "Copy, Bloodhound. Move in. Let's get this done."

Her hands shook. "Kroner, take us forward."

Bloodhound started to move, Crichton's chair bouncing as the tank rolled over the debris-strewn surface. Mae fired again, heat from the barrels washing back into Crichton's face. There.

Flashes.

The thwacking sound of bullets shattering on *Bloodhounds* armor filled the cabin. Crichton rotated her scope. The enemy was tucked in right along the river bed. From that angle, they had perfect range on the pedestrian walkway. She entered the coordinates.

She looked up "Mae, some idiots for you. Bring the rain. Kroner, move us along one side of the bridge. Keep the infantry covered."

The cannons fired again, and Crichton pressed her eyes shut, the intense light of the detonating shell painful in the night vision. She opened her eyes again. The enemy position was on fire, secondary explosions from the shots rippling across the bank. She wished the sponsons were available. The machine guns would have eaten those bitches alive. Unfortunately, she had disabled the warning and hadn't checked when they'd had the opportunity to reload.

Idiot.

The scene playing out in her periscope view was perfect. The combatants were breaking, pushing and shoving each other as they scrambled up the bank, discarding their weapons in the panic of escape.

Crichton re-centered the main gun's firing solution. The next shell detonated at the crest of the bank, showering the running enemies in flame and shrapnel.

Bloodhound rocked, turning slightly to the side as its treads pulled it up onto the bridge, its massive forward armor smashing the wall that separated the road from the pedestrian path. She could hear the engine throttle up as Kroner pushed *Bloodhound's* speed.

She turned her scope around, her night vision illuminating the Alliance infantry. They were running, flowing towards the far side of the bridge, but falling behind. Heat from the main gun surrounded her again, just as Mae hollered to let her know he'd hit his target.

She turned back. "Kroner, ease up. Don't lose the infantry. I don't want to get stuck by ourselves. We have this!"

Crichton was pushed into her chair, her head snapping back hard. The computer in front of her sparked and smoked. Machine gun fire peppered the hull like rain on a roof. Her eyes watered as the acrid smoke of the burning computer filled the compartment.

Something big had hit their forward armor.

She flipped on the exhaust fans. Mae and Kroner were shouting and cursing, searching for their attacker.

Crichton pressed her eyes into the scope, searching the terrain. She let her gaze follow the machine gun tracers back to their source.

Her eyes caught the flat tank, speeding upslope towards the bridge. It was covered in a camo sheet, its lights off. Behind it, tucked into the edge of the woods was a mobile artillery piece, an old 75 judging by the size. Concealed machine gun nests surrounded its position on both sides. The gun wasn't a threat to Bloodhound's composite armor, but the infantry and the bridge itself were vulnerable. If they blew the bridge, Marshall would be trapped and her crew...

They had to take out both targets.

Fast.

She coughed, rubbing her tearing eyes. "Anti-tank in the one-oh-five, now."

The seventy-five fired. *Bloodhound* rocked to the side and lurched to a halt. Crichton's hands shook and mind raced as she pulled up the diagnostics screen. That gun shouldn't be big enough to hurt them. Even a Jackson's armor should have been too thick.

She was tossed back again, her helmet slapping into the bulkhead behind her. The flat tank had hit their front armor. Warning sirens wailed, their flashing indicator lights bathing everything in a deep red light.

One problem at a time.

She targeted the flat tank's forward armor.

The hull barrel traversed toward its target.

"Firing!" Mae's shout vanished beneath the roar of the gun.

Crichton watched as the flat tank tried to turn, but couldn't move fast enough. *Bloodhound's* shell hit the smaller tanks turret, tearing it off in a wave of flame and metal shards.

Crichton whipped the periscope back to the edge of the forest. Mae had already fired once, but had missed the cannon. The trees were on fire, and one of the enemy machine gun nests was in pieces.

Crichton glanced at her diagnostics. Her heart slammed against her chest.

The treads.

The Legion had gone for their treads. *Bloodhound* wasn't badly damaged, but it wasn't going anywhere.

Marshall's voice cut through the sound of the main gun firing again. "Bloodhound, move up. They are coming from behind. We need cover."

She hit her mike. "Berserker Six, we've lost our legs. The old girl's done."

Marshall's response was delayed, his voice low and tense. "Abandon her. Set explosives to blow her. We'll run for it."

Crichton looked back through her periscope, watched the small arms fire dance off the armor, sparks cascading along the tank's metal sides. If she hadn't known it was bullets, it would have been pretty.

Abandon her.

How could she leave the hound?

Another 75 slapped into the bridge by *Bloodhound's* side. Crichton steadied herself as the bridge swayed beneath them.

There was no way they could get out of the tank alive. Even with the wall, those machine gun nests would gut them. If the enemy was coming from behind, they would be surrounded. Someone had to stay behind, hold off the Legion until the rest of the detachment could get to the woods beyond. If they could do that, they could cover her crew's escape.

If any of them made it that long.

Crichton took a breath. "No, sir. Request permission to cover your withdrawal. *Bloodhound* can cover your retreat. When you reach the tree line, you can cover mine."

"Ours," Mae and Kroner said at the same time.

Marshall's voice was emotionless. "Permission granted. Be ready to move as soon as we hit the woods."

Crichton shook as adrenaline hit her, her head light. "Yes, sir." She swiveled to face Mae and Kroner. "Alright. Smoke from the one-oh-five, now. Get that damn gun with the main turret. Kroner, get outside and take the fifty. Keep those bastards back."

"Yes, ma'am," her crew shouted in unison.

The hydraulics whizzed as the tank's weapons swung into position. Crichton turned back to her controls and typed in the self-destruct code, forcing herself to take deep breaths. She fought down her emotions. This wasn't the time to feel.

She watched the smoke shell land in front of the bridge and belch its dark cloud. She keyed her mike. "Berserker Six, go. Now!"

Crichton watched Marshall's troops run, crouching behind the wall. Machine gun tracers cut through the smoke, hitting the concrete barrier. The main gun fired, and this time it was on target. The enemy cannon detonated along with its spare shells, its barrel hurled backward out of sight.

Crichton pumped her fist in the air. "Fuck Yeah! There we go. Shrapnel. Hit those machine guns."

She turned her scope back to Marshall's group. They were stepping off the other side of the bridge now, moving into the wafting smoke screen.

They could still do this.

Kroner had stopped firing the fifty. She looked up. Kroner was dead, his hands still gripping the machine gun's handle.

Crichton choked back a wave of emotion as goosebumps danced over her skin. Her throat constricted.

Nothing you can do.

She turned back to her periscope, pivoting to face the enemy. The hostiles were approaching quickly from behind, would be on top of them in minutes. They couldn't wait.

Crichton's thoughts went to the fifty-cal. "Alright, Mae. Get your rifle and go." Mae opened his mouth to say something, but Crichton raised her hands, cutting him off. "No argument. I'm right behind you."

He nodded, his face pale and glistening with sweat. He popped the driver's hatch open, and slid outside, pulling his rifle behind him.

She grabbed her own hatch lock, popping it with a quick turn. She pulled herself up the ladder, careful to keep her head down. The cool night air hit her face. She gasped, scrambling to the fifty-cal. She pulled it free of Kroner's grip, forcing herself to ignore the warmth still in his skin. She settled herself into as much cover as she could.

Rifle and machine-gun fire was still skipping off the tank's armor, filling the air with razor-sharp metal fragments. The smell of swamp water, smoke, and blood filled the air. Her hands were shaking uncontrollably, her stomach churning.

Crichton fired in bursts, rocking her machine gun on its mount. Her eyes were still adjusting to the dark, but she could make out the scrambling shapes in front of her. The screams helped her adjust her aim as she swept it back and forth over the bridge's entrance.

Something tore into her leg, pushing her backward. Pain lanced through her, her head swimming. She could feel liquid running down her leg.

Blood.

Crichton gritted her teeth, using the gun to hold herself up. Tears ran down her face as she held the trigger down. She couldn't let up.

Something hit her in the shoulder and stomach. She lost her grip and toppled down, rolling off the tank. She hit the ground, the impact driving the air from her lungs. Every nerve screamed with pain, her limbs heavy and cold. She couldn't see, her vision fading in and out of focus.

The thought hit her. She was going to die here. Alone. On the terms of these fucking traitors.

Not like this.

She shook her head, forcing her eyes to focus.

Not like this.

Crichton reached out, pulling herself up *Bloodhound's* forward ladder. Her body seared with pain as she hauled herself up each wrung. Her fingers wrapped around the top step, and she slid onto the top of the tank. She let herself fall through the gunner's hatch.

She landed on her damaged shoulder with a cracking sound. White spots danced across her vision, but she refused to lose consciousness. She focused her mind on a single thought.

Not like this.

She reached up, pushed the buttons to tell the autoloader to select an anti-tank round. The autoloader sounded distant, quiet. Crichton pushed the controls to lower the hull gun, pointing it directly at the bridge's supports. She could hear the sound of voices and the tapping of feet on the hull. Someone was pulling on the hatch above her.

The fire station light turned green.

"Hope you can swim, fuckers."

Crichton pulled the trigger.

MAJOR MARSHALL WATCHED in horror as *Bloodhound's* hull cannon fired. A ball of fire shot into the air, followed a second later by the sound of an explosion. The bridge wavered back and forth momentarily before collapsing in a tidal wave of cement and steel. *Bloodhound* tipped sideways, falling into the rushing water. Legion soldiers fell thrashing and screaming alongside the tank, their bodies swept down the river. The steady stream of fire from the enemy positions on the other side of the river stopped, the gunners no doubt transfixed by the spectacle before them.

Bloodhound was motionless for a moment, its turret like a boulder in the center of the river. The vehicle's self-destruct went off, a jet of flame and water shooting into the air.

Marshall's head spun. His chest burned. He fought to catch his breath, forcing long, deep calming breaths into his lungs. He had been in the military since he'd turned eighteen. He'd never seen an operation botched like this one.

Polis had been right to ask for orders in writing. Intelligence hadn't done their job. Young hadn't done his due diligence, either. Someone had to pay for this.

The enemy machine gun fire sputtered back to life, bullets ripping into the tree line around Marshall. He threw himself back into to the thicker underbrush, his nerves raw.

There had to be a reckoning.

There had to be justice.

Assuming any of them escaped to pursue it.

Corporal Marc 'Snake' Masters
1ˢᵗ Infantry Regiment
Cross City
36 hours until evacuation

MASTERS CRAWLED FORWARD on his stomach toward the ranger lying still in front of him. He reached out, pressing his two fingers onto the man's neck.

Dead.

He shook his head, pulled the man's extra ammunition from his belt. Sliding the magazines into his knapsack, he wriggled back into cover.

Spud pulled him up. "Snake, what the fuck are we playing at?"

He pushed his fingers to his lips. "Keep it down, you idiot. What the fuck we supposed to do, brother?"

Spud shrugged his shoulders. "Get the fuck back to the port?"

Masters rolled his eyes. "How you suppose we gonna do that? Flap our wings and glide there?"

Spud shrugged, exasperated. "If we have to, mother-fucker. You wanna die here?"

He handed Spud his knapsack. "And the wounded we have rescued? Fuck 'em? Leave 'em to die?"

Spud sighed and passed the knapsack to the three soldiers behind them, Privates Omar, Berma, and Melvin, all from the 3rd. The soldiers divvied up the meager ammo between themselves.

Good fellas, brave.

They hadn't signed up for this.

No one had. They were up shit creek without even so much as a stick. When the enemy counter-attack had started, they'd been trapped behind the lines.

Stranded.

It just made sense to Masters to keep doing his job, help the wounded. If he'd been hit, if he'd been lying in the dirt bleeding, barely holding on to life, if he'd been roasting in the sun, praying for a drop of water, someone would do the same for him, right?

So, far they hadn't found many. The enemy was combing the area for wounded.

And they weren't taking prisoners.

Masters drew his pistol. "Let's sweep the next block and get back. Sun's coming up."

He got off his belly and crouched behind a pile of rubble that ran the length of the street. This was crazy. The area was flattened. Almost every one of the cheap wood and adobe structures had collapsed and burned. It reminded him more of disaster relief than a combat.

As a kid, he'd read about the wars that had led to the Exodus, seen pictures of the nuclear waste zones that had been China, America, and Russia. Hell, he'd even seen videos of planetary bombardments from during the Empire Period, but it had seemed impossible. Ancient history.

Modern warfare was surgical.

Quiet.

Masters crossed the square, legs and back burning with the effort of staying low. He stopped, pressing his back against a low wall. He looked out. This street was filled with bodies, mainly Legion combatants. Even in the low light, he could see the impact craters from the helicopters' rockets.

From the looks of it, the enemy had been trying to get past a small, collapsed building sticking into the street. Someone had tried to use it as a choke point. It was a good place to look. He pointed, saw Spud's gaze follow his finger to the building.

Spud nodded his head in agreement, pulling his knife.

Masters studied the scene. Nothing was moving besides the rats picking through the corpses. He crept out, threading his way through the bodies. The Legion hadn't left any of their wounded behind so far for him to find. He was grateful for that. If he'd been faced with saving one of those animals...

He didn't know if his resolve would hold.

No one had needed to die here. There was no reason for violent conflict. These bastards were traitors, murders. They'd killed so many of his friends. They were probably going to kill him. He'd taken an oath to ease all suffering, but this was something he could never have anticipated.

Masters squeezed into cover in front of the protruding mess of a building and craned his neck to get a better look. The structure had collapsed. He couldn't help anyone in there. He looked out, saw the bodies of a dozen or more Alliance soldiers strewn along the corridor leading down the street.

Shot in the back, killed in the retreat.

Masters hurried to the first body and fell to his knees beside her.

Dead.

He didn't need to check a pulse to tell she was dead. She was on her back, her eyes were open but vacant. A part of her cheek missing, rodent teeth marks covering what must have been a beautiful face.

Snake closed her eyes. He wanted to cover her, stop the rats from their purpose, but he couldn't. It would alert the enemy that someone was alive behind their lines.

He moved forward to the next solider, a lieutenant. His body was crumpled, stomach pressed into the ground against a wall. Snake reached down to feel for a pulse. His heart leaped. It was weak but steady. The man was hot, feverish, his skin clammy and caked with blood. He was probably in shock.

From the hole in his armor and blood trailing down his back, this guy had a stomach wound that had gone clean through. He'd lost a lot of blood, but they didn't have time to get plasma in him. The sun was coming up, and they were too exposed in the middle of the street.

Snake took a compression bandage out of his kit and pressed it into the wound. He bit off pieces of tape to secure the bandage. The first priority was stopping the bleeding. They could attend to the niceties back in their basement.

He rifled through his bag and drew out a shot of morphine and another of antibiotics. He pressed them into the wounded officer's thigh.

The man moaned quietly.

Masters waved at Spud. "Help me turn him over. Stomach wound."

Spud hurried over. "Alive?"

Masters grabbed the man's arm. "Yes, dummy. Any others?"

Spud helped him roll the lieutenant over. "Na, no one. Lots of ammo, though. Which is good, I guess."

Masters unclasped the man's armor, then pulled open up his uniform shirt. "Shut up, numbnuts, and help me."

The dirt had mixed with the blood, stopping the bleeding. It wouldn't hold once they got moving. They could clean it later. He plucked another compression bandage from his bag, tossed the wrapper aside, and pressed it into the wound.

Spud grabbed his shoulder.

Masters fought down his irritation, looking up. "Help me with him. I don't want to set up shop here—"

Spud looked white. "Snake, its Landro."

CHAPTER FOURTEEN

Captain Derek Hiltabrand
10th Recon Marines
Alena Bridge
33 hours until evacuation

Hiltabrand yawned, drank from his near-empty canteen. The sun was cresting the horizon, mist rising off the blood-soaked grass. They needed to get moving.

The Legion hadn't attacked Alena Bridge for four hours, but their strikes against Nijmegen Bridge had continued like clockwork, the constant sound of gunfire a testimony to their stubbornness.

Hiltabrand had sent Lieutenant Flay, the ammunition, and the majority of his own soldiers to reinforce Baxter's position at Nijmegan. If the Legion attacked Alena now, he wouldn't be able to offer anything beyond light resistance.

For the moment, the plan was to take Nijmegen without running dry on ammunition. Then he could think about escaping Nijmegen Bridge. Even if they could do that, they'd still have to cross the seven miles to the port and get across Remagen Bridge.

Assuming it was still standing.

Hiltabrand looked up at the bridge, its metal suspension cables running in pairs up to one of its two spires. It was beautiful, its gold paint glinting in the early morning light.

He clenched his fist, anger boiling to the surface. So many people had died over this piece of shit. A cold, worthless piece of metal.

Pointless.

Every marine understood death was in the job description. The few had to be sacrificed to preserve the freedoms of the many. It was an honor, but to sacrifice so many to rescue one man...

It was illogical.

It was crazy.

It was wrong.

Private Walsh was setting the final set of explosives. Hiltabrand was ready to watch this damn bridge burn. A god-damned piece of shit.

"Captain?" Private Scott's voice broke his thoughts. "Captain Hiltabrand, Major Marshall is coming in hot."

Marshall? Alive?

Hiltabrand's heart skipped a beat.

His own marines were running towards the bridge, their guns raised. Just coming around the bend was a group of Alliance soldiers, dirt, and clumps of grass shooting up from the ground around them.

Hiltabrand dropped his canteen and scooped up his helmet from the rock on which he'd laid it.

Fuck.

He slipped it on, keyed his mike. "All forces, fall back across Alena. Approaching Alliance forces, don't stop."

He sprinted towards the bank, adrenaline pumping into his system. His feet hit the gravel and slipped out from beneath him. He toppled down the bank.

Hiltabrand's head spun, sides ached. He scrambled along the bank, pulling himself up. Private Scott was firing a pistol, detonator in his hands.

Hiltabrand pulled it free of his grip. "Get into cover. I'm blowing this fucker."

Scott darted away.

Hiltabrand pushed himself down, crouching behind a wall of sandbags. He stared up through the grating. The first of the Alliance soldiers hit the bridge, the sounds of their boots echoing against the river banks. Bullets whizzed past them, skipping off the metal railing.

Hiltabrand popped open the trigger, forcing himself to breathe. The last two soldiers backed onto the bridge, firing short bursts from their weapons towards the pursuing enemy. His heart pounded against his ribs.

Just run.

He watched the soldiers work their way backward, leapfrogging between points of cover. His own detachment had opened fire now, the noise of the battle deafening. He rested his wrist on the sandbag.

The first of the Legion soldiers had reached the bank. They tried to enter the bridge but were cut down by the more accurate fire from the marines. The final Alliance soldier stepped off the bridge, turning to run towards the system of foxholes Hiltabrand's troops had dug in front of it.

Hiltabrand squeezed the detonator and dropped into cover.

An explosion thundered through the air. Bursts of fire and smoke rippled down the bridge, its golden cables whipping in all directions. Bits of wood and metal rained into the river. The bridge's supports swayed for a moment before collapsing, massive pieces of steel and concrete vanishing beneath the swift current.

Hiltabrand turned and crawled up the bank. Marshall was at the edge of the forest, waving everyone to him. The major didn't look well, his face sunburnt and eyes surrounded by black circles, his helmet missing.

Hiltabrand hit his radio. "Alena team, Tiger Three-Six. Fall back to Check Point Baker. Squad leaders, radio silence."

The trek back to Nijmegen checkpoint took longer than Hiltabrand had thought, and was far more uncomfortable. The heat from the rising sun beat down on the exhausted troops, even through the trees. The smell of salt water and the humidity didn't help.

Hiltabrand's muscles ached as he climbed up towards the island's pinnacle. His stomach cramped, growling loudly. Hiltabrand should have spent more time at PT and less time enjoying the officer's club.

The Alliance force crept silently through the underbrush. He wanted to pick up the pace but knew they couldn't. The gunfire from Nijmegen Bridge had escalated again. According to the last report, the Legion hadn't attacked Nijmegen from this side, but that didn't mean they weren't lurking nearby.

Sweat poured down Hiltabrand's back. He wanted to pull his chest plate off, let the breeze hit his skin, but it was too risky. His mouth was dry, his throat sore from thirst.

He missed having a full canteen.

Marshall came up behind him, speaking in between breaths. "What do we know?"

Hiltabrand swallowed, his voice cracking. "Bullshit with a side of rumor. I got lucky, held onto my sector by my fingernails. The other bridges are in the Legion's hands, at least according to the survivors that trickled in."

Marshall pushed a branch aside. "This is a furry fucking hairball. You can worry about counting failures later. You've done good, son."

Hiltabrand's stomach tightened. "Anderson's dead, at least according to the survivors from Remagen, and the spaceport is under attack. Don't know how they are faring. Goddamn radios won't connect, except for short distance laser links."

Marshall frowned, wiping his brow. "Anderson's dead. Crap. Things just keep getting worse. I noticed the radios."

Hiltabrand continued. "We have a good number of marines to work with, three hundred, give or take."

Marshall glanced down at his wrists. "There's a win. It won't be easy getting across Remagen, and our time is running out. The Hercules will be entering orbit in twenty-three hours. Anyone not at the port will be trapped on this shithole."

Hiltabrand tried to keep his face passive, fear running up his spine. "Let's cut through to the road."

The woods were thinning as the hill eased downward. They couldn't be more than a few minutes from Baxter's forces. Hiltabrand tried to swallow, but he had no salvia, the inside of his mouth the texture of sawdust. His knees and legs ached with each step. He braced himself on a tree, lowering his feet past the loose rock.

I am never going to hike again.

Utica had seen to that. Hiltabrand had spent hours as a kid hiking old neglected trails like this. Dirty trails, stone paths had been adventures, challenges to overcome. He remembered enjoying them. Granted, he hadn't had body armor, supplies, and a rifle then. This was anything but fun.

His team stepped out onto the road. Hiltabrand swept his rifle back and forth as he walked carefully forward, his squad following in tight formation.

If some fucker were here, he wouldn't make it easy for them.

The sweet sound of songbirds and rustling leaves overpowered everything, except the sound of distant gunfire. Nothing was moving, aside from the lines of Alliance troops leaving the woods. He felt the collective sigh as the soldiers and marines entered the cool shade cast from the hills behind them.

Marshall pointed to a row of unopened drop pods lining the ditch. "Check them out, then we'll keep moving."

A couple nearby soldiers broke formation, shouldered their weapons, and started picking through the pods' supplies.

Hiltabrand watched, the corner of his eyes stinging. These pods hadn't opened, the large black flak holes in them making their occupants' fates clear. He shouldered his rifle, trying to concentrate on covering the road.

The search parties finished, covering the pods with their emergency blankets. He should have told them to stop. If any of the Legion combatants crossed the river or were hiding nearby, the blankets would tip them off that Alliance troops had passed by.

But he couldn't give that order.

Marshall didn't say anything, either.

Captain Lauren Divina
10th Recon Marine Division
Cross Spaceport
21 hours until evacuation

DIVINA PUSHED Private Seltzer to the ground, tumbling alongside him behind a pile of rubble. The spot where they had been standing burst into flames.

Fucking helicopters.

Even without the door, this entry was a great choke point, the structures outside funneling the enemy to her marines, Erga's heavy weapons, and the tanks.

Those four goddamn whirly bids had fucked things up. Their rockets had taken out the tanks before Divina had even seen them.

She pulled Seltzer back to his feet. "Eyes up."

He nodded, hands white against his rifle. Divina leaned out and squeezed off several rounds. The Legion grunts were making another run.

Erga's mortars popped and the two pack howitzers boomed, their shells exploding onto their pre-measured targets. The ammunition was getting low, and Erga still hadn't managed to take down the helicopters.

At least he hadn't run yet.

If they couldn't take those fuckers down before the transport came, they were hosed. If the enemy pushed them back, they were hosed.

She fired again, finishing off the magazine and knocking two of her enemies down. Her only saving grace was the army was in good shape on the other side of the facility. The Legion was concentrating their efforts here, on the marines.

Lieutenant Gormelli, the highest-ranking army officer remaining, had begged to let him go out and break out the hundreds, possibly thousands of soldiers trapped beyond this wall. She had seen the desperation in his eyes. They all knew the Legion wasn't taking prisoners.

She'd refused.

The Legion had swarmed out of nowhere, engulfing the entire remaining 6th Regiment and two platoons of rangers in a matter of hours. As inexperienced as they were, the enemy had set the perfect trap, luring out Anderson's detachment with a trapped company, then using Anderson's survivors as bait to lure out the 6th.

The enemy was using their values against them.

Even with the elements of the First and Third Divina still had, it wouldn't be enough to do more than harass the Legion.

The port was everything.

One of the helicopters came into view, its machine guns strafing the opening. Seltzer collapsed, his face and chest a bloody wreck.

Divina crouched down behind the wall. "Erga. Clear my damn skies!"

She heard the telltale popping of the Howler P1A7 launcher, seconds before she finished speaking. The Helicopter's motor roared. She glanced out in time to see the chopper move, banking hard to the left. The small rocket whizzed by harmlessly.

She slammed her weapon's butt into the wall. "Fuck! Erga, you asshole, don't waste—"

The helicopter exploded.

Another Howler round had hit it dead center. It fell slowly, its rotor cutting into the charging Legion forces, flame showering them as they tried to avoid the wreck. The smell of burnt flesh and plastic clogged her nostrils as the sound of agonized screams filled the air.

She wretched, popping in a fresh magazine.

Erga's voice was dripping with mirth. "You were saying?"

She fought down a pang of guilt. "Stay focused. We still have incoming."

One down, three to go. The helicopter had forced her teams into cover long enough to let their infantry slip past the howitzers.

She exhaled, popping out of cover.

Divina pumped the trigger, firing from the hip. She didn't need accuracy, the attackers were shoulder-to-shoulder, pushing through the entrance.

Combatant after combatant collapsed.

Someone tossed a grenade just behind the entrance. Its dentation shredded the mass of enemy soldiers.

The attackers broke, turning and running back down the street. These bastards were determined, but they didn't like bloody noses.

Divina lowered her weapon.

Corporal Vener sat down, his back to the wall. "Last grenade, ma'am."

As long as Divina could hit the enemy hard each time they attacked, they'd run. They didn't have the stomach for an extended fight. Too green.

She looked at her watch. Twenty hours until help would arrive. It was now a race between the *Hercules* arriving and their ammunition running dry.

Divina hoped the cards fell her way.

Major Jeff Marshall
7ᵗʰ Ranger Battalion
Just above Remagen Bridge
15 hours until evacuation

MAJOR MARSHALL RUBBED HIS SHOULDER, trying to calm the spasm in his neck. Every one of his muscles ached. His eyes were heavy, fighting to close. He blinked, trying to clear his watery vision.

He pressed his eyes into a pair of binoculars. He studied Remagen Bridge. The Legion was dug in, sandbags and temporary walls surrounding the bridge's entrance. Similar makeshift defenses ran the length of the bridge. From the looks of it, the enemy had foxholes both along the bank and around the defenses.

Marshall had expected panic. It hadn't taken much to drive the Legion off at Nijmegen Bridge, the enemy crumbling as soon as the Alliance troops had counter-attacked. The enemy hadn't secured their flanks, hadn't set up more than a few tents for sleeping. Marshall had hoped to find the same lack of preparedness here.

This was going to take a major coordinated assault. There was a lot of movement by the base of the bridge. They were no doubt wiring it with explosives. Whoever was in charge had a bit of grey matter between their ears. They knew an attack was coming.

Marshall lowered the binoculars, looking up. "Thoughts?"

Hiltabrand flipped up his visor. "Tough nut to crack."

Baxter was still staring. "They have it wired, and our entire approach is easily visible."

Hiltabrand nodded. "Bastards will blow it at the first sign of trouble. We have three emergency boats in the ammo truck. Let's send a team to knock it out."

Baxter looked up the bank, pointing. "There are some flat spots up river we could use. It's always easier to take a bridge from both sides at once."

Hiltabrand smiled. "We'd only be able to get fifteen people on those boats, and they won't be able to take much with them in the way of heavy weapons. Who knows what is lurking in those trees. See them there, on the left, just behind that little hillock?"

Baxter cocked his head to the side. "I don't see any signs of movement, but this ain't the angle to look."

Marshall raised his binoculars, gazing upstream. There was a long flat landing a mile or so up the bank with trees leading almost all the way down to the water. It was exposed and within range of the enemy's weapons. He looked over at the treetops Hiltabrand had seen. They were dicey. The hill completely blocked their view, but he could see a fairly large square wall that looked like it might have been an old church foundation.

It would give them cover if there was something nasty in those woods and trap the Legion combatants on the bridge.

Baxter continued. "Best bet would be to hit them around midnight. Let our people sleep. It'll also let the attack group hike down there and get ready."

Marshall tucked his binoculars into his pocket. "Agreed. We'll wait till nightfall. One team will go in at midnight and disable the explosives. They'll take one of the RARs we can send without sinking themselves. Once they've disarmed the charges, they can set up in those ruins and pop some of those fuckers from behind. Baxter, your idea, your command. Pick your team fast and get going."

Baxter raised his visor. "How will you know when we're in position. A flare?"

Marshall shook his head. "Strobe. We salvaged a few from some drop pods. Preserve the element of surprise."

Hiltabrand frowned. "This bridge is still going to be tough. I think we should separate. The beach isn't as fortified. I can attack head-on and grab their attention. You can take a second team down on the right and come up from the behind."

Marshall lowered his binoculars. "Good idea, but you can lead the attack from the beach. I'll take them head-on."

Both his subordinates opened their mouths.

He turned back towards camp before they could say anything. "We have one shot at this thing. If we fail, it won't matter who led what. We'll be stuck here. Now get going, and get some rest."

CHAPTER FIFTEEN

Lieutenant Patrick Baxter
10th Recon Marines
Remagen Bridge
19 hours until evacuation

Baxter waved his team forward. "Shut it. Push off."

The first raft slipped into the water with three soldiers in it — Sergeant Guarna and Privates Burk and White. The three men dipped their oars into the water as they pushed away from the bank. The boat moved smoothly and quietly towards the far shore.

Baxter had split his team into two groups. The first two boats would go straight to the other side with the big guns and ammunition. The last one would float downstream and disable the explosives. They had no black clothing and that bridge wasn't dark. All it would take was one Legion shit bag to look down, and they'd be fucked. At least none of New Utica's moons were full.

Baxter nodded to Corporal Donavan.

The second boat slipped into the water as Donovan and his team — Privates Gerard, Shelford, and Frand — waded into the water, hopping in one after the other. They quietly paddled after Guarna's boat, disappearing into the darkness.

Baxter stepped into the river, suppressing a gasp as the icy water crept up his legs. He hoisted himself into the boat, and Sergeant Johns and Privates Horner, Arnett, and Willard crawled in beside him. Baxter flipped down his visor and activated his night vision.

The raft drifted away from the riverbank, pulled by the current. Baxter and his team lay flat in the boat's bottom. They had to be still, not draw attention to themselves. This operation wouldn't work against a Milipa unit. Number one rule of guarding this kind of bridge was to watch the water.

The Legion had been smart enough to fortify the beach, but they had done it up near the top, facing the woods. He looked out at the beach wall. There were enemies there, but they were crowded around fires, laughing and talking.

There were a few hostiles on patrol, one along the beach, well back of the rest of the unit, and the other two on the bridge, one partially covered by a beam. They were standing still, watching the woods and road, laughing.

Baxter glanced at his armband. Four minutes to midnight.

The person patrolling the beach had to go.

Baxter pulled out his suppressor, screwing it onto the rifle he'd borrowed from the company designated marksman. He pressed the butt into his shoulder, worked his arm into the rifle's sling.

He lined up the scope's reticle with the sentry's head. The raft rocked back and forth slowly, making it difficult to hold his aim.

But he had to wait. The woman was walking slowly down the beach, kicking a stone. It would take her a few more steps to get far enough from the others that they wouldn't notice her fall. She stopped, brushing the hair from her eyes. She looked up at the sky, breeze hitting her face. She smiled.

Even though Baxter's night vision, she was beautiful. Slender, big eyes, and amazing dimples. A wave of guilt hit him, his chest tightening.

He took a deep breath, trying to focus. She was the enemy. A traitor. She had participated in the slaughter of his unit. His friends. She wasn't a beautiful woman, nor a piece of ass for him to chase and play with. She wasn't even human.

She had chosen her fate when she'd joined these monsters.

He exhaled, his heart beating faster. He squeezed the trigger. The woman's head jerked back, and she collapsed in a heap on the sand.

Baxter watched the group by the fire. No one moved. He leaned back, lowering his rifle. The raft turned round, slowly spinning. They were close. If their observations were correct, only the middle brace was rigged with explosives.

Light from the bridge illuminated the area, forcing Baxter to deactivate his night vision. He signaled Willard to get the rope ready.

The enemies on the bridge were moving towards the railing, their voices light and happy, laughing about something Baxter couldn't quite catch. They learned their backs against the rail. One of them lit a cigarette.

If they looked down...

No one on the raft moved. Everyone's gaze locked upwards. Baxter could hear his heart beating, could feel the boat moving.

Come on! Drift faster!

The team crossed beneath the bridge.

Baxter's shoulders relaxed. Willard tossed the hook, which snagged on the rock by the bridge support. They pulled the raft against the rocks, and Sergeant Johns clambered onto island. Johns climbed up to the hanging packet of explosives. He started working without a word.

Baxter checked his wristband. Half past midnight. This was taking too long. He felt helpless. He wanted to climb up next to the sergeant and help, but what the fuck did he know about explosives?

He turned his night vision back on, examining the bridge's structure. Nothing was there, besides a few bird's nests. At least they had been correct. The Legion had only put up a single set of explosives.

Johns jumped into the raft and put up his thumb, smiling.

Baxter pulled out the strobe, flipped it on, and dropped it into the river. Marshall and Hiltabrand would see it momentarily.

Baxter shouldered his rifle, whispering. "This ain't over. Cut us lose."

Willard cut the rope, and the raft drifted back onto the river. They'd have to wait to gain enough distance before they could paddle to the bank and rejoin the rest of his team.

The night air exploded with gunfire and tracers from Marshall's position. Hiltabrand would be moving soon. The first part of the mission was complete. He unscrewed his suppressor, readied his rifle.

It was time for the next challenge.

Major Jeff Marshall
7ᵗʰ Ranger Battalion
Remagen Bridge
18 hours, 30 minutes until evacuation

MARSHALL THREW HIMSELF FLAT, his bruised body screaming in protest. Another burst of machine gun fire swept the field, and a marine in front of him collapsed.

He rolled and stood back up. "Take that damn gun out."

The lack of cover was worse than he'd predicted, the narrowing approach to the bridge funneling the Alliance troops forward. Even the inexperienced gunners of the Legion couldn't miss. The screams of the wounded echoed against the hill and riverbed.

If Hiltabrand didn't move soon...

The lieutenant in front of him pulled a grenade and chucked it into the nearest machinegun nest. Marshall aimed at the nest, waiting for a target. One of the Legion soldiers popped from cover, trying to escape the grenade's blast radius.

Marshall fired, hitting the man in his side. Instinctively, the enemies next to him pulled back. They died instantly, the shrapnel ripping them apart, the grenade's pop drowning out their shouts.

Marshall ran forward, heart pounding in his chest. They weren't even halfway to the barricade. They couldn't let up. He paused only to fire, wishing for his helmet and its night vision. Tracers from the enemy machine gun burned through the air.

The Legion soldiers stood, yelling and cursing. Most were firing carelessly from the hip, their bullets slapping the ground in front of the advancing Alliance troops.

Marshall skidded to a halt and took a knee. He raised his rifle, picking a target. It was time to teach these arrogant fucks what marksmanship was.

His first shot hit a tall fucker between the eyes. The people around him jumped, their expressions masked by the darkness. He picked off all three in quick succession.

Several of the marines around him were following suit, their well-aimed, coordinated fire facing off against the angry, random volley of the traitors.

The nearest enemy positions were breaking. The pressure was working, death and blood cracking the nerves of the combatants.

Marshall stood, waving his troops forward. He sprinted the last few yards to the ruined machine gun nest. He slid into the first foxhole, his bayonet glinting in the light from the bridge.

He pressed himself into the cold, blood-soaked ground, forced himself to breathe deeply, easing the pain in his chest.

The Legion was still an untrained mass of angry workers. That was his best advantage. Marshall couldn't forget that. The enemy clearly had strategists and engineers somewhere, but the people executing the plans and manning the defenses didn't measure up.

The sound of Baxter's RAR wafted over from the other river bank, its staccato bark overpowering the screams of battle. Marshall peeked over the edge of the foxhole, could just make out Baxter's tracers blistering the other side of the bridge. The Legion defenders lining the bridge turned, exposing their backs.

The tone of the battle had changed, the bold firing from the hip replaced with desperate panic.

Marshall looked down towards the beach. The enemy defenses there were intact, enfilading the hill behind him. The Alliance soldiers still streaming down towards the river were taking serious fire.

Marshall slapped in a fresh magazine and got to his feet. He waved his troops forward.

Time to whack the wasp's nest.

Captain Derek Hiltabrand
10th Recon Marines
Remagen Bridge
18 hours, 30 minutes until evacuation

HILTABRAND CREPT along the bank of the river, the sound of gunfire covering his group's approach. The bridge was alive with enemy activity. Some of the traitors were firing on Baxter, their rounds chipping into the thick stone wall. Some were firing back at Marshall, the machine guns on the beach cutting holes into the lines of charging marines.

Those MGs had to be his first target.

The defenders on this side were focused on the ridge, their guns firing steadily. The two machine guns were close to the rear on small raised platforms. The enemy infantry, maybe fifty, were tucked into a shallow trench that curved back towards the trees.

Just in front of the trench was a series of foxholes and walls. Each one had three or four people firing up at the exposed Alliance forces.

Hiltabrand stopped his column. He signaled his orders, pointing to five marines. He pulled his knife, inching forward. The enemies in the machine gun were loading a fresh belt from a can of ammunition.

The gun was old, an antique, probably from the stores of the territorials.

Or maybe a private collection.

Hiltabrand's heart was beating fast as he pulled himself up behind the steps, his second team moving to the other weapon, a few dozen yards away. Hiltabrand held his breath, waiting.

The second team reached their target.

Hiltabrand nodded.

He launched himself up the stairs. He grabbed the closest enemy by the throat and stabbed upward in the man's lungs. The man opened his mouth to scream, but only a sickening gurgling sound escaped his lips.

Hiltabrand swiveled around to check on Private Nita, saw she had been just as successful. The private crouched, lowering the machine gun towards the trench. Hiltabrand craned his neck to look toward the other nest in time to catch his troops tossing aside the bodies of their opponents.

Nita finished loading the belt and opened fire on the Legion positions. A few seconds later, Hiltabrand's troops in the other nest joined the volley. The enemy fell in droves, scrambled to escape, trapped in their own narrow trench.

A few of them turned, faces pale and bloodless. They fired back, their shots killing a few of Hiltabrand's own as they sprayed fire at the marines.

The enemy's resistance didn't last long, the traitors dying in an overwhelming hail of fire.

"Come on!" Hiltabrand shouted. "Move up!" They still had the element of surprise. If they could get onto the bridge quickly they could break the backs of the defenders. Each marine killed was too many.

Hiltabrand's troops surged forward, shouting and firing at the bridge.

The enemies on the railing caught sight of them, turned to fire down at them. One of the enemy machine guns peppered the beach, making a mess of a few marines to Hiltabrand's right.

Hiltabrand pulled a grenade from his belt and tossed it among the defenders on the bridge. A big man with a bushy beard kicked it off. It detonated in mid-air, showering the enemy with shrapnel.

The big man twitched and fell backward as marines surged onto the bridge and down the walkway. Marshall's team had broken through, the enemy falling back across the bridge in a panic. Hiltabrand ran, using his rifle butt to help him to keep his balance in the mud. He set foot onto Remagen's first wooden planks.

He ducked, pressing himself against a beam as enemy fire hit nearby.

The Legion still had some unwavering defenders. They had at least one well-placed machine gun tucked in where the marines couldn't hit, several walls blocking their line of site.

Some of Marshall's force was going after the other beach, but for the moment those bastards were also firing up at the marines on the bridge

"Keep up the pressure. Don't stop."

Hiltabrand turned toward the source of the voice, saw Marshall coming up behind him. He looked out at Baxter's position. Tracers were firing in all directions. The edge of the woods was burning, muzzle flashes exposing the presence of the Legion defenders there. They had to get to Baxter. His force was small, and fighting in two directions.

He pointed. "We need to break through before—"

"Focus on the now, Captain." Marshall cut him off, reloading. "I am going to take a small group and go head on for the machine gun turret on the left. I should be able to draw their fire. Take it out."

Hiltabrand nodded, plucking another grenade free. "Go."

Marshall rushed forward, running to the other side of the bridge. The marines followed closely behind him, firing as they went, their bullets pinging off the metal barricade. Hiltabrand could just see the barrel of the enemy machine gun tracking the path of Marshall's force.

It opened fire. Bullets ricocheted everywhere, metal splinters and sparks flying in all directions. One of the marines took multiple shots to the chest and fell sideways off the bridge. Another toppled backward, convulsing on the ground.

Hiltabrand and his team ran forward along the bridge's opposite side. He pulled the pin and tossed the grenade.

Pain shot through his leg, and he toppled forward, his rifle skidding away. He covered his head and second later his grenade went off. He looked up in time to see the machine gun flying off its mount and into the river.

Hiltabrand's team kept moving, firing as they went.

He closed his eyes, pressing his hand against the wound on his leg. Blood seeped through his fingers, warm against the cold air. He moved his hand and looked down.

He laughed, his entire body relaxing. It was a graze — deep, but not fatal. He pulled some gauze from his personal medical kit and wrapped it hastily around his leg.

Hiltabrand looked for his rifle. Unable to see it among the debris and bodies, he drew his pistol. He started forward, but stopped in his tracks before he'd taken a step. His stomach turned, bile rising into his throat. Lying five feet to his left was the body of a man, his eyes wide and mouth open, a gaping wound in his chest.

God, no!

Major Marshall.

Lieutenant Patrick Baxter
10th Recon Marines
Remagen Bridge
18 hours until evacuation

BAXTER TOOK down another two charging Legion soldiers with his rifle. The woods were bristling with hostiles. Waves of screaming people were throwing themselves at his position, though his three RARs were holding them back.

Barely.

The ruins were excellent cover, better than he'd thought. The old church walls were very thick, reinforced in the center by some kind of thin alloy. Even the enemy machine gun on the bridge wasn't able to punch through.

Apparently, Uticans took their praying seriously.

Baxter was lucky the Legion hadn't fortified here.

Private White's head snapped backward, his body sliding in an unnatural position to the grass. Baxter didn't need to check his pulse to know he was dead. He ducked back into cover and took the two grenades from White's belt. He crawled to the opposite side and looked out.

The enemies on the bridge were panicked, fleeing in terrified bunches. Sergeant Guarna and Corporal Donovan were picking them off with their rifles. He waited until he could see a larger group coming towards them. The fleeing mass seemed to ignore them, running down the bridge's left side.

He pulled the pin and tossed the first grenade.

It landed, rolling in front of the retreating soldiers. The detonation tossed their bodies backward, and over the edge of the bridge.

Baxter could just make out Marshall and Hiltabrand's forces entering the bridge on the far side. The number of fleeing fuckers was about to pick up.

"Reloading," Private Gerard called out from behind him.

He turned. "Covering fire."

Gerard's RAR lowered.

Another wave of screaming idiots charged out of the woods. He picked out targets, the other RARs cutting down the assholes as they crossed into the open.

Incoming fire struck into the wall, spraying sharp bits of stone and mortar over the Alliance troops.

Burk screamed and grabbed his chest, blood covering his front. Frand set down his rifle, pressed his hands into the man's wound to stem the bleeding. A second round caught Frand in the head, killing him instantly.

A bullet hit just to Baxter's left, the chipped stone cutting his face. He looked back down the field. The Legion forces were too close.

Baxter fired until his bolt locked. He pressed the magazine release, letting the empty magazine fall. His hands mechanically slapped in fresh load. Gerard popped back up, his weapon barking.

Donavan and Guarna were yelling for him, but he ignored them.

The enemy was still moving forward. He couldn't keep track of the number of people he'd killed. They were falling in piles, tripping over each other as they came. If Baxter and his troops couldn't stop this charge, it wouldn't matter what was happening behind them.

The RARs weren't discouraging them any longer.

He pulled the pin off the final grenade and lobbed it into the middle of the charging crowd.

"Bayonets ready." Baxter pulled his blade.

The troops carrying rifles stopped firing and slid their bayonets into place. The RAR handlers backed up, letting those with ready steel move forward.

The Legion soldiers were feet away. Baxter stood, firing point blank into the enemy. One jumped the wall and Baxter shot him in the chest, toppling him.

Another woman clambered over the wall and tossed herself at Willard. The two fell to the ground, fighting over a small knife the woman had. Horner stabbed the woman in the back, kicking her off Willard.

Horner spun around, cracking another Legion soldier in the face.

Shelford was firing from the hip, using up his rifle ammunition, the Legion soldiers in front of him throwing themselves down on the other side of the wall.

Someone behind him was screaming.

Baxter turned this head to look. He felt something hit him on the side. He twisted as he fell, using his elbow to knock his attacker in the chest. When he hit the ground, he rolled to his left, stabbing down with his knife.

The blade caught his attacker in the stomach. The man kicked, screaming, trying to pull it free. Baxter twisted the knife, bringing his pistol down onto his skull with a sickening crack. His opponent stopped moving.

Baxter pulled his knife clear, and turned to face the fray.

Horner was down, covering his face, two Legion soldiers kicking him. Baxter fired twice, killing both. Shelford was using his rifle like a club, his bayonet broken off in the chest of a burly Legion officer.

Willard was standing in front of the wall yelling. He skewered a buff woman as she hopped the barrier, his bayonet pulling him to the left as her body fell. The enemy next to her fired point-blank range at the marine.

Willard screamed as the bullet hit him. He kicked the dead woman free of his bayonet, then used his rifle to shove his attacker into the wall before stabbing the bayonet into his opponent's chest.

Willard let his rifle fall, stumbling.

Baxter emptied his pistol, pushing the enemy off his injured troops. He reloaded, pausing as he realized the sound that was missing.

The RARs had stopped firing.

A fresh wave of Legion soldiers came over the wall. Baxter met the bastards head on, knife and fists moving on instinct. The first woman stumbled, falling over the wall, her neck spitting blood.

This was it.

Baxter kicked the next man in the jaw. He stumbled as he righted himself, preparing for the enemy assault.

It didn't come.

The remaining hostiles were running for the woods.

Baxter's head swam, his lungs aching. He fell to his knees coughing, sweat and blood trickling from his face. He tried to focus. The bastards had nearly overrun them. Why give up now?

A chorus of shouts from his left drew his gaze. Marines from the other detachments had broken through, their rifles and numbers pushing back the determined enemy.

It wasn't shouting.

His troops were cheering.

They'd won.

Remagen Bridge was back in Alliance hands.

CHAPTER SIXTEEN

Captain Derek Hiltabrand
10th Recon Marines
Half a mile from Cross Spaceport
11 hours until evacuation

Hiltabrand fought to keep his face passive. Even through the painkiller, each step was difficult. Pain coursed up his leg, his thigh muscles seizing each time he put weight on his leg.

Idiotic flesh wound.

He was in charge now. He couldn't show weakness.

He was in charge.

Marshall's broken body came back into his mind, the man's cold, empty eyes staring through him, the bloody, leaking hole in his chest.

Hiltabrand closed his eyes, blinking the image away.

I should have died. I should have led that attack.

Hiltabrand took another step, his hands starting to shake.

Goddamn it, asshole, pull it together.

This was not his first taste of combat. He was a life taker and a heartbreaker, not some wet-between-the-ears grunt. A hard-charging officer.

A lifer.

He reached down, double-checking that both the .38 he'd picked up and his Colt were in place. It was strange not having a Heinlein on his shoulder. With his leg, he couldn't carry the weight of a rifle and keep his speed up. They didn't have time to waste. But if he still had his Heinlein, he could manage.

The *Hercules* was less than eleven hours from pick up. The Legion had space superiority. Any captain worth his salt wouldn't risk coming after stragglers who weren't in position.

Hiltabrand's troops didn't seem worried about this fact.

Up and down the road, the marching Marines were celebrating. Laughing, singing, clapping each other on the back, carrying on like it was Friday night back home. Hiltabrand wanted to yell, tell them to shut up. There was no guarantee this road was clear, but they needed to let off some steam.

He swallowed, focusing on the movement, on putting one foot in front of the other.

Oren was beside him, his face passive, his uninjured arm swaying as he walked. The weathered sergeant wasn't joining in the celebration. Hiltabrand wished he knew what the man was thinking. Things kept getting worse. If the spaceport wasn't under Alliance control...

Hiltabrand took a deep breath and let it out slowly. He couldn't do this. Couldn't fall into a rabbit hole of nasty possibilities. Until he knew for sure what they were facing, all he could was follow the plan, prepare for a fight to retake a facility he'd never seen.

At least he had the schematics in his command files. Hiltabrand would have preferred first-hand info or real-time images. He had the lives of an entire division in his hands.

Or the remains of one.

Pain that had nothing to do with his wound filled his chest. So many friends were dead. His priority was getting as many soldiers as he could off this hellhole.

He looked at Oren. How could the man stay so calm?

Hiltabrand forced a smiled. "How's the wing, Sergeant?"

Oren chuckled. "I'm not flying south for the winter, that's the fuck for sure. But it'll heal."

"I bet you'll be flying before you know it, unless we miss our ride."

Oren glanced over. "Miss our ride? Not a fucking chance. I can already see the port."

Hiltabrand looked up. The tallest point of the spaceport was breaking over the treetops, the glass on its tall landing platforms glinting in the rising sun. Smoke rose from its far side, and he could just make out the sound of distant gunfire.

He glanced over, noticed the sergeant was still staring at him. "The Legion isn't going to let us fly into the sunset. We still have some major shit left to walk through."

Oren raised his eyebrows. "I brought my boots. Shit's part of a marine's life."

Hiltabrand let out a sigh. His stomach ached and his hands trembled. He wished he could feel that confidence.

Oren put his arm out, touching Hiltabrand's shoulder. "You're doing fine, son. Focus on the objective. You can't escape death. It catches up with all of us. Just keep it for tomorrow."

Hiltabrand's eyes burned, his throat going dry.

He coughed, trying to cover his reaction. "Thanks, Sergeant. These bastards are everywhere. How the hell do ya stop something like this?"

He rubbed a hand over the stubble of his beard. "Same as anything else. One foot, one bullet, one damn thing at a time. No one is better equipped than Recon. Tip of the spear. Edge of the knife."

Hiltabrand nodded. "Oorah, Sarge."

Oren lowered his hand. "Marshall picked you for a reason. Don't forget it. Leaders see things in us we can't see in ourselves. Command can fuck with you. I've seen it eat people for breakfast."

Why the hell *had* Marshall chosen him?

Hiltabrand looked back up at the spaceport, clenching and unclenching his hands. If he wanted to have the chance to ponder that question, he needed to focus on that building. The fate of everyone under his command was tied to the spaceport.

Live or die.

Captain Lauren Divina
10th Recon Marines
Cross Spaceport
10 hours until evacuation

DIVINA SHOT off her final rifle rounds into the oncoming enemy. A mortar shell exploded directly in front of her, the heat of the flames singeing her face and showering her with dirt. The Legion soldiers turned, falling back towards the exit.

She set down her empty rifle. "Lay it on 'em!"

The fire from her detachment intensified, bullets ripping into the backs of the retreating traitors. This was insane. The Legion hadn't stopped hitting their position since nightfall.

It was a miracle Erga's guns weren't dry. Once the big guns went silent, the enemy would walk right in and set up camp.

Divina had been rotating troops in and out of the fight all night, trying to keep her people fresh. It wasn't enough. There just wasn't enough ammunition to go around.

Even the sunrise had brought bad news. The helicopters were hitting them again full force. Erga had managed to take out another, but unless he could knock out the last two before they fell back...

Two would be enough to cripple their escape.

As far as Divina could tell, she had less than a thousand soldiers left to defend the entire facility. The army had fortified common areas, but hadn't gotten far enough. She needed to go inspect things herself, get them organized. Too many inexperienced lieutenants at the helm.

The biggest win so far was the explosive work. She had gotten the engineers to collapse the hallways on either side of the entry room. They had also rigged a deadfall trap that would clog the corridor with stones and debris. Last but not least, she'd hidden anti-personnel mines throughout the courtyard.

These preparations wouldn't stop the enemy for long, but they didn't need to. There were only ten hours before the *Hercules* was in range. It was all about delaying the enemy now.

Divina drew her pistol. "Check for ammo. We only have a few minutes."

"Jaguar One-Six, Tiger Two-Six. That was my last mortar." Erga coughed into the radio, no doubt choking on the thick smoke. "Time to go."

Heat flashed through Divina's cheeks. "Tiger Two-Six, ready to tuck your tail and run? We need to get those choppers. Do you have any rockets left? Howitzer shells? Heavy machine guns?"

Erga's voice was steady. "Ma'am, all of the guns are low. Without resupply, we will run out in minutes. You ordered me to inform you—"

Divina cut him off. "Switch to TAC-13."

She waited a few second giving him time to switch over to the empty channel. "Tiger Two-Six, as long as those helicopters are in the air, it will be open season on our soldiers when we hit those platforms."

"That's not what this is about." Erga's voice cracked. "This is your personal crap. Your opinion of me. This is about our last drop. It is my duty as company commander to advise my commanding officer of our situation. We are out of ammunition, and our position is untenable. We must fall back now or risk serious, unnecessary casualties."

Another flash of anger hit Divina. How dare Erga accuse her of putting her feelings over the mission? Typical Erga. The world always revolved around him. Fucker. What had she seen in him?

She took a breath. "Lieutenant, I gave you a direct order. When your guns run dry, join the infantry on the ground. Bring all your remaining rockets. We are not falling back until those choppers are shrapnel or we truly cannot hold."

Erga didn't say anything, but she could hear him barking orders at his mortar teams, heard them arguing back. Her anger broke. He might be right. They wouldn't last long without his guns. Maybe they should cut and run now before more lives were sacrificed, take their chances with extraction.

She looked up at the open platform.

No, as long as they could hold she had to go after these damn choppers.

A burst of machine gun fire cut off her thoughts.

Here they come.

She could hear yelling and the sound of the helicopter's rotors growing closer again. The men around her dropped into cover.

Already?

Her heart started beating faster. She checked her pistol and clicked off its safety. She couldn't see anything through the dust and smoke. She held up her hand, waiting. They had to save their ammunition until they had clear targets.

The howitzers opened up, booming steadily. A second later, the shells exploded about a hundred yards in front of her position. Tracers from enemy machine guns cut through the smoke, crackling through the air.

Erga's heavy machine guns joined the howitzers, their short bursts following the tracers back to their owners. The first of the Legion bastards broke through the smoke.

Divina squeezed the trigger.

The entire courtyard exploded with the sound of small arms fire. She saw dozens of attackers jerk and fall. A howitzer round hit directly in the center of the oncoming horde, tossing crumpled bodies into the air. The enemy seemed to collectively run for cover, the ferocity of their attack momentarily blunted.

Erga's voice cut through the noise. "Howitzers are dry. I strongly suggest we fall back."

Damn it!

The machine guns were not far behind. Their gunners were trying to stretch out their last ammunition, their bursts short, targeted. They'd have to fall back, fortify the hallways and wait it out.

A burst of machine gun fire from one of the choppers cut off her train of thoughts, its massive guns blasting apart the forward-most Alliance position. The helicopter dodged left, narrowly avoiding a rocket. She had her shot at one of the choppers.

She had to take it.

She fired another round. "Take that thing out, and then we'll fall back."

The enemy crossed into the courtyard, ramming right into her soldiers. She picked out her targets, only popping out of cover long enough to fire.

It wasn't doing much good.

The combatants were swarming over the courtyard, the chopper clearing their way, its guns cutting clear a single path.

Out of the corner of her eye, Divina saw Erga and two of his troops slide into cover behind her, each with a rocket launcher.

Erga's face was a blotchy red.

His mouth was moving, but Divina couldn't make out what he was saying.

The three marines got to their feet, aiming. The man on the left crumpled, a bloody hole in his side. Erga and the other marine fired, their shots going wide.

Bullets slapped the ground all around them. Egra shook his head and slammed another rocker into the tube.

She met his gaze. She recognized that look.

He was scared.

Her chest tightened.

She'd never seen Erga scared before.

She clicked her radio. "Cover fire, all teams. Protect those men. Let's bring down that bird."

Divina jumped up, emptying her pistol. Rifle fire slammed into the charging enemy line like a wall. This was more like a game than real life. She couldn't miss.

They just kept coming.

Erga and his final man popped up. They fired, trying to get the chopper pilot to run into a round. The helicopter banked hard, nearly hitting one of the walls as it avoided the rockets.

Erga's shoulder jerked backward. He toppled from his feet screaming. Divina yelled, goosebumps running up her arms.

The other man bent down, reaching for Erga, but a bullet caught him in the neck. The man fought to stem the blood pouring from his wound, his life fading away rapidly

Divina didn't know she was running until she was halfway to Erga, rounds and chips of stone like a swarm of hornets around her. She collapsed into cover next to Erga and reached for him. He turned, coughing, a dazed expression on his face. She looked at his chest, saw a small but noticeable dent in his armor.

She let a breath, pulling him up and back into cover.

He looked at her, his eyes softening. She felt an all too familiar burning in her cheeks. She forced herself to stay stern. She had never let feelings take over.

She wasn't about to start now.

He smiled. "Too close."

She pushed the launcher into his hands. "Not close enough."

Erga's lips fell. "Sorry, ma'am."

She held his gaze. Her hand lingered on the launcher, almost touching his.

Divina looked away, guilt welling up inside. The helicopter had turned, its tail swinging towards them. They wouldn't get a better chance. She opened her mouth, but he was already on his feet.

He fired.

The rocket hit the Legion machine directly on the tail rotor. It spun out of control, thick black smoke pouring from its devastated tail.

She grabbed Erga by the shoulder and pulled him down.

The helicopter vomited fire over her position, detonating as it hit the ground. They were both thrown backward, crashing into the jagged stone flooring.

She shook her head, clearing her vision.

He'd really come through. She hated sucking crow, but she had no choice.

There was still one left, but there was no way to hold this landing now.

It was time to go.

The destruction of the helicopter hadn't slowed the Legion infantry. They were everywhere. Guns firing into the back of her battered forces. Divina's troops hadn't waited for the order. It was all she could do not to panic, run desperately to reach safety.

She turned. "Alright, Erga let's get out of here. I'm sorry for what I said earlier. This was top notch work. Amazing—"

Divina stopped, her gaze falling on him.

Erga was leaning against a small fractured wall, a jagged piece of helicopter rotor sticking out from his chest.

She let her pistol fall. "Ben!"

Divina grabbed him, pushing away the debris around him. She shook him, trying to get him to move. The corner of her eyes burned, tears blurring her vision.

He was dead.

She'd killed him. Not the enemy.

Divina looked up. Her team was dying one by one in the relentless hail enemy bullets. She had known they wouldn't last once the heavy weapons went dry.

Her fears were coming true. They were being slaughtered.

She'd let her bravado and desire to get those choppers win out.

She grabbed one of the discarded rocket launchers and dragged it to her. Hoisting it onto her shoulder, she stood. She aimed and fired at the oncoming Legion combatants.

The rocket exploded, ripping a fiery hole in the mass of attackers.

She dropped down next to Erga's body and keyed her radio. "Do it now. Blow the door."

Seconds later, an explosion split the air. It grew into a deafening thunder as the mines detonated all around her.

Divina watched the doorway collapse. She pulled Erga's body into her arms, his blood still warm. She held him for a moment, no longer holding back the tears.

The shock had already worn off the enemy. Their rifle fire was picking up again, skipping off the rubble around her. She looked up, saw there were maybe two dozen Alliance soldiers trapped with her.

She waved to them, and they ran over to her. Their faces were gaunt, white. A few of them were shaking. Surrender was written in all their eyes. She knew the Legion didn't take prisoners. The thought hit her like lightning.

She was about to die.

There was nowhere to go. No rescue coming. She doubted anyone even knew they were still alive. She stood, letting go of Erga's body.

She picked up his rifle.

Divina and her team met their enemy with bullets and steel. It took the Legion nearly twenty minutes to finish them off. When the smoke cleared, the Alliance soldiers were dead, surrounded by hundreds of their opponents.

No one would know of their bravery.

No one would know of their sacrifice.

Forever remembered only as names on the Wall of the Fallen.

———

Captain Derek Hiltabrand
10th Recon Marines

Cross Port – Control Tower
8 hours until evacuation

COME ON, Derek. Keep climbing.

Energy surged through Hiltabrand as he sprinted up the stairway. Ignoring the pain in his leg, he took the last flight of stairs to the control tower by twos. For the moment, the Legion was stuck outside. A blocked entrance on one side and a locked-down gate on the other. If those obstacles held, they'd be free and clear.

If they didn't hold, he had almost twelve hundred troops with which to hold the port.

The army had secured the main hallway with barricades, allowing Hiltabrand's marines to cover the tight spaces. The barricades he'd inspected were impressive, especially since the soldiers had built them out of the shit they'd found lying around.

The fleet engineers couldn't have done better.

Hiltabrand's plan revolved around these defenses, focused on letting the inexperienced enemy bleed themselves dry in the narrow, claustrophobic halls. When the Legion attacked, Hiltabrand's force would defend each barricade in succession. The Alliance forces could hold each area until they were either overwhelmed or out of ammunition and then fall back towards the platform farthest from the entrance.

He'd had the army rig explosives into the walls along the key junction between barricades. They'd buried the remaining mines under the damaged flooring. As each team fell back, they would detonate the explosives in their area. The blasts wouldn't be big enough to seal the hallways or collapse the building — the spaceport had to be standing for the landers to reach them — but it would kill a whole lot of Legion assholes and make them think twice before entering a new section.

It would be attrition.

It would be bloody.

It would buy the time they needed.

Hiltabrand entered the control tower. The small circular room was filled with shitty, subpar computers. Everything was without power, including the lights. Several marines, including Oren, were working on the port's beacon system. Another officer, an army lieutenant he didn't know, was staring out at the burning courtyard.

Beyond the great view of the enemy movement on the battlefield, the tower made a handy meeting facility. He'd called all the highest-ranking officers remaining to meet and prepare for an attack.

Hiltabrand had hoped a more senior officer would have survived, but none had. He was stuck in command. He needed to get the juniors he had on the same page.

They had one other major concern. Unless Oren and his team could get the beacon going, the *Hercules* wouldn't know they were alive and kicking. If they couldn't get a signal out, the ship may just leave, avoid the risk of an assault for a force that had been destroyed or was too far out of position to help.

If the *Hercules* abandoned them there, they were fucked. Their ammunition would run out and they'd be killed like trapped rats, staving as their enemy waited for their food and water to run out.

If Hiltabrand had to die, he'd take a bullet over thirst.

He crossed the room to the window. He raised a pair of binoculars to his eyes and zoomed in on the courtyard that held the young lieutenant's attention. There was the helicopter the army had reported. He had no way of counting the number of hostiles sitting, watching a wall in front of them. They looked like ants moving about before a rainstorm.

He caught sight of a large area of rubble.

That had to be the collapsed entryway. He couldn't tell exactly what they were doing, but it wasn't a good sign. They were active, clearly not wasting any time in their attempt to break in and finish off the Alliance force.

The young lieutenant raised his visor. "How the hell do you stop something like this?"

Hiltabrand switched his own visor. "It'll take a few hours for those fucks to dig through that mess. We'll be ready."

The man sighed. "That's not what I mean. They will break through. We will fight them, and, God willing, we'll be lifted off this trash pile before they wipe the floor with our bodies. I meant how do you face something like that? The Legion?"

Hiltabrand gritted his teeth. Even without the magnification, he could see the destruction. If he hadn't been shown images of city before the operation, he never would have imagined these piles of debris were once that — a thriving, industrial city. The massive enemy army reminded him of the elk herds covering the mountain meadows back home.

He looked over at the lieutenant. "I don't know. I never thought there'd be so many of them, but there are. It'll take a lot of firepower to knock these fuckers off."

The man shook his head, his expression dazed. "It's not the numbers. It's the hate. How can anyone hate so much? I grew up in a town like this. I remember hearing anti-government blather. I thought it was a joke, a bunch of assholes in suits trying to make money. No one can indiscriminately hate other human beings like that." The lieutenant's faced flushed. "But they can. They have throughout our entire history. It's easier to point a finger and spew shit rather than try to work for change. Real change. For everyone."

Hiltabrand felt like arguing, but how could he? He'd never fought an enemy like this. No one alive had.

He met the younger man's gaze. "This won't last. We will overcome this. Good people like you won't let this rest. Evil can only triumph when the good stay silent. We'll come back here, take back New Utica and anywhere else these bastards are. Set things right. We—"

The lieutenant cut him off. "We'll beat them, suppress this movement. But bullets can't kill ideas, can't curb hate. If we don't learn from this, it won't change anything."

The room was beginning to fill with the other platoon leaders.

Hiltabrand laid a hand on the man's shoulder. He fought back the twisting in his stomach.

Whatever this fight was about, it didn't matter right now. What mattered was keeping his people focused and getting the hell off this planet. He couldn't let himself think that way.

Even if that reality haunted him for the rest of his life.

CHAPTER SEVENTEEN

Lieutenant Patrick Baxter
10th Recon Marines
Cross Spaceport
3 hours until evacuation

Baxter leaned back against the cold stone wall, letting his eyes close. The sound of the guard's footsteps echoed quietly in the corridor. Most of his marines were sleeping. Why wasn't he? Baxter wasn't even sure how long it had been since he'd slept.

The *Hercules* was only a few hours away.

He forced his eyes open, shifting his weight. His eyes felt like gravel, and his heart was racing. He pushed himself up to a sitting position. He had been hearing voices from the Legion side of the rubble for the last hour. It wouldn't be long before those bastards broke through. This wasn't the time to sleep.

Hiltabrand had trusted him to hold the first barricade.

Baxter wasn't going to let him down.

He ran his gaze over his defenses, forcing his tired eyes to focus.

This corridor was the widest in the facility, almost twenty feet across. The army had torn apart one of the escalators, welded it to what looked like thick metal baggage carts. Packed dirt and rubble covered the wall. They had cut good gun ports just below the top of the barrier. Although the openings were too small for machine guns, they did give his marines a good view of the hallway. On the downside, they would only have their Enfields to counter whatever the fuck came down the hall.

Someone had strung a thin net from the ceiling to the top of the barricade. It should prevent grenades from coming in above the wall. Baxter doubted this particular net would hold long. It was waving noticeably in the breeze from the air purifier.

From the Legion's side, the barricade looked like a small dirt hill that extended about five feet into the air. With any luck, the fuckers would focus on the gun ports and wouldn't notice the weakness of the net. If not, he'd make them pay for this room.

He was going to make them bleed for each inch they took, teach these fuckers a lesson in warfare.

Baxter's eyelids and limbs felt heavy. He let his eyes close.

Wake up, asshole.

Baxter's eyes bolted open. He shook his head and pushed himself to his feet. He bounced slightly on his heels, trying to loosen his muscles. His whole body ached, his legs burned. He ran his hands through his hair and pulled his helmet down.

Baxter walked to the wall and ran his hands over it. Even this mass of metal and cement wouldn't stop these traitors. They were like a bulldozer, crushing everything in front of them.

Fuckers.

His gaze fell to his own hand. It was shaking. He stared for a moment.

Why was he shaking?

He couldn't feel it. The world slid out of focus. His vision swam, his stomach tightening, his heart slamming against his breastbone. He clasped and unclasped his fist, trying to ease the spasm in his fingers.

He leaned against the wall, closing his eyes. He swallowed a gulp of air, counted down from ten.

There was no time for this crap.

Baxter forced his eyes open, relaxed as the world came back to normal. He glanced through the nearest gun port, grounding himself in the situation. The crushed corridor was shaking, smaller bits of debris cascading down to the floor. Whatever those fuckers were doing, it wouldn't be much longer. He spun around, watched his troops sleeping, leaning in groups along the bullet-riddled walls.

Should he wake them already?

This was the last bit of rest these leathernecks would get. If something went wrong, if the Legion stopped or destroyed the *Hercules*...

He wasn't going to wake them before this storm.

They'd earned that.

Captain Derek Hiltabrand
10th Recon Marines
Cross Spaceport
2 hours until evacuation

GODDAMN SISSY.

Hiltabrand gritted his teeth, transferring his weight off his injured leg. These stairs had seemed so easy coming up. He leaned his weight against the wall and opened his medical hip pouch.

One more dose.

Fucking flesh wounds.

He'd better wait. When the shit hit the fan, he would have to move his ass to the platform, Legion dirtbags chasing him the entire way. He'd have to tough it out till then.

He closed the pouch, easing his weight down to the next step.

On the bright side, Oren had activated the beacon. As soon as the *Hercules* hit the system, they'd pick it up. The other win was the army officers accepting his command without argument. He had expected some objections from them because his rank was a field promotion.

He didn't even have a captain's gold coronet pin to prove the promotion had taken place.

If the situation had been reversed, Hiltabrand would have found it difficult to accept an officer as his superior based only on that person's word that they'd received a field promotion. Especially with an entire army of traitors bearing down on his ass.

He reached the bottom of the stairs, letting out a breath as he settled his leg on the tile walkway. His platoon was spread out in what had been the boarding terminal. They were going to be the final line of defense before the landing pad. About three-fourths of his troops were positioned on the opposite side of the building.

The two landing pads on that side were larger, with shorter staircases. Its exits were still intact — if *Hercules* didn't get through, it would give them a better escape route into the woods.

He eased himself down near Corporal Gomez. The woman was cleaning her rifle, her hands steadily wiping down the hefty receiver of her RAR.

Escape routes.

Hiltabrand had a hole in his leg. Gomez had a wound on her shoulder. Nobody on his team was without injury. They were all caked in dirt, hungry, and exhausted. Hiltabrand hadn't had anything other than water today, and he doubted any of the others had any food left, either. Hiltabrand almost laughed. Here he was, waiting patiently to be ripped into bits by a gutless group of traitors, and all he could think about was escape routes, tactics.

Knock that shit off, Derek.

This could be his last quiet moment before a sudden and probably gruesome death, and he couldn't shut his brain off.

What was the point of obsessing?

His stomach hadn't stopped aching since Marshall had suggested he get command of a combat sector. He couldn't stop focusing on his inadequacy, his lack of preparation. The lieutenant in the tower hadn't helped.

Bullets wouldn't stop the hate. Soldiers couldn't hold the line against ideas. Escaping with his life wouldn't put him in a position to resist evil.

He leaned his head down, trying to hide the smile that had forced its way across his lips.

What the hell would worrying do about any of it?

He certainly couldn't stop those bastards from attacking, couldn't ensure the *Hercules* made it through whatever blockade was waiting in orbit. It wasn't his job to stop the hate.

It was his job to get as many people out of this mess. He loved the Alliance and what it stood for, but no one except the biggest idiot would say it was perfect. The asshole politicians had gotten them into this. Someone smarter than he was would have to get them out.

Oren slid down next to him. "What's with the smile?"

Hiltabrand forced the grin off his face. "Just sitting. Waiting. Longest few hours of my damn life."

Oren snorted. "Least it isn't the Milipa. Those lanky, monkey-faced bastards would have stuffed us already. And not in a good way."

Hiltabrand laughed. "Shit, Sarge. If this was the Milipa, I'd have surrendered. Those fucks have more honor than these turds. The Milipa would have the decency to lock us away after a little torture. This time, it was intelligence that fucked us. No courtesy spit. Assholes."

Oren laughed, drawing the gaze of a few marines nearby. "That's what the infantry's for, brother. I don't ever remember a time those nitwits at Whitehall even considered the possibility of being wrong, let alone the consequences. In the dictionary under irony, it says, 'See Military Intelligence.'"

Hiltabrand chuckled. "Depends on if it's an election year. Nothing like a vote to delay suicide missions."

The radio crackled, and Hiltabrand turned the volume on his helmet up.

It was Lieutenant Baxter, the tension and fear in his voice obvious. "Tiger Five-Six to all units, the enemy has broken through. We're under heavy attack."

Captain Jordan Duncan
Bridge of the Hercules

CAPTAIN DUNCAN BRACED himself as the *Hercules* jolted beneath him, the transition from translight rocking the ship. He glanced over at his command screen, saw the image of his escorts pop onto the screen.

Collision klaxons blared.

Duncan was thrown forward, his chest belt cutting into his shoulder. That felt like a missile strike.

He refocused on the screen, scanning the warning messages that appeared on it. "Connelly, status."

"Torpedo impacts on the aft quarter," His executive officer responded. "Magnetic ordnance deflectors threw off the majority of them."

Ensign Ricky piped up. "Escorts are requesting orders."

The enemy had fifteen vessels in high orbit above them. The ships were spread out, their bows facing directly downwards at his formation. The small group of destroyers were stationary, guns firing into the gravity of the moon they were orbiting.

Hercules was positioned in the center of his force, with *Horizon* and *Simcoe* to either side. The *Montalban* and *Tupu* were directly above them, absorbing the majority of the fire. Their ventral defenses already read under fifty percent capacity.

Duncan cursed under his breath.

They hadn't been set. Why hadn't he preprogrammed a defensive move for immediately after deceleration? No one was stupid enough to fall for the same trick twice.

He entered his commands, sending them quickly to the escorts. "Get our drones in the air. I want eyes on New Utica."

The *Hercules* accelerated towards the far side of the planet, guns firing upward at the stationary enemy. The ship shook as she fought to overcome the moon's gravity. They needed to get out of range before the enemy reached full acceleration.

The last thing Duncan wanted was to be trapped between two enemy fleets. He had one goal: reach New Utica, pick up Polis, and get the hell out. The less he slugged it out with the enemy fleet, the better. Polis's team could be under attack.

Ensign Ricky's voice cut through his thoughts. "We are receiving a beacon from Utica. It's weak."

He tore his eyes from the screen. "Status of the ground force."

Ricky shook his head. "Unclear, sir. All I'm getting is they're under attack."

That wasn't a good sign.

The sensor drones broke out of the atmosphere, and the first images of the system filled Duncan's screen. The debris from their previous encounter was spread out in front of them, several partially destroyed hulks delisting directly in their path. The Legion hadn't even attempted to clear the system. The wreckage was full of undetonated shells and torpedoes and partially functioning power cores. There were also escape craft with doors open, their occupants probably having been retrieved.

The mess would make combat maneuvers more difficult, but it would also give them some level of cover — assuming they didn't run into something explosive.

The enemy fleet was spread out, small groups of ten to fifteen in high orbit of each of the nearby planetoids, their engines powered down. Duncan was thankful they hadn't learned that lesson yet. It would take time for each group of enemy ships to detect the Alliance force, power their engines, and come for them.

The nearest ships were already firing up their engines, turning towards New Utica.

He turned his eyes to the planet on his screen, saw it nearly undefended. Six cruiser-size ships hung in high orbit, a smattering of destroyers covering.

Duncan plugged in the numbers, ran a few projections on his screen.

If they could engage and defeat those ship before enemy reinforcements caught up, they'd have their window to launch the Banshees.

He watched the scenarios play out one by one, tweaked the details here and there.

It would be tight.

No matter how he calculated it, the enemy had the advantage. Duncan's force was surrounded, outnumbered, and the enemy knew their goal. Even from standing still, those ships weren't going to take all that long to come after the Alliance fleet.

Hercules shook again, a torpedo snaking through her defensive batteries.

Duncan turned half of the remaining combat drones backward, directing them at the pursuing ships. They were the first obstacle. They had to be slowed down or destroyed. He formed up the drones, aiming their formation slightly down toward the planet. He plugged in the last-minute maneuver and turned control of the drones over to Connelly.

Duncan entered the targeting vectors for the six ships blocking his path. He took a deep breath, ordered the escorts to accelerate.

This was it. All or nothing.

The deck lurched as the *Hercules* picked up speed, her nose angling towards the Legion ships defending the planet. He watched his targets begin to move, their guns turning upwards, flashing on his screen.

Duncan leaned back. "Full throttle, Gordon. Let's get our people off the hook."

CHAPTER EIGHTEEN

Lieutenant Patrick Baxter
10th Recon Marines
Cross Spaceport
1 hour until evacuation

Baxter leaned forward, aiming carefully at the nearest enemy, the one leading the others. The man's bushy red beard swayed as he waved his force towards the Alliance position. The enemy had assaulted the wall six times, but had failed to break through.

Bullets skipped off the front of the barricade, forcing Baxter to duck. The rounds ricocheted loudly in the small space. A bullet whistled through his gun port and the private to his left collapsed, blood streaking the wall as he slumped to the floor.

Fuckers.

Baxter stood, reacquired his target. The red-bearded man was laughing, a grenade in his hand. He pulled the pin.

Baxter squeezed his trigger.

The man fell, gripping his chest. His grenade fell to the ground, detonating among the Legion horde. A wave of gore sprayed wall, and panic gripped the enemy's front line. The closest living hostiles turned, fleeing headlong into the oncoming horde of comrades behind them.

Baxter took advantage of his enemy's confusion. He re-centered his aim, firing in quick succession at the front of the scrambling throng. Five more of the enemy went down before Baxter dropped back into cover to reload.

He fished in his pouch for a fresh magazine while, Sargent Johns emptied his rifle out of the gun port. The screams from the other side of the barricade told Baxter the sergeant had hit his targets. Baxter glanced up and down his own line. This was working. His troops looked focused, alternating turns at the gun ports as they kept up their rate of fire. There were sporadic casualties, but not many.

Beyond, he could just see the next barricade, the Alliance troops behind it just visible over the smaller, thinner wall.

Johns dropped down beside him. "Thick as swamp flies out there."

Baxter charged his bolt. "Thank God for these government-issued fly swatters." He stood and fired rapidly into the oncoming enemy. The bastards were noticeably closer, trampling the bodies that covered the ground.

How many more were there?

He hit one woman in the shoulder, toppling her over. A short, fat man took a round in the stomach. This was more like target practice than combat. Even when he fucked up his trigger pull or aim, his shot still found an enemy to kill.

It was almost comical, surreal.

Before the Legion, Baxter would never have imagined killing another human being. Now he couldn't even count how many he'd killed. He glanced back at the detonator behind him. If they got much closer, he'd have to consider falling back.

One of the enemies tossed a grenade at the barricade. It sailed up and out of sight. Baxter braced himself. A second later, the grenade exploded somewhere forward and to his left, drawing a chorus of screams.

Not behind the barricade.

He looked out. The grenade had rolled between a group of Legion troops trying to scramble up the wall. The net had held, and the grenade had shredded the enemy instead. Their bodies had been thrown clear, right in front of—

Oh, shit.

Behind the torn bodies of the enemy was a group of hostiles holding a rocket launcher. From the markings on the scumbag's stolen armor, it was one of the Tenth's own. The man holding the weapon was aiming at the barricade's center.

It was loaded.

Baxter aimed his rifle at the man, pulled the trigger.

Nothing happened. He was empty.

He yelled just before the rocket hit, his words lost in the explosion.

Baxter was thrown off the wall and slammed into the ground a few yards back, driving the air from his lungs. His ears rang as he pushed himself up, scrambled toward the detonators. It was time to blow the tunnel's explosives, knock the enemy force back.

He had been sure they would be able to fight as long as their ammunition held. How the hell had the enemy got that Howler?

Baxter's people couldn't hold this many attackers back forever, not with a hole in their barricade.

Baxter reached for the detonator and pulled it against his chest.

Several of his troops retreated past him, firing from the hip as they moved backward, their faces white with fear. The enemy was already behind the barricade.

He didn't have long.

He flipped the switch, activating the system.

A sharp pain tore through Baxter's back and chest. He tried to scream, but couldn't. He looked down. A bayonet blade was protruding from his chest, blood running down from a fresh hole in his armor.

He tried to breathe, but choked on the bubbles gurgling in his lungs, an unbearable pressure filling his chest. He couldn't move. He wanted to push the blade out but his vision was glazing over, his mind cloudy. He focused on the detonator. He could just feel his fingers wrapped tightly around the cylinder.

He was pushed forward by the force of an unseen attacker. He felt his body falling. He knew he was on the ground, but hadn't felt the impact. The images around him were dark, seemed far away.

Baxter wiggled his fingers, the cold hunk of metal still in his palm.

He pressed down on the trigger.

Captain Derek Hiltabrand
10th Recon Marines
Cross Spaceport
40 minutes until evacuation

HILTABRAND'S TOES vibrated as an explosion ripped through the building, a wave a heat billowing up the corridor. The first barricade was down.

Baxter was in retreat. He had to be. If the Legion had broken that barricade, it wouldn't take much time to subdue the others.

He tried his radio. "Tiger Five-Six, Tiger Three-Six."

Static was the only reply. Could Baxter already be...

Hiltabrand tried Flay, at the second barricade. "Fox Two-Six, Tiger Three-Six. What's your status?"

More static.

Lieutenant Melvin answered. "Tiger Three-Six, the second barricade is under heavy—"

The line went dead.

Son of a bitch!

The goddamn Legion must have a mobile version of their radio blocker.

Who the fuck are these guys?

Even the Milipa didn't have a transmission jammer that efficient. He looked down the hallway. He'd have to wait until Baxter made it up here to find out what the hell was going on.

A second explosion ripped down the corridor. The sound of gunfire was growing louder, echoing down the narrow hallway.

That couldn't be the next barricade already?

Flay was better than that. His barricade had machine gun ports that should have easily repulsed the enemy's initial attacks.

He met Oren's eyes, saw the same worry he felt in the sergeant's eyes.

There hadn't been more than a few minutes between detonations. He had more than three hundred troops at the forward barricade. If the Legion had already forced the second barricade to detonate their explosives...

Time was no longer on Hiltabrand's side.

He tapped Oren's uninjured shoulder. "Get up to the platform. Be ready."

Oren stood, stepped forward. "Be safe. I don't like heroes."

"Go." Hiltabrand grabbed his last shot of painkiller, and stabbed it into his thigh. A cold tingle pulsed over the wound, relief spreading quickly through his body. He pulled his Colt free from its holster and clicked off the safety.

Hiltabrand watched the hall, waiting for any sign of moment. He checked his armband. Another twenty minutes had flown by. Even with his shit leg, he could have walked the distance to Baxter's position by now.

Where was he? They couldn't all be... Surely, some of them had to have survived.

At the very end of the hall, a large group, maybe fifty in all, was running towards him. Hiltabrand strained his eyes. It wasn't Baxter's marines. Those were army uniforms.

Terror was plain on their faces, their weapons slung or missing. Some were pushing past their peers, clearly desperate to reach the stairs.

Another two explosions lit off almost simultaneously.

Hiltabrand's heart caught. If he was right, the Legion had taken all but the final defenses before his own. Something catastrophic had happened.

The first of the terrified soldiers hopped the barricade. They didn't stop, but sprinted towards the stairs. Hiltabrand reached out, catching a sergeant by the arm, stopping her in her tracks.

She turned, caught sight of his rank. "We need to get the fuck...The stairs." She panted, speaking between breaths. "We... it's our best... Only thing to do."

Hiltabrand held her still. "Slow down, Sergeant. What's going on? Where's your lieutenant?"

She pulled against his hand. "Dead. All dead. They have rockets and flame units. The walls aren't helping. The halls aren't enough to keep them back."

He let her go.

Howlers and flame units. These assholes were crazy. The first time Hiltabrand had fired a Howler, his drill instructor had pounded it into his head to never use it in a confined space. The heated back blast could kill, rip skin right off the bone.

Flamethrowers weren't much better. They were considered obsolete by most in the military. He'd never even seen one used. If it wasn't for clearing the occasional Frontin nests, the Alliance wouldn't even make them. They were bulky weapons of terror that posed risks for the user as well as the enemy.

In the academy, the debate about their use had centered on the political ramifications. The horrific way they killed was hard to justify, even against the Milipa.

Apparently, the Legion had fewer scruples.

Hiltabrand cursed himself for not planning to face them.

Flamethrowers were perfect for Legion tactics, deadly in close quarters and good for burning out bunkers and rat holes. These corridors would funnel the flame towards the Alliance positions. They still posed a huge risk for the operator, but...

Since when did the Legion care about casualties?

The enemy seemed more intent on causing horrific damage than achieving any obvious military objective. The hall was still crowded with panicked Alliance troops, and Hiltabrand could see fire in the distance. The final barricade must be putting up a fight in an attempt to let as many retreat as possible.

In a moment, Hiltabrand would have to do the same for them.

Hiltabrand raised his voice over the din. "Gomez, Scotts, Bartllet, Dalair, Warren, Monforte, Kilwan, and Heartford, you're with me. Everyone else, get up to the platform."

Corporal Gomez stood, her RAR above her shoulder. "What's the play, boss?"

He pointed down the hall. "Flamethrowers and at least one Howler are coming up at us. They're expecting us to be defending the wall. I aim to disappoint them. We need to buy time for our people to get out of here and then blow this hall."

The group nodded, their faces set in determination. A twinge of guilt hit him. This was all that was left of his platoon, minus Oren. He doubted if any of them were going to walk away from this mess.

Hiltabrand gestured with his pistol to a pile of rubble in front of the barricade. "Gomez, Bartllet, and Scotts, take that position. Light them up, and keep them back. Kilwan, Heartford, and Monforte, man the wall. Aim only for anything that looks like a rocket launcher or flame unit. You guys will engage first. We want to draw them in."

Warren pursed his lips. "And me? I am a goddamn better shot that Monforte."

Hiltabrand ignored him. "Warren, Dalair, you are with me. See that outcropping opposite the mess? We are going to light 'em up. This is about time. We need to shock them, get them on their heels. If your position is threatened, do not wait or go to steel. Fall back. Kilwan, if they get to the wall below the hall, high-tail it up to the platform."

An explosion rippled in the distance, flames licking the ceiling.

Hiltabrand and his group were all that was left.

Hiltabrand ran as best as his shitty leg allowed. He gritted his teeth as he tucked himself into the small outcropping. His marines dispersed to their positions. The explosives had done their job, killing or pushing back the Legion. He waited, forcing himself to breathe carefully. Warren was right next to him, silent, still.

Another group of soldiers ran by, slightly better organized than the last one. At least they were still armed.

The first Legion soldier appeared at the end of the hall. A tall man, with a large backpack on. Definitely a flame unit.

Several more hostiles came into view. They were shouting, firing wild, half-aimed shots at the wall. This was either the recklessness of victory or inexperience. Either way, Hiltabrand would make sure they paid for their error.

The tall man shot a jet of white flame into the air. It stretched half the distance to the marines.

One of Hiltabrand's marines fired a single round. The bastard with the flamethrower fell to his knees, wrestling with the straps of his weapon. The enemies around him flocked to his aid.

The fuel tank detonated, showering the people behind it with liquid flame. Screams filled the narrow corridor, the smell of burning fuel and flesh hitting Hiltabrand like a wave.

Hiltabrand gagged, his stomach turned. He aimed down the hallway, waiting for the Legion to keep coming.

They always kept coming

Sure enough, the other enemy troops moved around their burning colleagues, firing at Monforte's position. Hiltabrand could see another flamethrower, its pilot light nearly lost amid the blazing fuel and bodies.

No Howlers yet, but the enemy had to know this hallway was

mined, like the others. They likely didn't want to risk it in the first wave.

Hiltabrand looked across at Scotts, Gomez, and Bartllet. They were ready. Gomez was tracking the forward enemies with her RAR.

They would be on top of Hiltabrand's position in ten seconds. He picked his first target and fired. The hallway erupted with gunfire as Gomez swept her light machine gun at chest level over the infantry, killing dozens of enemies. The riflemen were pickier, firing quickly but expertly. Hiltabrand emptied his pistol, aiming at any of the enemies who seemed to be in charge.

He wanted confusion.

The second flame unit exploded, thick black smoke billowing from its burning remains. Hiltabrand coughed, his eyes tearing. Those goddamn things were dangerous.

He reloaded, searching for a target through the fumes.

Bullets slammed into the front of his cover. Warren pitched backward, hands flailing as he collapsed, blood pouring from his mouth. Hiltabrand aimed at the muzzle flashes. Gomez was doing the same, her bursts slow, controlled.

Hiltabrand couldn't see Scotts or Bartllet, and from the sound of it, their rifles were silent. He couldn't risk losing Gomez or her gun. It was their best way of clogging the stairwell with enemy corpses. He waved at Gomez, signaling her to pull out. She nodded, then disappeared back towards the barricade.

Hiltabrand loaded his last magazine. He looked up just as the barricade exploded, the smoke trail of a rocket still visible through the fumes.

He fired, knocking down the Howler's gunner. He didn't wait, but forced himself to his feet. He started running, thankful for the painkiller. Dalair was right on his heels. Bullets popped and twanged off the stone floor and walls.

Dalair screamed. Hiltabrand looked behind him. The private was dead, part of his face missing, his body shaking on the floor. Hiltabrand jumped over the wall, heading for the stairs. Monforte's body was crumpled at the base of the rubble. Kilwan had the detonator in his hands, his eyes wide.

Hiltabrand nodded. "Hit it."

He hit the dirt next to Kilwan, the concussive sound and heat telling him the explosives had gone off. He glanced up the stairs in time to see Gomez starting upward, Heartford right behind her.

"Private, go!"

Hiltabrand fired down the corridor, covering Kilwan with the last of his ammunition. His slide locked back, and he started up the stairs, tossing his pistol aside, Kilwan a step in front of him.

Hiltabrand took the stairs as fast as he could. They were narrow, just enough room for three or four people at a time. His leg burned, but he refused to let up.

He could hear footsteps behind him.

Blinking, he ran onto the platform through a set of double doors. A group of Alliance soldiers were there, their weapons pointing down the stairs, ready. He tossed himself to the side, rolling out of the way.

The soldiers fired, and bullets whizzed past him down the stairwell. The enemy screamed as they hit the wall of Alliance fire.

Hiltabrand pulled the thirty-eight revolver and pointed it toward the stairs.

He squeezed the trigger, blasting the first person who appeared on the landing below. The old gun felt good in his hands. He finally understood why the old timers loved these things. He emptied it, claiming several more opponents.

Movement caught Hiltabrand's eyes, and he saw Oren pointing. Hiltabrand's gaze followed the sergeant's finger. A Banshee was breaking through the clouds, its landing jets firing.

He turned, reloading his last cartridges. "This is it, we are almost out of this. Give them everything you got!"

The pad was crowded, hundreds of survivors firing at anything that moved in the doorway. The enemy was charging, waves of reckless soldiers popping up through the opening, falling back over each other as the Alliance troops cut them down. Gomez was still firing careful bursts, bolstering the volley of remaining defenders.

Hiltabrand's heart leaped.

They had this.

As long as their ammo lasted, the Legion wasn't going to get up those narrow stairs.

Thank God for architects.

A loud burst of machine gun fire came in at them from the side. People toppled around Hiltabrand. One fell from the platform screaming while another twitched helplessly, bleeding out on the ground.

He turned, and his mouth dropped

The Legion helicopter rose up in front of the platform, not forty feet away, its engines roaring.

For fuck's sake!

He'd forgotten about it.

Time slowed.

People were yelling, the rotor's backwash whipping over them. The helicopter's machine gun fired another burst. The soldiers around him scattered, diving to the ground to avoid the fire.

Hiltabrand knees locked. He couldn't move.

He stared at the chopper, his heart pounding. A surge of heat ran up his spine.

Things would not end like this. He would not die cornered like a rat. Hiltabrand yelled, firing his revolver at its glass.

The bullets bounced harmlessly away.

"Sir," Gomez was shouting, her voice far away. "I'm almost dry!"

Hiltabrand fired again, emptying his final rounds at the helicopter.

It turned towards him. He could see its guns spooling up.

It exploded.

Shrapnel and chunks of rotor fell from the air as three Alliance combat drones banked away, back towards the sky. The first Banshee's ramp clattered open.

Everyone besides Hiltabrand, Gomez, and Oren turned and ran off the platform into the lander. Hiltabrand's team backed up slowly, covering the top of the staircase.

An enemy appeared on the platform, a grenade in hand, but a burst of fire from Gomez's RAR knocked him down. A second later, flame and debris burst from the staircase.

When Hiltabrand felt his boots hit the ramp, he turned and dived into the lander. He hugged the metal grating, breathing the clean, recycled air, his heart pounding.

Hydraulics whined as the ramp shit, and the Banshee's engines roared, its frame shaking as it pushed away from the platform.

Hiltabrand sheathed his revolver, and surrendered to his exhaustion.

A smile crossed Hiltabrand's face.

He'd done his job.

Gotten his people out.

New Utica would be someone else's problem now.

CHAPTER NINETEEN

Corporal Marc 'Snake' Masters
1ˢᵗ Infantry Regiment, 4ᵗʰ Division
Cross City
10 minutes after evacuation

Masters couldn't look away from the Banshees. The last couple landers were pulling away from the platform, rapidly shrinking into the distance. His heart was pounding. He and his people were stranded, left behind.

Abandoned.

Masters swallowed. They'd lost. This rabble of unorganized traitors had made easy work of *his* infantry regiment. The assaults on the outpost worlds had been shocking, but it wasn't hard to believe the Alliance forces there could be overrun. The Legion's ruthless surprise attacks had come up against poorly equipped backwater garrisons.

Not here.

This should have been different. The landing force had lost with surprise on their side. Masters' regiment was made up of top-notch professionals, decorated combat veterans. Most of the people in his unit had made a dozen drops together. They were well-equipped, well-supplied badasses.

None of it had mattered.

The sheer weight of the enemy's numbers had ground them down. The communication blackout hadn't helped. The enemy had used it along with the Alliance's policy of not abandoning their own to murder them. He doubted if any of the Alliance personnel who'd escaped even realized Masters and his group were still alive. Everything after the landing had been such a cluster-fuck.

No one had seen the territorials. There was no sign of the regional or planetary government. Hell, even Cross Industries' internal goddamn security was absent. This planet was in the Belestock Defensive Line. Its armaments should have been strong enough to hold off a sizable invasion. If the Legion hadn't taken the planet completely, they certainly had this part of it on lockdown.

The final lander vanished into the clouds, black smoke hanging in ribbons behind it. Masters eased back through the crack he was using as a door, careful to avoid snagging himself on the jagged adobe. He pushed the pile of debris over the crack in the wall, sealing them in.

This drop was supposed to be his curtain call before civilian life. Instead, he was stuck on this shitty world, trapped in this shitty wreck of a building. Unless one of these traitors put a bullet in him.

Or he starved.

At least he'd done some good.

He picked his way across the sunken room. It was quiet. The ever-present sound of gunfire and explosions was gone, replaced with the muffled moaning of the wounded. Most of these soldiers — seventy-nine in all — would have died had he not found them.

If they could avoid the Legion and starvation long enough for some of these guys to recover, they'd have enough troops to annoy the enemy, eat away at the bastards.

He lowered himself down next to Lieutenant Landro. He didn't look good. He was clammy and pale. His skin gaunt, eyes dull and sunken. If he'd found the lieutenant much later, he would have died, bled out in the street, half buried in rubble. Even with his team's intervention, Landro had taken their entire remaining stock of O-negative blood.

Spud was checking Landro's dressing. "Tough as nails, brother."

Landro nodded, his voice barely a whisper. "Na. I just like it when you save my ass. Gives me the warm fuzzies."

Masters tapped Spud on the back. "That's it. They've bugged out. No help is comin'. We are on our own."

Landro looked over. "Water. First priority. Then ammunition. Get a team together—"

Spud laughed. "Look at our boy, Snake. Still giving orders, hole and all. Ammo isn't an issue. Legion didn't strip it from the dead. They were too busying winning."

Masters nodded. "We can't risk going out there right now. Too hot. We all need to rest. With the supplies we have here, we can rest."

Landro's face contorted as he tried to push himself up. "No. We need to be able to hit these fuckers, break their fucking backs."

Spud restrained him gently. "Rest now. Fuck them up later."

Landro shook his head, closing his eyes, a tear in its corner. Masters felt his own eyes burn with emotion.

He'd lived with death his entire life. He'd watched the life drain out of soldiers as he'd fought to save them. None of it had taught him to ease this kind of pain.

Masters reached out and took Landro's hand. "I promise you, we are going to make them pay. Together."

Even if it killed them both.

Captain Jordan Duncan
Primary Landing Bay
RAS Hercules

CAPTAIN DUNCAN KEYED OPEN the door to the landing bay, his body numb.

Polis, dead. Snider, dead. Marshall and Anderson, dead. That asshole Cross, dead. Everything had gone fucking sideways.

Snider...

Snider had commanded the 10th for six years. He and Duncan were friends. It was not hard for a dropship captain and his detachment leader to get to know each other. It was the nature of the position, especially when the dropship was a division's permanent transport.

Duncan's stomach turned.

So many of the 10th were dead. The *Hercules* and the 10th were connected. He almost couldn't bear to see those marines now.

He'd read the preliminary reports from the ground teams. It was unbelievable. Everything had happened faster than he'd imagined possible. The enemy didn't know they were coming, and it hadn't slowed them. They hadn't run or fallen back. They'd fought. Polis had worried about this, but despite his own trepidation, Duncan had felt confident in the outcome.

He'd allowed *Hercules* to deliver 9,702 of the Alliance's finest down to New Utica without objection. Only 1,100 had escaped that death trap. Of those, only ninety of the Tenth had returned. That was assuming all the wounded survived their injuries.

This operation had been a massacre.

Duncan stepped through the door. The landing bay was hot and loud, the moaning and screaming of the wounded audible over the engines of the Banshees. Ragged troops wandered like zombies towards the exits. They were caked with dirt and blood, their faces pale and eyes hollow. Duncan knew the look.

It was defeat.

He picked his way towards the back of the bay. He wished he could avoid eye contact with the wounded, but it was his duty. He was master of this ship. They needed his confidence. The looks in each of their eyes stung. Guilt burned in his chest. Duncan should have refused to land the force when he had seen the size of the fleet in orbit.

The deck chief, Ensign Charlie Gammon, should be waiting with whoever had been left in charge of the ground forces. Duncan wanted to see this man ASAP. From all of the early accounts, the young captain had kept the survivors organized and fighting, maintained discipline despite the odds against them.

It didn't matter how mad Admiral Young was going to be. If this officer had done what it appeared he had, he deserved a medal.

The deck was littered with wounded. Medical staffs from all four of his ships were darting about, trying to get hold of this debacle.

"Clear the way. On your left, on your left."

Duncan flattened himself against the side of one of the landers. A gurney pulled by two medics raced by. They were restraining a struggling woman, blood trailing behind them.

He stared for a moment at the expanding pool of blood. He pulled off his jacket and knelt. Mechanically, he wiped up the blood and tossed the stained jacket aside. He wiped his hands on his uniform shirt, trying to clean his hands.

He pushed himself up, moving out of the way of another rushing medical team. He moved up along the front of the landers, forcing his feet to keep moving. Duncan couldn't count the number of times he had walked this bay after a mission. This wasn't the first time he'd searched for a commander after a defeat, and it wouldn't be the last. He'd never seen anything like this, though.

More than 8000 dead and missing, including those from the *Hercules* crew and that of the escort vessels. Even during the war, he couldn't remember such a one-sided defeat. There was nothing he could say to this man, whoever he was, to make that better. Bile welled in his throat. Maybe if he'd waited longer, sent down escorts for the landing... Done something besides follow orders...Maybe he could have spared some of those troops.

Duncan crossed into the rear of the bay. Charlie was standing awkwardly in the front of one of the Banshees. A few marines were sitting on the ground in front of him. One of them had his leg up while a medic treated a nasty wound.

No one was talking. They were staring ahead, gulping down water, the same look of exhaustion on their features.

Duncan nodded to Charlie. "Where is he?"

Charlie pointed to the lieutenant whose leg was being bandaged. "Here, Captain."

The man looked up. "Cap — Lieutenant Hiltabrand, sir."

Duncan stared for a moment. A first lieutenant in command of an entire ground team. Where were the captains? The army colonels and majors? How could they all be dead?

Duncan forced a smile. "Lieutenant, you were in operational command?"

Hiltabrand grimaced, his voice sharp. "I'm as high as it gets, sir."

Duncan kept his face passive. "I was told I was looking for a captain. No offense was intended, Lieutenant."

The older sergeant next to Hiltabrand smiled, placing a hand on the man's shoulder. "Field commission from General Polis. We'd be dead if it wasn't for the *captain* here."

Hiltabrand tensed at the words, shirking off the man's touch. He looked trapped, guilty. How could he not? To watch so many others die would affect even the hardest chargers.

Duncan held up his palms, kept his voice calm. "At ease, Sergeant. I wasn't suggesting otherwise. I just wanted to make sure I was talking to the right man. Were you in operational command, Captain Hiltabrand?"

The sergeant nodded once, his lips still wearing a smile.

Hiltabrand's voice softened. "Yes, sir. I had operational control after Major Marshall..."

Duncan extended his hand. "Then you're the man whose hand I need to shake. If the reports are correct, you're a hero."

Hiltabrand took Duncan's hand, his expression numb.

Duncan pointed back toward the exit. "Can you walk? Admiral Young is waiting to debrief you."

Hiltabrand's voice was cold. "Yes, sir."

The medic finished tying off a fresh bandage, then Duncan pulled Hiltabrand to his feet.

Duncan turned to head back the way he'd come. "You can give me your report, fill in my blanks on the way." He let his smile drop as he walked back through the bay, listening as Hiltabrand recounted the battle in a low, monotone voice. The young man was in shock, still stuck on that planet. If Duncan had a choice, this would have waited for later. The man needed rest. A good meal.

The trip back to Earth would take time.

Young was insistent.

Duncan knew the admiral was searching for a scapegoat to protect his political ambitions, his career. He'd argued with that unpleasant Colonel Tramo the entire trip. This mission could wreck anyone's image.

Especially when it had been undertaken without Parliament's consent.

Duncan's stomach lurched. Maybe that's what made this defeat worse than any he'd survived. It wasn't the causalities or the loss of so many great leaders. Death was part of a warrior's life. He hated it, but understood it. It wasn't even the utter failure of military intelligence. It wasn't even facing humans in battle.

That was all bad enough, but it wasn't what had made this operation so horrible.

It was the same thing he hadn't been able to shake since the very first briefings. This whole mission had been about a single man. An entire debacle over an individual. It didn't have to happen. It *shouldn't* have happened. This mission didn't hold back the enemy or cut their throats. It was never meant to win back the planet or even to win a strategic prize.

This was all political ambition and intrigue.

Cross had chosen to stay here when the fighting had come. He'd had the means to escape. He hadn't. Cross should have been the one to bear the consequences of his actions. Instead, because of a few men's political goals and Cross's cash, the landing force had paid in blood. To top it all off, Cross hadn't even survived the extraction, a victim of the same insane suicide attacks that had killed Polis.

Duncan wasn't about to let Admiral Young cast the blame on this officer or anyone else. He owed the fallen more than that.

And so did Young.

Captain Derek Hiltabrand
Captain's Office
RAS Hercules

HILTABRAND LET OUT AN EXASPERATED BREATH. How many times would he have to tell the same story?

Admiral Young was pacing back and forth in front of Captain Duncan's desk, his face a mess of splotchy reds and purples, his hands shaking behind his back. Another colonel he didn't recognize was standing behind him.

What did they want?

Hiltabrand couldn't change what had happened on New Utica. Maybe if Polis or Marshall had survived the suicide bombers...

Suicide bombers.

Who in their right minds could have prepared for that? Young didn't want to admit this was his fault, but he'd given the orders to land. It was his responsibility.

Hiltabrand forced his eyes to stay open. His lids were heavy, and his leg throbbed. He let himself sink into the soft leather of the chair. The captain's office was brightly lit and comfortable, every bit the working space of a career navy officer.

Young turned away. "So that's it? That's your explanation? Blame bad intelligence, bad luck, and enemy surprises? This is asinine. I want the truth. Who fucked up?"

Duncan cut it. "Admiral, bad intelligence is a given. I lost eight birds to flak cannons. We have video confirmation of this. We already have enough proof—"

Young wheeled back around, throwing up his hands up. "I don't need you to quote me the obvious, captain. It might have been an uphill battle, but things go wrong in combat all the time. Why didn't Polis take action to correct the situation? Or Marshall? Why didn't they change the plan? Go for another option? These were—"

Heat pulsed through Hiltabrand. "What the hell could they do? What fucking options did they have? It's easy to stand here and whine about the decisions of others, but you weren't there. We were in a fucking hornet's nest. We got separated during the drop, and we didn't have air support. We were outfoxed."

Admiral Young turned towards him. "I didn't give you permission to speak, Lieutenant. You are out of line."

Hiltabrand's hands started to shake. "You're out of line. I won't let you smear the dead. Those people died heroes. They did their jobs, and you failed them!"

Young's face went purple. "Heroes? You can't speak to me like that. Shut your mouth, or I'll have you thrown in irons."

Captain Duncan stood. "Admiral, calm down. The lieutenant may be out of line, but he's right. The Legion was ready. We need to regroup, lick our wounds, and mourn our fallen. We can't lose ourselves in this."

Young didn't move. "Captain, I appreciate your opinion, but—"

Duncan pulled something from his pocket. "It isn't an opinion. Here is the official written order you gave to Polis along with his objections. I also have a sworn affidavit from the other dead senior officers given to me in case they didn't return."

Hiltabrand was missing something. Why would anyone do that? What the hell was in those papers? He studied Young, whose pallor had gone from purple to a sickly pale color.

Young lowered his voice. "Hand me those, please."

Duncan sat back down. "Negative, sir. I have previous orders from General Polis to turn these documents over to Second Fleet

Command only. Those orders were confirmed by Vice Admiral Knight yesterday."

Young crossed his arms. "That was an order, Captain."

Duncan nodded. "I understood that, sir. However, I cannot be compelled to violate the orders of my fleet commander without good cause. You may, of course, file an official reprimand, but I will not surrender these documents."

"Captain..." Young trailed off. "When people find out about what happened here, there will be panic. We have to know who's at fault."

Duncan put the packet back in his pocket. "Let's focus on the real enemy. The Legion. They are obviously a much bigger threat than we imagined. The Admiralty tried to get ahead of it, but couldn't. Lieutenant Hiltabrand — or Captain, if you confirm the promotion — is a hero. Polis, Anderson, Snider, Marshall and every one of them died defending our soil from traitors. That is what matters. That is what people need to know."

Young nodded. "And I have your support on that."

Duncan smiled. "Of course, Admiral."

Young looked at the colonel. "And yours?"

"Of course, Admiral."

Young turned back towards Hiltabrand, a thin smile on his face. "*Captain* Hiltabrand, I apologize for my words. Tensions are high. I don't know about you, but I'm distraught. It sticks in my craw, losing so many people. You should be proud. I will see to it that you have your own company and the medal you deserve."

Hiltabrand grumbled a thank you, not sure what to say.

Young patted Hiltabrand's shoulder for a second before leaving the room, the colonel on his heels.

Hiltabrand stood. "Permission to leave?"

Duncan was staring. "Granted."

He turned to go.

He stopped. "Sir, what is going on?"

Duncan leaned back. "Politics and war don't mix. Unfortunately, they tend to sleep together. Nothing to worry about."

Hiltabrand shook his head. "Those people gave their lives for us. Young can't smear them. I won't let him. I—"

Duncan put up a hand, rocking in his chair. "They did. Their sacrifice will be remembered in the proper light. You have my word. Right now, focus on your achievement and your marines. You got them home. Be proud of that. The rest is for others to obsess about."

Hiltabrand nodded. "Thank you, sir."

Duncan stood. "We'll be back. I promise you that."

Hiltabrand nodded and left the office.

He made his way towards the barracks deck, his muscles stiff as he moved, the pain in his leg a dull ache. He yawned.

Duncan was right. Hiltabrand needed rest, and so did his marines.

They'd done their job.

The Admiralty and the politicians would have to do theirs. The Legion had caught everyone off guard. It was logical to assume they would all struggle with it in their own way. Hiltabrand was not a politician, and he would leave them their worries.

He had his own burdens.

What mattered now was healing himself and getting back into the fight. He had to make the Legion pay for the lives they had taken.

He owed it to Marshall.

He owed it to those who died under him.

He owed it to himself.

CHAPTER TWENTY

Remagen Village
Leader Joshua Miles
4 days after evacuation

S corched houses. The stink of explosives. Burnt flesh. Decay and death.

The smell hit Joshua Miles in the face, filled his nostrils as he opened the door of the personnel carrier. His throat constricted, trying to gag, but he suppressed his physical reaction. He couldn't act fragile in front of his people, the heroes who had faced the military and won.

"Leader?" The voice of Tonya, the driver, drew his attention. "Are you alright?"

Miles met the woman's gaze and worked a smile onto his face. "Perfectly. Thank you." He turned, stepped out of the vehicle, and hopped down to the ground.

Good God.

The scene in front of him was worse than any of the descriptions he'd heard. Every building in sight was wrecked, their walls peppered with bullet holes or punched through by more powerful weapons. Rubble filled the streets alongside—

Bodies.

Government troops and his own people heaped and contorted on the ground, their dried, blackened blood pooled and spattered around them. There was a faint buzzing in the air, and nearby, a dozen or so of his soldiers were moving bodies and equipment. They'd arranged the Legion's own dead shoulder-to-shoulder, covered with bedsheets, tarps, and torn fabric. The Alliance troops were in a pile next to a growing stack of rifles, machine guns, and other weapons. There was a swirling grey cloud in the air above the mass of bodies, and Miles realized with a start what they were.

Carrion flies. The source of the buzzing.

He swallowed, his stomach turning.

You did this.

Miles shrugged off the slimy feeling in his chest. The government had forced his hands, sent a massive invasion force against the movement, sided with that villain Cross. Victory and justice required sacrifice and pain. Until the Legion triumphed, he would have to fight many battles like this, plan other victories.

Then get used to the smell.

"We should be shooting instead of doing this bullshit," one of the Legion soldiers was saying to another as they both hauled the stiffened corpse of an Alliance ranger major between them. "If there are more of them out there, I want to be ready."

The other grunted in agreement as they tossed the body onto the pile.

"I know." A third soldier walked up, a battered military-issue Colt pistol in his hand. "We'll do both." He raised the gun and fired a couple shots at a corpse. It jerked, its mouth open in a silent scream of horror.

The other soldiers on the street spun around at the gunshots, then joined in the dark laughter of their three comrades.

"That is enough!" Miles' temper exploded, and he closed the distance to the three soldiers. "Are you an army or a bunch of thugs?"

The closest soldier, the one who'd fired, sneered. "What's it to you?"

"Yeah," added another, a stocky woman with curly hair. "I don't think I saw you here when we took on the military. Who do you think you are, talking to us like that?"

"Joshua Miles."

The soldiers' eyes flew wide, and they stepped back, stammering.

"Leader, I—We... I didn't know!"

"Now you do." Miles crossed his arms. "Save your ammunition and your hatred for the real enemy. The industrialists still in their forts. These men and women were workers, like us."

"Yes, leader," they blurted out together. They turned around and scrambled back to join their comrades up the street, who were staring at Miles, open-mouthed.

Miles shook his head. The stories were true. Crowe hadn't exaggerated.

"Leader?"

Miles turned around to see Tonya standing next to the personnel carrier with another soldier, a tall man with dirt and ash covering his clothes.

"The Supervisor is this way." Tonya pointed off toward a low-slung building with the words *Cross Laundromat* written across a bullet-ridden sign over its entrance.

"Lead the way." Miles followed the other two as they picked their way through the wreckage of the town, his anger festering in his chest. The Legion's infancy was over. It needed discipline, order, or it would devolve into a gang, a destructive horde. There were already reports of Legion soldiers looting the destroyed towns, and of assaults against the neutral civilian population. If those soldiers' treatment of the military's dead were any indication, the other stories had to be true — the reports of murdering the wounded, killing prisoners.

Thank God for Crowe.

If the Legion was to succeed, it would need to grow up, and fast. Miles would need many more people like Crowe at his side if was to make this into a proper army.

A military to be reckoned with.

They stepped through the entrance, ducking below a tumbled-down ceiling beam and passing between two rows of washing machines.

"Insert change or payment card. Please, insert change or payment card." An automated voice was playing from one of the machines. Miles stopped and looked down at the washer, the spray of bullet holes across its front, the pile of clothes abandoned on top of it.

"In here, Leader."

Miles turned to see Tonya pointing inside a back room, past a door with a sign that read *Staff Use Only*.

Miles slid past Tonya, but a hand on his shoulder stopped him. The soldier who'd led them here was looking down at him, a hand extended toward him.

"Leader... I... without you, we'd never have..." The man seemed to struggle for words, his eyes filled with emotion. "Thank you for our great victory."

Miles looked back over at the washing machine.

"Insert change or payment card. Please, insert change or payment card."

Miles took the man's hand, but didn't say anything. He nodded at Tonya, then entered the room.

It was dim inside, the only light spilling in through a small hole that had been punched in the ceiling. In the corner was the wrecked hulk of an ironing robot, its darkened approximation of a face in stark contrast to the bright words painted on its chest that proclaimed complimentary pressing and stain removal. Kline was sitting on a table next to a medic, who was packing away her equipment. There were a couple sutures on his back and shoulders, a bruise on the side of his cheek, his normally smooth hair tousled and messy. He was rubbing his face like a man from one of those shaving commercials, a razor and a bowl of water next to him.

Miles stood perfectly straight and cleared his throat.

Kline turned and saw Miles. "Leader Miles! Welcome!" He stood, reaching for a shirt beside him.

"Supervisor." Miles nodded. In the past months, he'd come to distrust the positivity and ebullience of the Supervisors. They were too much — too much show and emotion coupled with too much aggression toward the enemy.

"Everyone is talking about you." Kline pulled his shirt over his head, then drew what looked like a comb out of this pocket. "Everyone wants to meet the man whose strategy defeated our enemy."

"What are you doing here, Kline?" Miles crossed his arms over his chest, refusing to be flattered. "You were supposed to be in Otego with me. We need you there."

Kline smiled as he slicked his hair into place. "You're only just getting started in the capital, and against territorials at that. I thought I'd be more helpful here."

"And in greater danger." Miles gestured at the medic.

Kline made his lips pouty, an exaggerated look on his face. "You were worried about me?"

Miles didn't give a damn about the Supervisors one way or the other. But the people admired them, loved them for having galvanized the movement. "I needed you in Otego."

"You exaggerate. You're fine without me." Kline tucked his comb away and picked something else off the table, a sparkling gold ring by the look of it.

Miles couldn't help but wrinkle his nose. What would a man with a ring like that have in common with factory workers? He changed the subject. "How did you get hurt?"

Kline waved a hand dismissively. "I helped lead our band of heroes in destroying the enemy tanks. Some of the shrapnel caught me."

Band of heroes.

Kline meant the suicide bombers. That hadn't been in Miles' plans at all. Yet another thing Crowe had warned him about.

Miles raised his chin. "Speaking of our heroes, I've heard our people have been killing the enemy's wounded. Is it true?"

Kline's expression fell ever so slightly. "You can't blame people for getting excited."

"Excited?" Miles turned to the medic. "Can we have a minute?"

The medic nodded and strode out of the room, shutting the door behind her.

"Goddamn it!" Miles slammed his hand on the table, making the water bowl and razor rattle. "I gave specific instructions. Why did you disobey me?"

Kline put a hand to his chest. "I didn't disobey—"

"Crowe heard you give the order." Miles took a step toward Kline.

"She heard me encouraging our soldiers' warrior spirit."

"Bullshit." Miles balled his hands into fists, resisting the urge to hit the table again. "You do not have the right to countermand my orders. Supervisors advise the people—"

"And the leaders command them." Kline rolled his eyes. "I've read the Legion Compact. I helped write it."

"Then I know you won't interfere with my operations again."

Kline laughed, and for once it didn't seem fake. "Your operation? I suppose everyone praising you for defeating the Alliance here has gone to your head. Let me explain things." Kline held his hands out to his sides. "You acted on intelligence which I provided and devised a strategy with soldiers that *we*, the Supervisors, have organized and inspired. We never would have stopped those tanks without *my* tactics."

"You mean your suicide bombers." Miles refused to allow this to become an ego contest. "We are trying to build an army, Supervisor. If we cannot act like disciplined troops, if we come across as blood-thirsty thugs, we will lose. Our victory is in winning over the people of this Alliance. My plans depend on it. What would the people of Earth, of Souville, think of this?"

Kline guffawed. "What will people think if the military crushes you on the battlefield?" Kline was in his face now, their noses inches apart. "A silly little worker's revolt, snuffed out as soon as the military decides it's serious. You're playing with fire, and all you've got are clerks and shopkeepers and janitors. The military will be back. You must meet the enemy with brutality, shock them, if you want to make people listen. They won't be caught off guard a second time."

Miles refused to blink. "We are not murderers."

"We—or you?"

That slimy feeling wriggled in Miles' chest as he held the Supervisor's gaze.

This is pointless.

Miles took a breath. "Come back to the capital with me. I require your leadership there."

"The great hero needs my help. How surprising." Kline picked up his bowl and flung the water out on the crumpled robot. He tucked his razor in it and gestured for the door. "After you."

Miles opened the door and stepped back out into the main area. Tonya and the other soldier were standing there with the medic, their eyes wide. No doubt they'd heard the shouting. And walking in the front door was—

"Crowe!" Miles couldn't help but smile.

She had a rifle slung over her shoulder and a dented military helmet on her head, a yellow slash painted on one side, a makeshift symbol of rank. Her arm was bandaged, her eyes darkened with fatigue. She grinned.

Miles walked over to her and held out his hand.

She saluted. "General."

Miles cleared his throat and returned the salute. "Colonel."

She winked at him. "I figure we could start with the ranks in front of that asshole," she whispered, gesturing over Miles' shoulder.

Miles opened his mouth to respond, but the sound of footsteps told him Kline was right behind him.

"Well, well. It seems playing soldier *has* gone to your heads."

Miles turned to face Kline, saw him staring at Crowe with his lips curved in a smile, contempt in his eyes.

Kline made an exaggerated salute. "I will remember to take you more seriously, young lady. It seems your word has a lot of pull with our leader."

"The *general* trusts me." Crowe put a hand to something on her side. Miles glanced and saw it resting over the hilt of a bayonet.

Kline's smile faltered. "Well, then, I trust you." He turned to Miles. "Let's get going. It's a long ride to Otego." Kline ducked under the beam and walked out into the street.

Miles watched Kline go. "Dana, round up soldiers we trust. Give them positions of leadership and transmit the list to me. I'll assign ranks."

"You mean I can't dump that asshole in a ditch somewhere?" Crowe stuck her thumb over her shoulder.

"I need you here to get this mess in order." Miles put a hand on her shoulder. "I want relief for the neutrals here who've lost their homes." The moment people began to blame the Legion for their suffering, they would lose any chance of gaining public support.

Crowe nodded. "Consider it done. I'll get to it you ASAP."

"Good. You can rejoin me in Otego when these troops are organized. I can't have them acting like brutes there. For my plan to work..."

Crowe held up a hand. "Understood." She saluted again, then turned on her heels and walked outside.

Miles knew her job wouldn't be easy. How could you make people act civilized again after they'd tasted their own power for the first time?

Tasted it, and won.

Miles rolled his shoulders, fighting away the tension there. The

Supervisor was right. The Alliance would be back. This was only the beginning.

But it *was* a beginning. The plan was in motion now, and the fight in the capital would soon be in full swing. Otego, Miles' own hometown.

And what will it look like when you're done?

Miles ran his gaze around the ruined laundromat, at the wrecked village beyond the shattered front windows. "Come on, Tonya. Let's get going." He ducked under the beam but stopped on the threshold.

Inside, the voice recording was still playing.

"Insert change or payment card. Please, insert change or payment card."

ALSO BY W. P. BROTHERS

Line of Battle Series

First Command

Outpost

Planet Fall

Legion - Coming soon!

ABOUT THE AUTHOR

W.P. Brothers grew up in Colorful Colorado, where he filled his childhood with made up heroes, villains, and incredible adventures in space, on the sea, and on smoky battlefields. A life-long fan of science fiction, his other passions include military history, fine cooking, competition shooting, and hiking and camping in the beautiful Rocky Mountains.

www.wp-brothers.com

www.ingramcontent.com/pod-product-compliance
Lightning Source LLC
Chambersburg PA
CBHW031713170626
46808CB00005B/1736